Registered in U. S. Patent Office.

| Volume 3 | CONTENTS FOR OCTOBER, 1933 | Number 4 |

EVERY STORY COMPLETE—NO SERIALS!

Published quarterly by the Popular Fiction Publishing Company, 2457 E. Washington Street, Indianapolis, Ind. Entered as second-class matter, September 8, 1930, at the postoffice at Indianapolis, Indiana, under Act of March 3, 1879. Single copies, 25 cents. Subscription, $1.00 a year in the United States, $1.40 a year in Canada, $1.20 in other countries. English office: Charles Lavell, 13, Serjeant's Inn, Fleet St., E. C. 4, London. The publishers are not responsible for the loss of unsolicited manuscripts, although every care will be taken of such material while in their possession. The contents of this magazine are fully protected by copyright and must not be reproduced either wholly or in part without permission from the publishers. All manuscripts and communications should be addressed to the publishers' Chicago office at 840 North Michigan Avenue, Chicago, Ill. FARNSWORTH WRIGHT, Editor.
Copyright, 1933, by the Popular Fiction Publishing Company
COPYRIGHTED IN GREAT BRITAIN

"The unbound fingers gripped his throat like iron bands."

Berber Loot

By H. BEDFORD-JONES

The story of a madcap adventure in Morocco, told as only Bedford-Jones can tell it—a story of thrills, romance, and sudden death, in a wild hunt for stolen treasure

HENNESSY was a tough egg, any way you looked at him, and at the present moment he was in a tough place.

His cap, his attire, his fingers, the silver Senegal coins he handed out, all showed that he was from the engine-room of the tramp. She had just arrived in Casablanca from Dakar. He was bronzed, efficient, scarred, with a warm but deceptive grin.

Croghan, lean and dark, sat beside him. They drank, and watched the Berber dancers whose thudding feet seemed about to tear the platform apart. Shipmates two years previously, they had met here in Morocco, by sheer accident, half an hour ago.

Croghan seemed at home here. This was the one place in Casablanca where they might have met. It was the new *"ville Arabe,"* expressly designed for pleasure. And it was the one place where Croghan could tell his amazing story in safety. The squealing fifes and fiddles, the monotonously beating drums, the iron heels of the Berber men thudding dust from the planks, all served to cover up his words.

The room was long and low. At one end, a platform held a score of Berber men and boys, the platformers. The trestles were crowded with girls of all shades from pitch-black to white, and with all sorts of men—Arabs, Berbers, French civilians and tourists. Occasionally one of the fuzzy-haired girls would approach the two men who sat talking together, only to be sent away by a negative gesture from Hennessy. Men and girls were coming in or leaving every moment, causing a continual flow of movement in the place.

As the police agents in the streets outside, and at the entrance gates, bore witness, this was a place created not alone for the native quarter, in this comparatively new city of Casablanca, but for every one—and for the amusement of every one. From down the street came other music, indicating Arab dancing, and the bustle and stir on every hand showed that the night had just begun for this Moroccan underworld.

Hennessy gave the dark Croghan a hard, level look.

"Are you talking stage money, Frog dough, or cold cash?" he demanded.

"All kinds, cash included," said Croghan. "The Berber who told me about it was one of this crowd right here. Met him here last night and he recognized me right off. He was going to meet me tonight. And half an hour after telling me, from what I can learn, somebody cut out his gizzard. I mean just that, too; you know, these natives think a knife is

meant to rip any one from the ribs down——"

"Keep to the point," said Hennessy. "How come this Berber recognized you?"

"I was running guns up into the hills last year. Rather, acting as agent for the main guy, and collecting," said Croghan. "That's all ended now, of course. Durell, the head of the outfit, is here in Casablanca now. I quit the game and have been running an auto stage to Rabat and Fez the last few months. Are you interested or not?"

"In fifty thousand dollars? Boy, you said it," Hennessy assured him.

"All right, then listen," said Croghan, dropping his voice. "During the troubles, this Berber and some of his pals raided the hill castle of a pacha; you know, the Berbers hate all the pachas, who are held in power by the French. They got the old boy's loot, got away, and then set in to kill each other off for the loot.

"This Berber of mine, and another named M'tel, double-crossed the rest of the outfit and cleared out with the loot. They ran afoul of a French column and were captured, but hid the stuff first. They were sent up for two years each, to different prisons, M'tel was sent to Marrakesh, but my chap went to the prison at Rabat. That's where I got next to him— he fixed it for me to get in touch with his people and so forth, about the munitions."

So Croghan had been in prison, then! Hennessy sipped his mint tea and said nothing.

"Day before yesterday, time was up for them both," said Croghan. "This bunch of Berbers met my friend in Rabat and came down here to keep their dancing engagement; I dropped in last night, and all was jake. The other one, M'tel, is in bad with his tribe. Most likely, he came along and knifed my friend. I had a hint he had thrown in with Durell, the same chap——"

"Say, listen!" broke in Hennessy abruptly. "Is this some pipe-dream or what?"

Croghan leaned forward earnestly, sweat standing out on his forehead, a snarl on his thin lips, his dark eyes blazing at Hennessy.

"Cash: bank-notes and gold! Is that a pipe-dream, you fool? I know exactly where it's hidden. I can get it."

"What I want to know," said Hennessy, "is why somebody——"

"I don't give a hang what you want to know," snapped Croghan. "I can answer every argument you put up, explain everything you don't understand; but not here and now. I've no time. I've got to get somebody to lend a hand with this job, because M'tel and that chap Durell will be after the stuff in no time. If you want in on it, say so—yes or no. A fifty-fifty split."

Hennessy grinned.

"Agreed," he said. "When do we start?"

"In an hour, if you can be free of your ship in that time."

"I can so," said Hennessy promptly. "All I have to do is get my pay from the Old Man and leave her. He can ship a dozen engineers here, and he knows it. Will you come to the dock for me?"

"Not much," said Croghan. "I'm scared, I tell you; I'll not monkey around the port at night! Hennessy, I'm plenty tough, and so are you, but let me tell you that we're up against a bad gang if Durell is in on this. Let's separate here and now. Meet in an hour's time at my hotel, the Bonaparte. It's a little joint, clean and honest, in Rue Bonaparte. I'll have my car ready."

"Okeh, feller," said Hennessy. "Your car? Where do we go, then?"

"A hell of a long way," said Croghan, and drained his glass. Then he started and set down the glass abruptly, and slid from the bench. His hand gripped Hennessy's shoulder for an instant. "Look there—the chap with the chauffeur's coat! That's Durell himself. So long."

Croghan was gone, through one of the several exits—gone like an eel.

HENNESSY drew down his brows and looked at the man swaggering in, seeking an empty place at the long table. He wore the white dust-coat of a chauffeur, and a cap pulled over one ear, but he was clearly no chauffeur. His figure was lean, spare, powerful, his high-boned face was framed by black hair, sideburns, and centered by a short black mustache. It showed hard and ruthless lines, an expression of cool effrontery and the nerve to back it up. It was plain that Durell was well known here. Some called to him, others glanced at him and muttered hastily to their neighbors. Durell waved his hand, sauntered along, and slipped into the place just vacated by Croghan.

Hennessy sipped his mint tea, and stared at a soldier and a half-caste girl opposite.

"If you know what's good for you," said a voice in faintly accented English, somewhere close at hand, "you'll get back to your ship and leave that rascal Croghan alone."

Hennessy glanced around, but no one was paying any attention to him. Durell had just given an order to the waiter and was breaking open a packet of "jaunes." As he selected a cigarette, Hennessy shoved a package of matches along the board.

"Thanks," he said. "Have a light."

Durell glanced up swiftly and met his

gaze. The dark, vivid eyes struck against the calm, laughing gray ones, and a smile curved Durell's hard lips.

"Obliged to you," he said. "Stranger here?"

Hennessy nodded. "You seem to know," he said amiably. Durell surveyed his clear, laughing eyes, his heavily built, strong features, his wide shoulders, and shrugged.

"Better take my advice, my friend. Croghan ignored it; he'll be sorry, within the next half-hour. Better take it."

"Thanks, I will," said Hennessy, and rose. "I'm back to the ship right now."

He started for the door that gave on the street. Half-way to it, two Frenchmen wearing the blouses, red sashes and voluminous corduroys of workmen, suddenly seized on a girl who was passing them—a girl whose tattooed white forehead showed she was a Berber. One grasped her hair, the other caught her arms, and the first tried to empty a cognac bottle down her throat.

Amid the rough horse-play all around, the scene was unnoted, except to provoke laughter, but Hennessy caught a glimpse of the girl's face, and the stark fright in it jerked him into action. With a shove, he sent the first man reeling headlong into the wall, and his fist smashed into the face of the second man, who was knocked sprawling. The first man came to his feet like a cat, a knife glittered, shrill screams went up; but Hennessy crashed in a blow that doubled the man up in agony.

Then, elbowing a way out, Hennessy left the tumult behind him and slipped into the night, well aware of the police consequences for using fists—something abhorrent to the French taste. He strode down the street to the entrance, whose significant posters on either hand indicated the character of the place, and so

to the line of taxicabs waiting outside the wall. Two minutes later, he was on his way back to town and the waterfront.

H E SETTLED back comfortably in the car and thought of Croghan. He knew perfectly well that Croghan was unscrupulous, hard as nails, and a distinct social liability; on the other hand, he was dependable and resourceful. Hennessy was no shining society light himself. Having knocked around the French and Mediterranean ports considerably, he had a working knowledge of impolite French; while his ability to handle recalcitrant men and at the same time take care of himself, resembled that of an old-time bucko mate. The engine room is not a school of polite manners.

That Croghan had been pursuing fickle fortune in Morocco for the past couple of years, doing everything from filibustering to killing jail lice, did not convince Hennessy that his yarn of Berber loot held any truth. What did appeal to Hennessy was the intervention of this Durell, and the fact that Durell had been keeping a watch on Croghan, as his words proved.

"He'll be having me followed, too," reflected Hennessy cheerfully. "So I'll stop long enough aboard ship to convince him. Then I'll slip off up the docks. Hm! Not far uptown, and this Rue Bonaparte isn't a great way off. I'll walk. If Croghan is waiting, I'll take a chance with him. If not——"

Would Croghan be waiting? He strongly doubted it. Durell's words showed that something was in store for Mr. Croghan, and something distinctly unpleasant. On the contrary, Hennessy was well acquainted with Croghan's innate abilities. The odds were about even.

Having been in port for three days, Hennessy was by no means loth to throw up his job and go careering off on a wild gold-hunt in Morocco. With Croghan as cicerone, there would be nothing tame about the trip— even leaving himself out. It might end in jail, or worse, but it would certainly not lack in excitement. Croghan certainly believed in the existence of this loot.

"It's plausible, anyhow," decided Hennessy, and dismissed further arguments.

Forty minutes later, without the least misadventure and without being followed so far as he could tell, Hennessy approached the Hotel Bonaparte on foot. It was a small hotel in a small street well down from the old Arab town. As he drew near, the lights of a car standing before the hotel entrance were flashed on, and he heard Croghan's voice.

"If that's you, Red, hop in and do it quick."

Hennessy, whose hair was not red but close enough to it to get him the name, quickened his pace. The car was a small but powerful Fiat sedan.

"Step lively," said Croghan. "Can you drive this outfit?"

"Me? I can drive anything," returned Hennessy.

"Then get under the wheel and let's go," ordered Croghan, his voice urgent. "Straight down past the docks to hit the Rabat road. Don't switch on any dash-lights, either."

Hennessy obeyed. As he settled under the wheel he was aware of Croghan's dim figure at his side, and sniffed.

"What you so blamed busy at? Smells like blood."

"It is," snapped Croghan. "Found two birds up in my room laying for me. They're still there and I've got repairs to make. Hurry and get out of here, blast you!"

The gears clashed. A moment later the Fiat went roaring down the street,

and Red Hennessy was off on the trail of Berber loot.

2

A FEW miles outside Casablanca, on the straight paved highway following the coast, Hennessy pulled out of the road and halted. Under the headlights of the car, he assisted Croghan in his repair job.

This was no elaborate matter. Croghan had suffered a number of slight cuts about the arms and hands, which momentarily interfered with his driving, and a life-preserver had given him a nasty rap over the ear, but he was quite content.

"You should see those two birds who laid for me!" he observed darkly. "Luckily, I knew Durell's little ways, and kept my eye peeled."

"No police around?" queried Hennessy. The other sniffed.

"Police? You don't know this country; anything goes! Between the native police and the French police, the double court and jail system and so forth, you can get away with murder. This isn't part of France, but a separate country so far."

Hennessy started the car again and related his encounter with Durell, touching briefly on the incident of the Berber girl. At this, Croghan cursed.

"Durell will have the cops after you for that, sure! Why didn't you kick, instead of hitting — don't you know the French yet? So he had you spotted, eh? Sure, I knew I'd been trailed for the past day anyhow."

"Well, produce some information," said Hennessy. "How do you know this money has been lying untouched all this time, huh? Why didn't those two Berbers send somebody for it?"

"Nobody to trust," replied Croghan. "You don't know this country. Anybody would cut his own brother's throat for a tenth part of that coin, Red! And the French would grab it in a minute if they caught on. No, that cash is lying under a boundary rock up in the hills, fifty feet off a road, an hour's drive outside Fez."

"Lying under a rock!" repeated Hennessy in scornful accents.

"Yeah. Boundary rocks don't get moved in those parts, without bullets flying. When these two chaps got caught by the French, they slipped the money under that rock, and it's still lying there, all right."

"Maybe. Once out of jail, why didn't either of 'em head straight for the spot? Especially if it was a question of which one got there first?"

"Why did my friend take me in on the deal? Why has the other chap, M'tel, taken Durell in with him?" responded Croghan. "Allee same need help to dispose of the loot; the country isn't what it was a couple of years ago. There's slathers of buried money, but not banknotes. An unknown Berber can't walk into a foreign bank with that amount of money and cash in on it, not without questions asked! But one of us can. Have you got a gun?"

"Two," said Hennessy. "Well, what's your program? How far is this place Fez from here?"

"Let's see. Ninety-two from here to Rabat; from there to Meknez, a hundred and forty; from there to Fez, sixty more. That's nearly three hundred."

"Miles?"

"No, you nut! Kilometers. About a hundred and seventy-five miles."

"That's easy," declared Hennessy, with a laugh. "No speed limit in this country, I hear. We'll tap your rock sometime tomorrow morning — it isn't eleven yet. Good roads, too."

"Sure. Only, Durell will know that we're on the way. He's got a Cadillac."

Hennessy stepped on the gas. The needle rose to a hundred, and passed it.

"We're doing sixty now, in miles. Suit you?"

"This is no race, Red," said Croghan bitterly. "Get that out of your head. Durell ain't in any great rush. He's got a pull, get me? All he has to do is telephone on to Rabat or Meknez, and have us pinched or else met by some of his gang."

"Well, what d'you expect to do? Fly?" asked Hennessy. "Can't we cut around those towns?"

"Not a chance. No network of roads in this country. Have you any papers?"

"Nary a one," said Hennessy cheerfully. "The skipper promised to leave the necessary documents at the consulate in the morning, with my pay."

"Then you're in dutch if the police hop on us. Maybe Durell will stick to his own gang, though." Croghan lit a cigarette, passed it to Hennessy, and lit another for himself.

"Well, what's your program?" asked Hennessy. "Crowd her through regardless?"

"You bet. Suit you?"

"Okeh by me, feller."

They swept on by hill and dale, once the coast was abandoned, then swooped down long valleys, leaving the occasional farms and old towers to right and left, the rolling boom of surf coming to them again to speak of the returning shores.

Twice they plunged across great chasms on suspension bridges, the road following the railroad rails with what seemed to be a dizzy lack of appreciation of any danger. They were ten miles out of Rabat when, topping a rise, the lights picked up a car stalled by the roadside below, two figures beside it. One of these stepped out and signalled frantically with a pocket torch.

"Go through," said Croghan. Hennessy slowed.

"Nope. Women. Have your gun ready, though."

"What the hell!" exploded Croghan. "Durell has women agents——"

THE brakes ground. Croghan, his gun ready, opened the window. Hennessy kept the headlights on the stalled car and its two passengers—a chauffeur in white dust-coat and cap, and a woman in a dark cloak. It was the latter who had signalled, and who now addressed them in French with a strong accent.

"*Messieurs,* can you have the goodness to help us in to the city? Our petrol has given out, and no other cars have passed to give us aid——"

Hennessy saw that her car bore a French license, indicating a tourist, as did the luggage piled on the top. It was a handsome car, a large Renault painted a bright blue, with brass trimmings; no hired hack.

"Certainly, *madame,*" responded Hennessy. "One moment, if you please." He turned to Croghan and spoke in rapid English. "Get out and look at their tank. See if it's a stall. I'll keep 'em covered——"

"Oh! Are you Americans?" came the quick exclamation from the woman. "So am I! And I took you for French! This is certainly a relief. You can give us a ride to the city?"

"Yeah," returned Hennessy. "Go on, Croghan! Take no chances. I've got an idea.—Miss, let me talk with you a minute. Come over here by the car. My name's Hennessy, usually called Red for short, and this here is Croghan, and we're in a tough jam."

He paused in astonishment. The ray of the electric torch fell for an instant on his face, while Croghan was getting out.

Then the woman who held it, flashed it on herself briefly. Hennessy had a vision of a laughing face, framed in masses of dark hair, and gasped.

"Lord! I thought you were an old hen," he exclaimed, as she came close. "Who are you?"

"Good sir, I am a poor wandering damsel out of gas but with plenty of madmoney," she responded merrily. "By name, Mary Gray. My chauffeur speaks no English, luckily. You look too bronzed and happy to be a tourist."

"Correct," and Hennessy chuckled. "Where you headed for? And why all alone?"

"Because I *am* alone," she returned. "I'm not as young as I look, Red, being thirty-one last week; so I don't need to be chaperoned, if that's your notion. I'm an artist, a painter of this and that, and I'm supposed to put in a couple of weeks at Rabat and have an exhibition and so forth. The luggage you see is mostly works of art. Now do you know enough about me?"

"No," said Hennessy promptly, "not near enough.—Croghan! Never mind; gather round and listen. This party's on the level, and I've got an idea.—Miss Gray, we need your car."

She broke into a laugh. "How'll you make it run?"

"Listen, this is serious!" exclaimed Hennessy. "Half of Morocco is or may be looking for us right now, having a description of our car. Chances are, we'll never get to Fez without trouble, unless we get another car——"

"Check," she broke in quickly. "Who's after you? The police?"

"No." Hennessy caught a growl from Croghan, and grinned. "She's straight, partner, so shut up. No, not the police, but they may be later. Right now, a bad gang is looking for us. We're looking for treasure, if you want it straight, and the gang wants it——"

The flashlight bit up at him again.

"No," she observed, "you certainly don't look drunk, Red! Does this car belong to you?"

"Belongs to me, miss," said Croghan.

"What we want," went on Hennessy quickly, "is to swap cars. We'll put most of our gas in your tank. You put your luggage in this car and go on to Rabat. Then later on, we'll bring back your car. We're responsible folks——"

"Yes, you talk like it," she broke in, with a silvery laugh. "Is your treasure hunt on the level?"

"Croghan has a few knife-cuts to say it is," replied Hennessy. "And if this cussed Durell ever catches up with us, they'll get paid back——"

"Durell!" came her voice sharply. "Not Carlos Durell, of Casablanca?"

"My gosh! Do you know him?" snapped Croghan.

"I've met him, to my sorrow; only a couple of days ago. Here, wait! Climb out of your car, both of you, and shift over some gas. Can you do it?"

"Sure," said Croghan. "I've got a rubber tube. Siphon it easy."

"Pull up beside us, then, and get to work," she ordered with decision. "I'll have Jules change the luggage. Where's yours?"

"We travel light," said Hennessy. "If we have luggage later, we're satisfied."

He drew up alongside the other car. Croghan was mouthing admiring oaths as he glimpsed the strategy in view, and leaped to work on transferring some gasoline.

"How'd you come to run out?" demanded Hennessy, as Jules shifted over the luggage.

"Came up from Marrakesh today," replied Mary Gray. "Thought we had

enough to go right on to Rabat, but there's something wrong with the gage. Where are you headed for?"

"Fez, or the other side of there," and Hennessy proffered a cigarette. She accepted. "Was Durell down at Marrakesh?"

"Yes."

To himself, Hennessy thought that this rather backed up Croghan's yarn, for the Berber M'tel had been in prison at Marrakesh. Durell had probably met him when he was turned loose and brought him on to Casablanca.

"There! Got enough to reach Rabat now." Croghan straightened up and turned to the woman. "Miss Gray, it's mighty white of you to let us use your car like this. Means a lot to us. If we win out, we'll sure let you know how much we appreciate it! Come on, Red."

"I'm going too," said Mary Gray abruptly. The two men stared at her in the starlight.

"You are not," spoke up Hennessy. She laughed lightly, and then he caught her arm and led her to one side. "Listen here," he said, "don't be silly, now. We don't want any woman along on this trip. It's not safe."

"So I judged," she returned coolly. "That's why I'm going. I'm interested."

"Well, get uninterested, then," snapped Hennessy. "Me, I'm a second engineer out of a tramp from Senegal. This guy Croghan is an ex-jailbird and gun-runner. Durell's gang——"

"Better and better!" she cut in. "But you listen to me a minute. I've met this Durell, as I said. And I'd give a good deal to meet him again, and help any one else give him a black eye. I'm going with you, and that's flat. Maybe I can help."

"You can't. You'd be in the way."

"Nothing of the sort. You can swear all you like; I can swear too, for that matter. I'm no tenderfoot, Red. I can drive as well as you, too. I use a chauffeur for looks and as a guide. Jules can take my things on to the Transat hotel at Rabat and wait for me. I'm going, so you may as well stop your protests."

The fire in her voice, the vibrant personality of her, conquered.

"All right, but when the shooting starts——"

"I have a pistol in the car, and a government permit to carry it."

Hennessy threw up his hands and strode to the Renault, where Croghan was still standing.

"Does she mean it, Red?"

"She does. And short of using force——"

"Let her come, then," said Croghan bitterly. "Damn it, we've got to be halfway decent, but for two cents I'd ditch her somewhere."

"Better not try it," said Mary Gray, who had caught the words, and laughed again. "Cheer up, Croghan! I'm not such a bad sort, really. Jules! Take the other car to the hotel in Rabat and say I've been delayed and will be along later. And keep your mouth shut."

"Yes, *mademoiselle*," responded Jules.

Croghan climbed sullenly into the Renault, and two minutes later, with Hennessy under the wheel, they moved off. As they got into speed, Hennessy chuckled. Mary Gray, who had the front seat beside him, gave him a sharp look.

"Well? What's the joke?"

"I was thinking that Jules might run into trouble with that car."

"Oh! Well, I was thinking so myself. That's one reason I'm in this car now."

Hennessy broke into a low laugh. She was all right!

3

AS CROGHAN admiringly stated, one had to admit that Mary Gray was a useful companion.

While the two of them huddled under a blanket on the floor of the tonneau, she got the Renault filled with oil and "essence", and drove off; then Hennessy resumed the wheel, and Croghan steered him out of town, knowing all the back streets of the French city that here, as in the other old Arab towns of Morocco, had been built adjoining the more ancient huddle of masonry and apart from it.

Then they went soaring on through the night to Meknez, the great garrison city, whose enormous ruined walls in which thousands of Christian slaves had been buried alive ran off across the hills for miles. It was two-thirty when Meknez fell behind them, and a quarter past three when the lights of Fez flashed into sight ahead.

Hennessy pulled out of the road and wakened his two companions, who were dozing.

"Conference, partners," he exclaimed gayly. "If you ask me, we've made time."

"I'll say you have!" said Croghan. "There's Fez. What you stopping for?"

"Orders. We need gas and oil, not to mention sleep. Do we go straight through, or break the trip here?"

"I need daylight to locate the right spot," said Croghan, doubtfully. "And you must be about done up. It'd be safer to go right through, but——"

"There's a new hotel in the French town, this side of Fez," spoke up Mary Gray. "Why not take rooms there, get an hour's sleep and an early breakfast, and go on about six?"

"The only reason why not," said Croghan, "is that we must give our names when we light, and fill out the usual police card. If any one is looking for us, they'll know it in twenty minutes."

"Well, no car has passed us, so Durell's not ahead," said Hennessy. "We've broken the back of the trip, and I vote to start fresh at six."

"O. K., then," assented Croghan.

Another ten minutes, and they halted before the Hotel Splendide. Here Mary Gray took charge, issued the orders, obtained rooms, and Hennessy thankfully crawled between the sheets and was asleep on the instant. The nerve strain of that night drive at top speed had been terrific.

He had no luggage except the clothes he stood in and a toilet kit. Wakened at five-thirty, he was shaved, dressed and downstairs ahead of the others, and went outside to find that the hotel had refueled the car. Over the ancient twin cities of Fez was hanging the usual morning mist of smoke, so that, with the hill forts on either hand, it looked like a scene from fairyland.

Hennessy turned back into the entrance, then halted. A big car was just coming up, a Cadillac with a Moroccan license. With sharp premonition, Hennessy drew back into the doorway and watched. The new arrival halted behind the Renault. Sure enough, Durell got out, stretched himself; he was followed by two other Frenchmen, and then by a red-headed Berber in a new white jellab.

Waiting to see no more, Hennessy strode back into the lobby and encountered Croghan.

"Hey, Red! She's in the dining-room. Hustle in and eat—what's the matter?"

"Durell's here. Looks pretty done up. Come along, take a chance on the dining-room. Damned if I want to hide from that skunk! If he doesn't come in, so much the better."

THEY passed into the dining-room, a small alcoved room highly decorated with tiles and carved plaster in Moorish fashion. And here Hennessy had his first real look at Mary Gray, as they came toward her table.

Again he got that impression of vibrant personality, of laughing energy. Dark hair and dark eyes, firm feminine features—nothing spectacular about her, until she laughed and spoke. Then her face lit up with animation, with eager interest in everything around her. Thirty-one? He would have set her down as little over twenty.

And she, looking up at Hennessy, warmed to his quick laughing blue eyes, his alert, crisply carven features, the touch of whimsical recklessness that set him apart. She gave the two of them a bright greeting, and waved her spoon at the chairs adjacent.

"Settle down, comrades. I've ordered for you. A real breakfast, not a French snack. Well? What's gone wrong?"

"Durell's here," said Hennessy, as he seated himself.

She was facing the door, and looked past him, then frowned slightly.

"Let him be here, then!" she exclaimed. "When did he come?"

"Just now."

Their words died, as the waiter approached with a laden tray. During their night ride, Mary Gray had heard the entire treasure story, by snatches, but had related nothing about her knowledge of Durell. Now Hennessy recollected it, and spoke.

"You seem downright set against poor Durell. What'd he do to you?"

Anger lightened her dark eyes.

"He kissed me."

"Shucks!" Hennessy grinned cheerfully. "That's no crime. That's merely following a perfectly natural inclination."

She gave him one furious glance, then broke into a laugh.

"You're—well, Red, you're a caution! Not only that, however; he was insulting about it, and I didn't like him anyhow. He came along when I was sketching the Koutoubia, down at Marrakesh; it was built by the architect of the Giralda at Seville, you know. He just naturally got his face slapped, and then he grew ugly, but Jules came along and he decamped."

Hennessy rose and laid down his napkin.

"I'll be back in a minute," he said. "Just thought of something——"

"Sit down!" she exclaimed sharply. "You hear me? Sit down! None of your nonsense, Red. I can read your mind. I won't have it, d'you hear? Leave Durell alone."

Before her determined words and look, Hennessy shrugged and seated himself. Croghan grinned.

"You'd better not be reading his mind, Miss Gray——"

"Hold everything," she said quietly. "Here he is. Please don't have any trouble in here."

The two men, seated with their backs to the entrance, exchanged a glance and fell silent.

Durell descended the two steps into the dining-room, glanced around casually, then came to a dead halt as his eyes fell on Mary Gray, facing him. Delight sprang in his eyes, and regardless of her cool stare, he approached and doffed his cap with a gay greeting.

"My lady of Marrakesh!" he exclaimed. "Come, this is nothing short of a miracle! What good fortune has brought you to me here?"

Mary Gray regarded him for a moment, then shrugged.

"A madman," she observed to Hennessy. "Pay no attention to him."

Durell broke into a laugh. "Ah, but——"

Hennessy came to his feet and swung around to face the other. Then Durell recognized him, glanced down at Croghan, and for an instant seemed frozen. His eyes hardened into cold pin-points. The recognition was an obvious shock.

"So, this is it!" he said slowly. "This is where you disappeared——"

"On your way," said Hennessy, curtly. "Did you ever hear of the bum's rush?"

Durell's gaze bored into him with a flame of hatred; then the man bowed, turned, and went striding out of the room.

With a grunt of disgust, Hennessy resumed his seat. "Eat fast," he said. "Pitch in, everybody!"

"And get away," said Mary Gray.

"Right. Everything's paid, including breakfast, and a lunch is being put into the car now. Quickly!"

No time was lost. Swallowing a hasty meal, all three rose and departed. They saw nothing of Durell. His two companions stood in the lobby, and by the door was the red-headed Berber, who looked at Croghan with a curl of his bearded lips and a flash of hatred.

"That was our friend M'tel, right enough," said Croghan, opening the car door. "Hop in! Durell's probably telephoning and raising trouble. Straight back to the highway, Red, and then follow it out to the left, around the walls."

A tip to the attentive garçon, and they were off with a roar, Croghan now sitting beside Hennessy in front. A long block away from the hotel, Croghan uttered a startled oath.

"Stop," he exclaimed. "In to the curb, Red——"

A MOMENT later he jumped out, glanced at the tires, and suppressed certain violent words.

"Nail in the right rear," he said, climbing in. "Ain't flat yet—there's a garage dead ahead, though I can't say much for it. May be open now. You can reach it."

"Right," said Hennessy. "Now we know what M'tel was doing outside, eh?"

"Yeah. He got the nail part-way in, which is some job, and before we rolled a block, the car did the rest. There's the place, over to the left. She's open, too! No use sweating around and wasting time with tools, when we can get it done quicker. I'll give the mechanic a hand. Looks like a native."

A native it was, who had just opened up the garage. The *patron* was here, he told them, but was at the telephone. Hennessy thought nothing of this, at the moment.

They rolled in. The proprietor, a greasy-faced Provençal, appeared with great expressions of his desire to serve them; and Croghan got the native mechanic to work. Hennessy, having taken for granted that this was entirely a scheme to delay them, was watching the work and talking with Mary Gray, who refused to get out of the car, when the proprietor appeared at his side.

"A thousand pardons, *m'sieu,*" he said with a smirk, "but am I speaking with M'sieu Hennessy?"

"You are. How the devil did you know my name?"

"A lady asks for you, *m'sieu,* on the telephone."

Amazed, Hennessy followed him into the office at one side, catching a laughing jest that Mary Gray flung after him. The Provençal threw open a door at the end, opening into another room.

"The telephone, *m'sieu,* it is there——"

Hennessy strode through. The door was slammed after him. A blackjack slammed into the door, as he sidestepped like a shadow. A moving streak had given him warning.

Two of them, on him hammer and tongs as he slipped aside; knife and slungshot lunging and falling venomously. No time for questions. Two brown shapes, lithe and active as scorpions, displaying all the marvelous agility of Arabs, despite their apparently clumsy robes.

Somehow Hennessy evaded the rush, side-slipped like a phantom. The pair were silent, deadly, their eyes glimmering with intensity of emotion; they meant to kill, and they were not wasting time about it. Hennessy ducked, took the blackjack on his shoulder with numbing effect, swerved aside as the knife drove in for his belt; then his foot slipped and he shot sideways, falling headlong.

The place was littered with old tires, disused implements, empty tins. Hennessy rolled over and over, came to his feet like a cat, and brought with him a Ford tire-tool. The knife lunged in, but his weapon slanted down athwart the brown wrist. The Arab screamed shrilly as the knife fell.

The second man was rushing in. Hennessy unexpectedly met him half-way, caught his swinging weapon-arm, and slapped him over the skull with the iron. He crumpled, and Hennessy swung about. The first Arab was picking up the knife with his left hand. Hennessy booted him under the chin, then gave him a savage blow across the skull.

"You asked for it, and you got it——"

He started suddenly, now aware of a frantic honking of the car horn. It ceased as he stood panting, listening. Hennessy caught up the blackjack; then the room door was flung open, and into the place came the greasy Provençal, dragging Mary Gray by the wrist.

"Come, pretty one, and join your

American friend," he panted. "Ah! Thunders of heaven——"

He staggered back under a stinging blow in the face from her fist. Then Hennessy came down upon him, just as the man was gathering himself to rush upon her. He swung the greasy fellow about, pinned him against the wall with one long arm, and slapped him hard, twice, with jarring force. Then, deliberately, he swung the persuader and put the man out for good.

"All right, Mary," he said, and grinned at her. "Hurt?"

"No. But they killed Croghan——"

"Come on."

Hennessy leaped into action. He was gone through the office like a streak, running swiftly, silently, his face a blazing mask of fury. There was Croghan lying beside the car on his face, the Arab mechanic rifling his pockets.

The native had no warning whatever until Hennessy was upon him. Then he straightened up with a frightful cry of terror. Hennessy caught him by the throat and shook him for a moment, lifted him and shook him again, then flung him down to the cement floor.

"Fix that tire and do it sharp! Or else——"

For the first time, recollecting his pistols, Hennessy jerked one out. The Arab let out a howl and bent over the half-completed tire job. Hennessy glanced around, and found no one else in the place.

"Here." He shoved the pistol into the woman's hand, and spoke in French. "Kill this man if he stops working."

Stooping above Croghan, he found that the latter was not dead, and had suffered nothing worse than a crack over the head. Mary Gray's voice struck at him, and he was astonished to find it perfectly cool.

"They struck him down before I knew it. I honked the horn; then they pulled me out of the car——"

"Thought you had a gun!" snapped Hennessy.

"It's in the car. By the driver's seat."

"Keep mine, then. Watch that bird, there!"

He lifted the inanimate Croghan and bundled him into the rear of the car. Two minutes later, as the last nut on the rim was tightened, the Arab mechanic came erect and bleated in stark fear as Hennessy strode at him. The slungshot darted out. The native slumped over and lay in a crumpled mass.

Abandoning the punctured extra tire, Hennessy stepped on the gas. Next moment they were out in the street, swinging on two wheels, heading out and away.

Behind them, the telephone in the office was ringing steadily, vainly.

4

"WASN'T that brutal?"

"Eh?" Hennessy glanced at the woman beside him. "Wasn't what brutal?"

"Hitting that mechanic. He was in deadly fear of you——"

"Sure." A joyous, savage laugh broke from Hennessy. "I aimed to be brutal. When you're caught in a jam and want to get out alive, young lady, don't sit around manicuring your nails. That's a free trip. Say, just how did all that mess happen? By accident?"

"I doubt it." She regarded him for an instant, fascinated by the fighting glow in his eyes, the splendid laughing eagerness of his expression. "That Berber put the nail in the tire. There was only the one garage, straight on our road——"

"I see," and Hennessy nodded, realizing the truth. "Say! That chap Durell is no slouch! He must have telephoned over; probably knew the garage man.

Those two Arabs meant to kill me, and no mistake——"

"Two Arabs? Where?" she exclaimed. He flung her a laugh.

"Didn't you see 'em, in that inner room? Too busy to notice them, I suppose. That was a fine crack you hit the grease-spot! Yes, Durell phoned from the hotel, framed up everything in a flash. How much law is there in this country, anyhow?"

"Depends on what you can get away with, I fancy; about like Chicago. Oh!" She stirred swiftly. "I'll climb over in back—I forgot poor Croghan——"

"Right. Wake him up. We need directions. Crossroad ahead——"

"Turn right," she exclaimed. "We go past Fez, anyhow. When you come to the walls, turn left. The highway circles outside the city."

They swung into the highway and picked up a small column of marching soldiery, for the camp and aviation field were close by. Hennessy waved his hand gayly as he swept past, and a chorus of eager replies broke from the Frenchmen —something in this laughing, eager man compelled a comradely greeting from them in the sunrise.

Without regard for dignity, Mary Gray climbed into the back of the car and opening a bottle of wine from the lunch-basket, poured some down Croghan's throat. The latter coughed, opened his eyes, and struggled to sit up.

"Hello!" he exclaimed. "What hit me?"

"The sky dropped on you, partner," said Hennessy, without looking around. "Wake up and watch the road! Looks like we go slap into that gateway ahead——"

"Turn left!" cried Croghan sharply. Directly before them loomed the high crenelated walls of Fez, a wide gateway

thronged with men, horses, mules, camels, soldiers. Hennessy saw the left-hand road, swerved into it abruptly, and sent the car roaring along.

"Sure we're right?" exclaimed Mary Gray. "If you're heading for Taza, Croghan, we should have gone to the south of the city——"

"We're right," said Croghan. "Straight on up the hill, past Fort Chardonnet, and then swing left on Highway 26. You can't miss the marker. Well, what happened?"

When he learned, his lean dark features contracted with anger; but he said no word, and after fingering his head and finding no great damage done, lit a cigarette and sat staring silently at the olive groves as they wound up the long hill slopes.

So they came to the shell-ruined tombs of the Merinide sultans. Now, below them, lay outspread the massive walls, the far-reaching twin cities of thousand-year-old Fez in the curving valley. Then all was gone, and they were sweeping past olives and cemeteries, circling with the twisting road, until they gained the fork and the six-foot section of wall that served as a marker.

So Fez fell away behind them.

THE empty road ahead drew in among the hills, apparently absolutely deserted and yet in reality filled with native life. Suddenly Croghan came to life.

"Hey, Red! Something wrong!" he exclaimed. "What's that knocking?"

"Search me." Hennessy slowed, then quickened the pace. They were passing a crossroad, where stood a neat little building corresponding to an American hot-dog stand. Presently, half a mile farther, the knocking became more distinct. Hennessy pulled out of the road, and Croghan uttered a groan of despair.

"Can't be the bearings, surely! Didn't they put in oil?"

Hennessy glanced at the gages. "Full when we left. Empty now——"

With a subdued oath, Croghan was out of the car. He dived underneath for a moment, then rose and kicked the front tire savagely.

"Broken oil line. Bearings burned out. This is a sweet mess!" he said. "Probably was broken last night and we got in without oil. Been losing ever since."

"Can't we go on regardless?" asked Mary Gray. Croghan gave her a bitter look.

"And have the rods bust through the pan? Not a chance. Ten miles to go yet —blast the luck! Just when we had him beaten——"

Hennessy lit a cigarette and regarded the others, whose dismay was complete.

"Facts are facts; no use blinking them," he observed coolly. "I suppose Durell must come this way? Or could he take another road?"

"No, he'll be along," said Croghan, frowning blackly.

"And he won't be wasting any time, either, once he finds what happened at that garage. Hm!" Hennessy puffed for a moment, his gaze darting around, scanning the road ahead. They had halted just around the bend of a curve. "Croghan, you hop out. Walk back to that crossroad; I saw a telephone line at the eating-stand. Get another car out here from the city. Can do?"

"Huh? Sure," responded Croghan, staring at him. "But by the time another car gets here, Durell will be digging up the stuff."

Hennessy grinned. "Not if he comes this way. You keep your eye on the road as you go, for if he comes along and sights you, you'll die of lead poisoning in a hurry."

"And what about you?"

"We'll be sitting here, partner. And if we have any luck, there'll be a Cadillac sitting here likewise, when you come along."

Croghan stared at him for a minute, the dark eyes a-glitter.

"You're a fool to chance it! What about her?" and he jerked his head toward the woman.

A laugh broke from her. "Never mind about us!" she said gayly. "You get going, will you? Trust Red."

"All right."

Croghan climbed out of the car, waved his hand, and started on the back trail without more questions. Hennessy met the merry, inquiring eyes of Mary Gray, and chuckled.

"You've got a lot of faith in me, young lady!"

"You deserve it. What's your program?"

"You'll see."

Hennessy started the clanking engine and ran the car a dozen feet ahead, then halted it half on the road, half off, as though it had run suddenly out of control. He pointed to the scattered boulders lining the sloping hillside to the right.

"You get up there and take cover—and keep it. Understand? No matter what happens, you remain out of sight. If anything goes wrong, stay hidden."

She nodded, her eyes searching his face. "And you?"

"I'm taking cover too, but closer to the road. This has come down to a real private war, and the less you have to do with it, the better. Promise to keep out of it?"

"Of course. But you've got to tell me what you mean to do——"

"You'll see that for yourself." Hennessy got out of the car and extended his hand. "Come along; I want to see you tucked away securely."

She shrugged, and obeyed.

Fifty feet up the hillside, Hennessy left her ensconced in a snug nest of boulders and cactus, completely hidden from the road below. The sun by this time was mounting well into the blue sky and was blazing down fiercely. As usual in upland Morocco, the landscape was precisely that of the California hills, with the exception of the huge cactus cultivated for centuries by the Arabs in place of fences or hedges. This was scattered wild over the hillside among the boulders, and came down close to the road. On the other side of the road was a steep descent, running off out of sight into a ravine.

Some distance ahead of the car, Hennessy settled down behind two small boulders, completely screened by cactus that hid him without preventing his observation, and composed himself to wait, pistol in hand. He was convinced that Durell would halt at sight of the Renault; if not, he would be halted anyway. As he well knew, no half-way measures would now be used, for he was dealing with Durell in person, and that made all the difference.

THE moments dragged. Every minute of delay now meant that Croghan was farther on his way to the crossroads; in fact, Hennessy calculated that Croghan must have reached there long since.

"No doubt whatever now, about that loot!" he reflected. "Improbable as it seems, this is a country of improbabilities, sure enough. Durell wouldn't be so cursed hot after it, if he wasn't certain. He's a slick one, too! The way he walked out of that hotel dining-room and then got his gang to work was a caution. Well, if I have any luck now, I'll pay him back

M. C.—2

for the tire he ruined, and with added interest——"

The hillside gathered and reflected the vibration of a car's engine. Hennessy gathered himself together, assured himself by a glance that Mary Gray was out of sight, and gave all his attention to the curve in the road.

An instant later, a car swept around this, going at high speed. It was Durell's Cadillac, and the Frenchman—though Mary Gray had intimated that he was half Spanish—himself was at the wheel.

As Durell sighted the stranded Renault, his brakes screamed. By his side was M'tel, the red-headed Berber; in the rear seat were the other two men Hennessy had seen at the hotel. All were craning out at the Renault. The Cadillac slowed down; then Hennessy saw Durell make a sudden gesture and pick up speed.

"Too smart to stop, eh?" thought Hennessy. "Doesn't like the deserted look of things. All right, mister——"

His pistol came up. He fired twice, rapidly. A third report made answer, as the right rear tire of the Cadillac was blown into ribbons. The big car lurched, swerved wildly, and just to make sure, Hennessy fired again and the other rear tire went out.

There was his mistake. He knew it instantly, too late to check his action. Instead of firing again, he should have held them under his gun. Even as he realized this, pistols roared from the halted car, almost directly opposite him. The cactus around him popped and split under a hail of lead.

Hennessy fired twice more, frantically, then fell forward and lay quiet.

Durell's imperious voice halted the fire of his companions. One of the two Frenchmen lay slumped in the rear of the car; Hennessy's last bullet had gone through his brain. Durell's gaze searched the hillside rapidly.

"No sign of the other two," he observed. "See anything, M'tel?"

"*Mais oui!*" responded the Berber at his side, after an instant. "Something moved in that clump of rocks and cactus up above."

"So? Croghan's there, hurt, no doubt; their car ran off the road," said Durell, and then spoke rapidly. M'tel nodded and wriggled out of his jellab. Durell got out with his remaining companion, on the far side.

"With me, Pierre," he said, then lifted his voice. "He's shot dead? Good! Come along and take care of him. Why the fool shot at us, heavens knows! Luckily we have two spare tires——"

He beckoned Pierre. They darted forward to where Hennessy lay, a trickle of crimson running over his face. Durell spoke rapidly, softly.

"Lift him to the car. Hurry. She is up there, you comprehend?"

Meantime, the Berber had slipped from his car, free of the jellab, and darted forward down the road. After a moment he began to ascend the hillside among the rocks.

Lifting Hennessy's body, Durell and Pierre carried him to the far side of the car. Then Durell flung himself on the American, with a snarl, and searched him thoroughly. Finding nothing of importance, he straightened up.

"He's not hurt; a bullet merely clipped his thick skull. Tie him up and shove him in; we can make use of him later. Leave Moreau's body among the cactus yonder, across the road. He's dead enough. We'll carry him over in a minute. I'll fasten his murder on this blundering American, you comprehend?"

"And the tires, *m'sieu?*" questioned Pierre. Durell made a sharp gesture.

"Wait. Watch."

He peered up the hillside. There, nothing was to be seen. Hennessy, firmly tied hand and foot, was bundled into the rear of the Cadillac. Pierre lit a cigarette, waiting. The road remained empty in the morning sunlight.

Suddenly a sharp cry broke from the hillside. The figure of M'tel appeared, and waved a hand.

"I have her, *m'sieu!*" he called. "She's alone."

5

THE men of northern Africa waste no time on recalcitrant women, whose value is that of a few sheep, no more.

Her whole attention fastened on the road below, caught entirely by surprize when M'tel leaped upon her from the rear, Mary Gray had no chance to use the pistol in her hand. M'tel knocked it away, and as she fought him savagely, clipped her over the head with a stone and picked her slim body up in one brawny arm.

He grinned as he came down to the car. He was a big fellow, blue-eyed like many Berbers, brutal and uncouth of expression. Durell came to him savagely.

"Have you hurt her? If you have, then——"

"A tap, no more. She fights like a man," said M'tel. "Tie her hands if you mean to take her along."

"No sign of Croghan?"

"None," answered M'tel positively.

"Then he must have gone for help— ah!" Durell started slightly. "He could telephone from the crossroads, back there! That's it. Well, to work! We have two tires to change. Let her wait in the car. Don't tie her up. I'll take her."

He took the woman in his arms, looked into her unconscious face, and laughed softly.

"So, my precious one! Your lips are too good for Carlos Durell, eh? We'll see about that, and if you want to fight, just try!"

He placed her in the tonneau, and went to work with the other two. The body of Moreau was tumbled among some cactus on the downhill side of the road, the two spare tires were slipped in place, and in high good-humor, Durell gave his orders.

"Pierre, you drive. Sit with him, M'tel, and show the road. I'll ride with the lady and the American. Now to finish it up quickly!"

"And the man Croghan, m'sieu?" questioned M'tel. Durell laughed.

"We'll attend to him. Forward!"

When Mary Gray opened her eyes, the car was bouncing over a rough hill road, and Durell, his arm supporting her, was smiling down into her eyes. She recoiled from him, and his arm tightened about her.

"Fight, little bird, fight!" he exclaimed delightedly, in English. "You have spirit, and when you learn who's your master——"

Her clenched fist struck him in the mouth, twice, so that the blood spurted from his cut lips. Again Durell laughed, drew her more closely despite her struggles, and pressed his lips to hers until his blood was smeared on her face.

"There, little one, you'll soon learn to love me!" he exclaimed, the two in the front seat glancing back and laughing heartily. "Come, be a sweet child. You won't?"

He winced as her fingers sank into his neck, driving his head back. With this, he struck her twice, as he would strike a man, so that she sagged limply back in the seat, unconscious again. A torrent of oaths rushed from him, and M'tel uttered a roar of laughter.

"That's right, m'sieu!" he cried. "You know how to handle a filly, eh? Better leave her as she is. We're nearly there now."

Durell wiped the blood from his lips, produced and lit a cigarette with a grimace, and then watched eagerly as M'tel pointed to the road ahead. He did not observed that the eyes of Hennessy, doubled up at his feet, were open a trifle, watching what passed.

"We'll just take no chances on her making a dash for it," he said, as the car slowed. He leaned forward and knotted his handkerchief about Mary Gray's ankles, then prodded Hennessy with his toe. "Awake, swine?"

Hennessy gave no sign of life, and Durell, laughing, swung open the door; the car had come to a halt.

To their right was an open field, sown in wheat. To their left, the hillside rose quite sharply. Part-way down it came a ragged hedge of cactus, ending at an irregularly shaped boulder of some size. No house was in sight, nor any living thing.

"There it is," and M'tel jerked a thumb at the boulder. His bright blue eyes were glittering with an eager light. "There's a hollow under the stone, into which it fits like a socket. Two of us can lift the rock."

"How d'you know it hasn't been lifted?"

"It is death to touch a boundary stone, m'sieu—that is, to move it."

THE voices receded. The three men strode away toward the stone, two hundred yards up the long slope.

Hennessy stirred, moved, wrenched himself around. Frantic desperation spurred him to herculean effort, but he was powerless to break the cords about his wrists. He strained upward, flung his voice at the woman on the seat.

"Mary! Mary Gray! For God's sake, wake up, Mary!"

That urgent, piercing voice broke through to her consciousness. Her eyes opened. She looked down at him blankly. Hennessy spoke again.

"Mary! Get the knife from my pocket —quick! Wake up! Get the knife, cut me free!"

The words registered. She leaned forward, fumbling at his pockets. He guided her with sharp words, twisted his head, looked out. Durell had left the car door ajar. Up the hillside, he could see the three men clustered about the stone there.

Then her hand had found the pocket-knife. She drew it out, opened the blade, and swayed over in the seat.

"I—I can't——" she murmured, and Hennessy feared that she was about to faint. Her face was bruised from Durell's blows, and blood-smeared.

"Cut my wrists free!" snapped Hennessy angrily.

The bitter authority of his tone drove into her. She blinked at him, and leaned forward anew. The knife-blade bit at the cords, bit at his skin, sawed almost blindly.

Then a low cry of helpless effort escaped her lips, and she collapsed again.

Hennessy swore in heartfelt desperation, as the knife fell to the floor beside him. He looked down at his bleeding wrists—and to his amazement, perceived that the cords were severed. One burst of straining muscles, and his hands were free. Yet he could feel nothing in them. So tight had been those cords that his fingers were purpled, the circulation was cut off.

He glanced up the hillside. The three men were returning, Durell was holding in his arms a brief-case, of all things. Desperately, Hennessy moved his right hand, caught the knife clumsily in his numbed fingers, slashed at the cords about his ankles. They were severed. He was free, but momentarily helpless. The knife fell by his feet and he could not recover it.

He hurriedly resumed his doubled-up posture, crossing his hands before him as before. He saw in a flash that he must gain time. If they knew now that he was free, they would shoot him without mercy. His hands and fingers were tingling with renewed circulation, strength was flowing into him. He felt no pain from his hurt head. His own fate and that of Mary Gray depended on him now, entirely.

The three were close upon the car. Their voices came loudly.

"She has not wakened, eh?" said Durell, with a laugh. "Excellent. Pierre, you shall have the honor of sitting with *madame*——"

"Stop! First, about the money," intervened M'tel, his voice ugly.

"You shall look into that while I drive," said Durell, "and count it. We know that money is here; nothing else matters. Take it."

"Good," replied the Berger. "There is that man Croghan——"

"I have thought about him," said Durell. "Get in, Pierre, get in! And don't forget poor Moreau. Here are three of us who can swear we saw this American try to hold up our car, shoot our tires, kill Moreau."

"If the woman tells a different story?" suggested Pierre, climbing in over Hennessy. Durell uttered a low laugh.

"She will not. She will tell no story whatever, because she is to be my guest for a long time; that is, until I grow tired of her. We'll not return as we came, but drive straight on to your village, M'tel. You keep her there. We'll arrange everything with the authorities and say that you were a witness. We'll come back tonight and pick her up and take her to Casablanca. You understand?"

The Berber grunted assent, as he settled himself in the front seat. Durell got under the wheel and started the engine, ordering M'tel to open the brief-case and count the money.

A low exclamation of astonishment came from Pierre. Hennessy, peering up through half-closed lids, saw the man staring down, saw him lean over amazedly. He had discovered that the cords were gone from Hennessy's wrists. He stooped down to make certain of this incredible thing——

The unbound fingers gripped about his throat like iron bands.

In the front seat, Durell was driving slowly along the hill road, with half an eye on the Berber beside him. M'tel had opened the moldy leather case, raking out to view thick packets of banknotes— American notes, Bank of England, Bank of France, Bank of Algiers and so on. Both men were utterly absorbed in their occupation, the Berber aflame with cupidity, Durell half watching him, half intent on the road.

Neither of them paid any heed to the rear seat. There was nothing to draw their attention, except a slight thudding as the wildly flailing hands of Pierre hit the body of Hennessy and the car floor. Pierre had been drawn forward, off the seat and on top of the American, as those clamped fingers sank into the flesh of his throat.

Presently his struggles became fainter, then ceased entirely.

HENNESSY drew clear of the man's body, came to one knee. His intention was to get Pierre's pistol, when he would have the pair in the front seat at his mercy. At this instant, however, M'tel glanced around, glimpsed the face of Hennessy behind him, and broke into a shrill cry of alarm.

The American's fist promptly smashed him under the ear.

Against two pistols, once they came into use, Hennessy well knew that he had not a chance. His whole idea now was to prevent a pistol being used. Durell instantly slammed on the brakes but could not abandon the controls. A flurry of banknotes spread over the whole front seat.

Driving another blow into the Berber's face, Hennessy flung himself on the man bodily, trying for a grip about his throat, twisting his own body over the back of the front seat. He kicked out viciously, and the car lurched wildly as his heel met Durell's cheek. A moment later, the car halted, still on the upper road above the stone marker.

In that moment, however, things happened rapidly.

Hennessy was sprawled above the two men, keeping Durell occupied with his feet, and giving his prime attention to M'tel. Hard as iron, apparently impervious to blows, the Berber put up a vicious fight, but Hennessy roughed him, and then, as the car halted, got a purchase and slammed his head and shoulders forward with terrific force.

M'tel's skull was smashed against the windshield frame, the impact cracking the thick glass. The Berber went limp. Hennessy had caught Durell's neck between his legs, and flung himself backward as the other frantically threw open the car door. Both men tumbled out in the dust together.

Durell came up with a pistol in his hand. It exploded, but the bullet went wild—Hennessy kicked at his wrist, knocked the weapon away, and flung himself on Durell.

He was met with a smashing crack that drove him sprawling.

Durell wasted no time trying to retrieve his pistol. He stepped into Hennessy's rush with a beautiful left from the shoulder that should have finished the matter straightway. Before the American could regain his feet, Durell was in upon him like a flash with a vicious kick to the face.

The engine room of a tramp, however, affords a wide range of education. Hennessy dodged that kick somehow, took another in the chest, then came to his feet, only to meet a storm of terrific smashes to the face and body. Durell could use his fists; he could use everything; and now he used all he had, to the very limit.

Hennessy had been up against many a battering in his day, but after the first ten seconds of this, he knew he had to fight with his head. He gave ground rapidly. Before him burned the snarling, bleeding, blazing-eyed face of Durell, alight with malignant hatred; the man was in the grip of an incredible ferocity. Hennessy evaded, ducked, parried, then got his balance, found his second wind, planted a straight left to Durell's belt and crossed over his right to the jaw.

Durell was halted. Like a flash, Hennessy bored in, beat the man back with a storm of blows, and landed one perfect crack flush to the chin that snapped back Durell's head and shook him badly. Panting, the Frenchman covered up, retreated, took another right and left that dazed him, and slipped in the dust. He was definitely mastered now, and realized it. Hennessy instinctively stood back to let him rise—then cursed himself for a fool. Durell, lying on one elbow, kicked savagely. Hennessy's feet were knocked from under him. The Frenchman flung himself sideways and his arm shot out. The forgotten pistol in his hand, he came to his feet, cat-like, just as Hennessy rose.

The pistol cracked. Hennessy staggered to the impact of the bullet. Then, surprizingly, he hurled himself forward. Durell fired again, and missed clean. Hennessy was upon him, knocking up the pistol, planting a final blow in that high-boned face—and then slumping down in a heap. Durell looked down at him, laughed, lifted his weapon.

Another pistol-shot reverberated from the naked hillside.

6

THIS shot came from the pistol of Croghan.

Wholly absorbed in that frantically savage battle for life, neither of the two men had observed anything around them. They had not seen the approach of the Renault, had been blind to the figure of Croghan leaping from it and running toward them. Not until Durell lifted his weapon to blow out the brains of Hennessy, did his eye catch the moving object. Then it was too late.

Croghan's one shot whirled him around and dropped him, for good.

When Hennessy came to himself, he was in the rear seat of the Renault, and Mary Gray was pouring wine between his lips. He spluttered, met the grin of Croghan, and sat up.

"What's this? Thought I was dead! Felt Durell's bullet hit me——"

He looked around in utter stupefaction. No sign of the Cadillac, of the hillside, of anything. The Renault was pulled up beside the gray-green mass of an olive grove, hot in the noonday sun.

"Good lord! Was that all a dream?"

"You'll know if you move around," said Croghan. "That bullet slapped your ribs, partner, and we've been patching you up for some time. Gosh, man!

What you did to those three devils was a plenty! You hardly left enough of Durell for me to shoot."

"You!" Hennessy felt under his shirt, found himself bandaged heavily, and comprehended. "You—shot him?"

Croghan nodded.

"Yep. We've got the loot we came after, and now we're going to get something to eat and drink. We all need it."

Hennessy met the dancing eyes of Mary Gray; they were no longer laughing, and their gay merriment was sobered, but the smile that came to her lips, the pressure of her hand, brought swift answer from him.

"And now we've got to pay the piper," he said, and then bit into the sandwich Croghan passed him. The lean, dark man nodded gravely.

A bite to eat, a bottle of wine, and the three regarded one another. Croghan was the first to break the silence.

"No use blinking it," he said. "Durell was a bad egg and no one will mourn him, but all the same, if we go back to Fez there's going to be merry hell raised over all this."

"No place else to go," said Hennessy. "We've nothing to be afraid of. See the thing through, tell the truth and shame the devil——"

"Not for me," and Croghan shook his head. "I've been in jail, remember. I've got a record here. We may get off eventually, sure, but they'll jail us and grab the money, and we'll not see a red cent of it. We've worked for that loot, partner."

"I'll say we have," said Hennessy, frowning. "What else is there to do, though?"

"Well," said Croghan, "I made a mistake. Got a man out from town, soldered up the oil line of this car—and she'll go. The bearings aren't out after all. I came

on alone with her. We can make the north highway and hit for Spanish territory, or get the railroad up to Tangier. There's an afternoon train. In a couple of hours we can be clear outside any zone of danger—or I can."

"I've no papers," said Hennessy slowly.

"Won't need any, until you get into Tangier itself. The consul there can wire the consul at Casablanca and fix up your status all right. There won't be any hunt for us if we do the vanishing act—they won't pin this on us, or connect it with us. In fact, there may not be any trouble at all, but I simply couldn't take the chance."

"I don't like Morocco anyhow," said Hennessy whimsically, and met the eyes of Mary Gray. He started slightly. "Hey! But what about you, young lady? If——"

"Let's all go to Tangier and see what happens," she said quickly.

"Nonsense! You have pictures at Rabat——"

"Pictures be hanged!" she exclaimed, her dancing eyes suddenly aglow with eagerness. "What are pictures? All aboard for Tangier! We can make the train, at least, and settle everything else by wire. Ready? Then, let's go! You take the first spell at the wheel, Croghan!"

Croghan twisted about in his seat and shied the empty wine-bottle from the window.

"O. K., then," he rejoined. "Want to sit in front, Red? Won't joggle you so much there."

"No, thanks," and Hennessy met the eyes of Mary Gray, and caught her fingers in his own. "I stay here—all the way! There's better and bigger loot than money. Right?"

"Right," said Mary Gray, with her old silvery laugh.

The Young Men Speak

By K. B. MONTAGUE

"He writhed up on his elbows and looked into their faces."

A gripping tale of head-hunting Filipino mountaineers, of the hateful Don Pedro of Pangasinan, and of the avalanche that roars in the night

THE old wise men of the Bontoc village sat in council. All morning they had squatted in the *Fawi*, whose walls hung with bobbing skulls and funnel baskets of jawbones taken in years past from their enemy, the Benguets. But the council this morning was not of enemy neighbors. Nor was it of Don Pedro of Pangasinan who, they hoped, was dead. The old men read the omens for a matter nearer to them today than Don Pedro, extortioner of gold.

All week the eyes of the village had turned to the mountain at the east. Close to Tulok village on north and west, the mountain walls rose in sheer cliffs, seamed by ledges where avalanches had stripped the rock bare. Above the cliffs were forests of Luzon pine, jungle of grass rank even in this year of the long drought, and tree-fern. One wall alone had earth and grass—the great mountain at the east. The grass of its huge paunch was burning dry now; and the earth was torn in long strips from its flanks by washes of the last wet season. Only one spot was green—the terraces of rice in the lap of the mountain, the terraces cut and leveled through the years by the village fathers and watered, all this long dry season, by endless jugs borne from the spring on the heads of the women, so faithfully cared for that even now, when the rice was well harvested, the terraces were alive with young camote plants.

For the drought was ending. Women skilled in signs of the weather augured that the purple heaviness in the southern sky boded the coming of the rains. Rain. Before another shrinking of the moon, rain, the *baguio*, the typhoon, would come. The young men outside the *Fawi* looked darkly up at the worn washes that flanked the terraces, and the old women's trembling lips shaped the syllables—"*boos-boos*". For the washes had cut deep into the mountain on either side. At the top, the earth was cracked in a great gash. Dirt and stones rattled down almost continuously from that crack. With the first heavy fall of rain, it was sure to come—the *boos-boos*, the avalanche. That great mountainside of earth, loosened by the washes on both sides and by the crack above, would come thundering down into the canyon. The village lay far enough up the canyon to escape the avalanche. But the terraces, treasured for years, were sure to be buried deep. No wonder the old men sat long reading the omens under the nipa thatch of the *Fawi*.

Without the *Fawi*, the young warriors paced the shaded court restively. Young Bontocs were used to spending their hours in fierce battle with wild carabao by the watering-places, in deadlier ambush for the head of an enemy. They hated waiting. Anangka stood under the heavy branches of the great mango tree by the spring—Anangka, son of Obtogan, the headman; Anangka, whose eyes saw more than his tongue reported, whose judgments, so the young men whispered, were shrewder than those of the fathers. He stood now under the mango, naked but for the blood-red gee-string of the Bontocs, his fine bronze body at ease in erectness, his far-seeing eyes to the south, where the box canyon opened narrowly to a long canyon that ran east and west. A stir was in the bamboo by the trail that wound out of the canyon.

"Tangpa!" Anangka's voice was soft and curt. "See who comes there!"

Tangpa, his cousin, who was seldom more than three spears' lengths from Anangka, skipped gleefully on Anangka's errand. With one lithe spring he was across the court and behind the banana trees that bordered the trail. But the stir in the grass was quicker than Tangpa. Banana leaves were brushed roughly apart. Up the trail came two husky Bontoc lads, pulling between them a man larger than they. They hauled him straight into the court of the *Fawi*. Breathless, sweating, laughing, they demanded, "The headman!"

But the headman was still at council in the *Fawi*. Anangka, frowning, walked up to the boys and their captive. The man stood, either sullen or listless, his head drooped forward on his neck.

"You are a Benguet," Anangka said, quietly.

THE black-matted head threw itself back, small weary black eyes met Anangka's survey.

"A Benguet," the rough sore voice admitted. "My name is Wigan."

"A Benguet from the village of Kubong." Anangka spoke almost in wonder. "The village that has warred with our village through the years. Yet you come into Tulok village. You were well within our land when these lads seized you. If they were old enough to carry a head-ax, instead of a camote bag, your head would not now be on your shoulders. *Where*"—he spoke sharply—"is your knife?"

The black eyes, black and small and round like papaya seeds, were curiously glazed, whether by fear, excessive weariness or by something worse than either, Anangka could not say. The Benguet's purple lips looked swollen. His raw voice spat out the words.

"I have no knife. I am a servant of Don Pedro of Pangasinan. I bring a message from him."

"Tchlk!" For all his training in control, the exclamation of dismay slipped from Anangka's tongue. Don Pedro—a message! He looked swiftly to the *Fawi*. Its door was yet closed. He had no right —neither he nor any young warrior who now crowded near had a right to take that message. And the door of the *Fawi* was yet closed on the council of the old men.

Anangka folded his arms and looked hard at the boy. The Benguet was only a boy, he decided, hardly older than the lads who had seized him by the camote patch. He was a Benguet of Kubong village, many of whose heads hung yonder in the *Fawi*. If Anangka had been behind the banana trees by the trail, this man's head would now lie at his feet. But Anangka had no wish for that head. The mention of another name made him gaze earnestly at the boy. The Benguet's skin was brown like his own. The matted black hair, the thick eyebrows, the strong cheekbones, the clean chin—they were all those of an Igorot, of the mountain people of Luzon. Benguet or Bontoc, who could tell one from the other against the glassy yellow skin, the curled mustachios, the

cruel colorless eyes of Don Pedro, the fiend for gold?

"You come from Don Pedro," Anangka said presently to the boy. "We had thought he was dead. He lives, then. And he sends you into the enemy's country without a knife, without an ax, without a spear."

"And without food," said the Benguet.

"He tried to steal our camotes," said Milas, the Bontoc boy of the camote patch, "but we caught him." He spoke jubilantly, executing with agile calves the leap with which he and his companion had taken the Benguet. Milas had not been sobered by the mention of Don Pedro of Pangasinan. He was too young to remember much of what the village had suffered at the hands of Don Pedro.

"You are starved," Anangka said to the Benguet. He glanced again at the *Fawi*. "Our fathers," he said, "are in council. You know, for you are an Igorot, that a council may not be interrupted. You know that only the fathers may talk with you of Don Pedro. Until the *Fawi* door opens, you had better sit by the spring. And the women may bring you food."

They brought him a crockery bowl of rice. The girls did not smile as they gave it, but neither did they scowl. Rice, in these last weeks of the long drought, was scanty, but then the man was starved. The women felt that Anangka was right in ordering food for an enemy who was thinner than a chicken. But the girl who brought the plate and the other girls who had come out from their quarters in the Olag, gathered in a little group in front of the Benguet. They stood with their chubby feet rather wide apart so that the oblongs of striped cloth wrapped about their thighs made triangles larger than the funnel-shaped baskets held on their shoulders by woven bands across their foreheads. Bontoc women of Tulok were nearly as large as Bontoc man, and in their spread skirts and huge baskets looked larger than they were. They completely hid the Benguet from view of the door of the *Fawi*, in case it should suddenly open. The old men in the *Fawi*, the women surmised, might be angry if they saw Bontoc rice in the hands of a Benguet. The girls lifted sly laughing eyes to Anangka from beneath the tangle of black hair on their shoulders, and saw no reproof in his face for their trick.

"Tst!" Fu-kan, Anangka's sister, made the sound sharply, and the Benguet let the emptied bowl slide into the spring behind him. The door of the *Fawi* swung slowly open. The old men came forth from the council.

2

To OBTOGAN, his father and the headman, Anangka led the Benguet. The old man's figure was shrunken with age; he stood half a head shorter than his stalwart son. But when he flung back his head, his grizzled locks streaming under the feathered Bontoc cap, his spear poised like a scepter, he towered as if high above the warriors in front of him and the old men behind.

"A Benguet!" His voice was raucous with scorn. "A Benguet stripling in a court of the Bontocs! Infants, weaklings, cowards!" His flaming eyes seared the Bontoc warriors. "When old men are in the *Fawi*, only women, it seems, are left to guard Tulok. If a man were among you, that Benguet's head would be tossed in a basket. He lives—a Benguet of Kubong—in the court of our *ato*."

"*Lockai!*" Anangka's voice, clear, resolute, was like the clang of steel after rattling of tin. "*Lockai*, reverent old one, graver matters are before us than the head of this Benguet. He comes as the messenger of Don Pedro of Pangasinan."

That name was like a quaking of the ground under their feet. The old men grasped their spears, but rather for support than in defiance. Their skin, leathery as carabao hide, looked withered; their naked shoulders shook. Over Obtogan's sinewy old frame a tremor ran, but passed. His eyes burned more darkly. For a moment he looked about to break into new rage. But he stood proudly still. He faced Anangka with the control of Anangka.

"What is the message?"

Anangka pushed the Benguet boy forward. Food had brought some vigor to the Benguet's listless body. He lifted his head boldly and looked into the eyes of the headman. He recited in distinct tones the message:

"*Let the Bontocs deliver five kilos of gold to Don Pedro of Pangasinan with the first rain.*"

Silence swept the circle, silence and then a snarl. Defiance, anger, mortification, the rage of years were in that snarl. Some one in the court struck a *ganza*, the war-gong, and warriors lifted their feet as if to fall into the war dance. But the headman raised his hand.

"Silence!

"You!" he thundered at the messenger. "You Benguet dog, have you sense to bear a message back to your wild pig of a master, Don Pedro of Pangasinan?"

The Benguet shrugged. His listlessness was not all weariness, Anangka saw. Nor was the boy by nature contemptuous, indifferent.

"He came to us faint with hunger," Anangka spoke for him to the headman. "And he has been tortured perhaps by Don Pedro, so that his spirit is broken. But he is not a fool."

"The Benguet who is neither a fool nor a coward is dead," Obtogan said, contemptuously. His sharp ears heard the

Benguet's teeth click on that insult. But the papaya-seed eyes met his unwinkingly. So a true Igorot met an insult, with no movement until the one movement of revenge. Anangka was right. The Benguet was not a fool. The headman slightly nodded.

"Listen, then, to the tale of our wrongs from Don Pedro of Pangasinan!"

The storm poured then on the messenger as if he were the hated one of Pangasinan. It was the story every Bontoc child knew by heart, that had been told at every *teng-ao* ceremony and twice at least at every *cañao* following a successful head-hunting. It began with the days, fifteen wet seasons back, when Don Pedro's men first rode into the mountains of Tulok. In trappings of rich red cloth and silver they had come, with strange knives and machines that spat forth fire. They rode horses such as no man had seen before, tall and white and smooth. The Bontocs thought them beautiful— men and horses. "Did we or did we not receive them into our villages with kindness?"

"We received them," said the clear voice of young Tangpa, who usually led the responses of the recital, "with kindness."

"We were poor. Of food we had only enough to last the season. Yet we heaped bowls with rice and camotes and gave them too of our *tapoy,* the treasured rice wine. We had no gifts to equal the lace and buckles of metal that they wore. But our best armlets and leglets, beads wrought with much cunning from the gold of our ledges, scarves and bags and robes woven through many hours by our women, we laid at their feet. Did they or did they not receive those gifts graciously?"

"They received them," said the bitter young voice, "with the manners of pigs."

"They tossed them about with contempt on the points of their knives. Then they thrust them into their saddle-bags. With no bow or smile or word of thanks they pocketed them. They pocketed them —for Don Pedro's men knew the glint of gold. Then they leaped to their saddles and galloped away. They bore that gold to Don Pedro."

"And he—sent for more."

"We gave them more." The headman's voice was heavy as if with the astonishment, the hurt, the weariness of those years. "We had much gold. We dug it at will from the ledges laid bare by the *boos-boos,* when the great spirit, Lu-ma-wig, dwelling in *chayya,* the sky, willed it to be laid bare. We shaped it in the days of the wet season into bands and beads and ornaments of beauty. We bartered those ornaments, when there was need, for pigs for the *cañao,* for cloth from other villages, for rice from the Ifugaos when our own terraces were ruined by the *boos-boos.* We knew not the value of our gold in those days. We knew it only when Don Pedro robbed us of it."

"He robbed us." Other voices now joined Tangpa's.

"His men came again and again. At first, they demanded more gifts, which we gave, though ever less willingly. Then they brought articles made in their land to exchange for gold—cloth, and beads of many colors, and strange water in bottles. The cloth was worthless, not able to endure one wet season's wear; the beads were of silly brittle stuff, and the vile water gave us evil sickness. We refused then to barter. We refused them gold. They came then—how?"

Another voice quite suddenly joined the litany. The Benguet said, promptly, "With whips."

THE headman stared at him a moment, then continued. "We had hidden our gold. We had buried it. They forced us, under lashes of great black horsewhips, to unbury it. They stuffed their pouches with our gold. They came for more, and there was no more. They forced our men to the ledges. They made them work night and day, digging, digging, digging, into the heart of the mountain. Long tunnels were driven. What had been play, in the days when we dug our gold and made it into things of beauty, became now work, blinding work, cruel work. Our old men bent under the cracking whips, stumbled and did not rise again. Our young men, penned in the stinking tunnels, had sickness of coughing and died, choked by blood. That our village might not altogether perish, we sent young boys into the hills to grow up like the wild deer hiding from the hunter. When the Spaniards came again, they found no men to dig for them."

He paused. The silence was sudden and sharp. All the circle knew the question the headman would not put.

Tangpa dully gave the response. "They drove our women to the tunnels."

Obtogan's teeth clenched on his silence. A Bontoc Igorot did not speak lightly of his women. The shining of a girl's eyes behind the handkerchief that she lifted in the courting dance, the swift sweet graceful movement of a woman's arm or foot, the trembling fingers of an old woman tottering along a path to bring her best food to a loved son or husband —they made the laughter and tears of a Bontoc's life, his joy and pain. Igorots were tender with their women; sensitive to the quick about them. Yet those Bontoc Igorots had to tell a tale—were now recounting before an enemy Benguet— the humiliation of their women. The headman's fury turned on the Benguet before him.

"And you, contemptible cousin of the dogs that fawn at Don Pedro's feet, you, whose men have been horsewhipped too, whose women driven to pound gold for the Spaniards even as ours—for in these last years, when he has left us in peace, we know well he has harried you—you come as the servile messenger of Don Pedro. Shame should lick your skin from your flesh as fire in the dry grass sucks the life from the cobra."

The Benguet faced him stolidly. "We are all," he said, "servile." Undaunted by the headman's glare, he went on, in tones harsh but no longer raw. "And why are we servile? Because you—the old men of my village and yours—egg us on to wear out our strength in useless fighting between the villages. Because, when we take the heads of your best young warriors and you take ours, no men are left to fight our common enemy. You, the old so-called wise men of the Igorots, have made us servants of the Spaniards."

Such insolence should have been met by another snarl of rage from the circle, but that snarl was hardly more than a murmur. The young warriors stood square on their feet, unheeding the throb of the war-gong. The old men, indeed, shook with anger. The headman raised a mighty voice. It poured in invective on the Benguet, who stood with eyes half closed, as if indifferent. But there were no rhythmic responses to this tirade of the headman's. It lacked drama and it lacked climax. In a desperate effort, he flung out the peroration.

"You, if there is a warrior among you, men of Tulok, take this man's——"

But Anangka's voice rode across his. *"Lockai!"* The steady young eyes forced the raging old ones to meet his. "My father, the message of Don Pedro awaits an answer."

The old man gasped at the affront. A youth to check an elder, a warrior to correct a councilor! But the young men of the village stood a solid group behind Anangka. Every Bontoc of the court looked to Anangka. The Bontoc, who was his father and his headman, loved him more than he loved his village. Yet he would never forfeit the dignity of the council of that village.

"The message of Don Pedro," he said, crisply, "awaits the council of the elders. Our message to him will be carried by a man of our own tribe. This Benguet," he forced his rage to simmer to contempt as he looked from the messenger, "let the weakest of you, unarmed, conduct him down the trail and past the camote patch. His head is not worth the dulling of your ax."

The lads of the camote patch danced forward to claim their charge. The old men moved in dismissal of the meeting. It was time for food, time for a brief rest before another long council in the *Fawi*. The result of the reading of the omens about the *boos-boos* was not yet told; and already another reading for the message of Don Pedro was upon them. But before they could turn away, young Tangpa had sprung forward.

"My uncle!"

The headman regarded him wearily.

"My uncle, you said one of us should go as a messenger to Don Pedro of Pangasinan. Let me be that messenger!"

Obtogan laughed shortly. "You, Tangpa? This is a dangerous enterprise."

"It is for that reason I wish it," Tangpa said, eagerly.

"No, no." Obtogan turned him off, impatiently. "You are only a boy. You have never taken a head from an enemy."

Tangpa, mortified, rubbed his smooth brown chin. Anangka was quickly beside him.

"Grant both of us the honor, *Lockai!* Tangpa for his readiness, and I—well, I have taken a head."

The long blue mark tattooed on his splendid square chin was sign of that achievement. The headman looked upon him with pride but with doubt. Anangka had long ago taken a head. But had he conducted himself today as a man who gloried in taking heads? Obtogan wrapped his striped robe about his skinny shoulders.

"That appointment, too," he said, testily, "awaits the council of the elders."

3

ANANGKA and Tangpa were on the trail that led out from the land of the Bontocs. Their walk was that of Luzon hillmen—less a walk than a swift skimming of the earth that their feet seemed scarcely to touch. Strong supple feet they were, the big toe and even the second one almost as detached from the others as thumbs from fingers. Their calves, round and hard and knotted, gleamed bronze as their naked thighs. The skin rippled over shoulders beautifully muscled and lithe as deer flanks. But for the tufted head-dress, the axes and bright women-bags hanging from their belted gee-strings, the hunting-spears and wooden shields slung from their shoulders, they could have passed for fine brown animals leaping naturally down the ravine between clumps of bamboo and banana plants.

Their alert black eyes, however, had a keenness beyond the watchfulness of wild deer. They had been granted the mission to Don Pedro of Pangasinan, granted it reluctantly by the father of Anangka, for the journey bristled with war spears in the enemy land they must pass through, and they faced no man knew what dangers in Pangasinan; yet it was granted inevitably to Anangka, bravest warrior of the tribe, the rightful bearer of the message. For their message to Don Pedro was one of defiance.

"According to the omens, they say, such must be the message," young Tangpa chattered, as after crossing the transverse canyon they wound up the mountain opposite on a footpath none knew but himself and Anangka, a short-cut into the land of the Benguets. "But what else could the message be, Anangka? After what Don Pedro has done to us in years past, what other message could go to him but one of defiance? Suppose old half-crazed Itliong, with his poor twisted head, had otherwise interpreted the omens, should we have borne some other message? Should we have meekly then lain down crushed under the feet of Don Pedro of Pangasinan?"

"It is the custom to learn the will of Lu-ma-wig by reading the omens," Anangka said, gravely.

"A-ah, custom." On Tangpa's tongue were questions of where custom had led them in years past, of the village weakened almost to breaking through years of following the custom of the fathers. But he knew Anangka disliked rebellious carping, and he clipped his tongue between his teeth. He could not keep, however, from the subject fretting them both. "And this message—the message that we bear to Don Pedro, what of it, my Anangka? Is it wise?"

Anangka slowly repeated it. *"Let Don Pedro of Pangasinan try to take five kilos of gold from the Bontocs with the first rain."*

"Aha—'*Let him try*'——" Tangpa's eyes snapped. That part of the message pleased him. But a quick gravity scat-

tered his grin. "M-m—'*With the first rain.*'"

That last phrase was no idle repetition from the message from Don Pedro. It was, although Don Pedro would not know it, the vital point of the message of defiance sent him by the Bontocs. The war council of the night before had chosen a plan of action that depended on the rain and on the *boos-boos*, the avalanche, that would come with the rain. The message sent was one that would surely entice Don Pedro into their canyon. By the help of Lu-ma-wig, dwelling in the sky, he should arrive there at the very moment of the *boos-boos*.

"Old Itliong, the soothsayer, has power to control the *boos-boos*," Tangpa ruminated. "He will plant his witch-stick on the mountain, and it will hold the *boos-boos* from falling until the appointed time. When Don Pedro rides into the canyon, Itliong will withdraw the stick and the *boos-boos* will fall. Don Pedro will be crushed beneath the mountain."

This scheme, greeted at the ceremonial fire the night before with war-gong, dances and shouts of exultation, young Tangpa in the clear morning light of the mountains recounted slowly, gravely. Anangka listened, intently, his brows also knotted.

"And it is true," Tangpa tripped along on his toes, like a suddenly thoughtful bird, "it is surely certain, isn't it, Anangka, that the *boos-boos* will obey the stick of Itliong and fall only when he wills it?"

"We can not be wiser than Lu-ma-wig," Anangka reasoned.

"No, of course not." Tangpa, for all his inquisitiveness, had the faith of his people in his people's religion. "But if something unforeseen should happen, if something happened to Itliong, that he should not be able to release the stick, or if he released it too soon or late—his poor eyes, you know, Anangka, are not always to be trusted—what then? Don Pedro will ride into our *barrio*, Don Pedro with soldiers armed with whips and knives and guns—with more soldiers than we have men. We are helpless against him. Once again we are beaten, tortured, our women driven to the tunnels. Our girls—your sister, Fu-kan——"

"Not," said Anangka, "while there is a Bontoc warrior to swing a head-ax."

"But how many warriors are there left?" cried Tangpa. "Oh, it was true what Wigan, the Benguet, said that day, Anangka. That our old men have wasted our strength in head-hunting within the Igorot tribes. Anangka," he made one of his sudden turns, "if you come upon a Benguet today, will you take his head?"

They had come out at a bend in the ridge where, unseen themselves, they could look out over the valleys and mountains of the Benguets. They did not speak of the dawn lights on the feathery hill slopes. Their eyes were too busily alert for any crackling of the grass, any spot of color to mark the gee-string of a Benguet. But the freshness of the morning, after their swift climb, was wine in their arteries. Young Tangpa stretched his arms heedlessly.

"Oh, Anangka, what is it like to kill a man?"

Another moment, and he almost answered the question himself. A *tling!* The whiz of metal through air, a crash and thud. Tangpa whirled, leaped into the cane brake behind, head-ax aloft, and grappled with his man. But he was thrust back. A strong arm against his chest moved him, with the force of pushing rock, backward. Another strong arm held back his enemy. Anangka stood between them. Anangka looked sternly into the eyes of Tangpa.

"Say again," he ordered, "what you said one kilometer back about wasting warriors in head-hunting. What old man eggs you on today?"

"It was his spear," shouted Tangpa. "It grazed my ear." And there was, indeed, a slight roughening of blood on his head.

"And you," Anangka turned to the other, "this is the way you repay the life we gave you in the court of our *ato?*"

It was Wigan, the Benguet boy, Tangpa now saw, the Benguet who had borne the message from Don Pedro. They faced each other, the Benguet haggard still, but armed now with ax and shield. His eyes, with their curious glazed dullness, turned slowly to Anangka.

"I did not know you," he said. "If I had known you, I would not have thrown the spear. I am very sad that I threw it."

"You knew the Bontoc head-dress. You would have killed a Bontoc. After what you said in our *ato*, you would have killed an Igorot."

"Let me kill him," Tangpa beat against Anangka's arm, "just for his falseness to his words."

The Benguet looked wearily and steadily at Anangka. "I, too," he said, "have never killed my man." But he showed none of the naive eagerness of Tangpa. "I have left," he said, "the service of Don Pedro. Though he kills me for it, I will never return to him. I have returned to my village, Kubong. And I have not been welcomed there. I need food, rest. The old men of Kubong laugh at me. They will not let the young men give me food. They tell me to come to the village when I have taken a head. It was for this reason that I would have taken yours."

"He, too, you see," said Anangka to Tangpa, "had a reason." In his heart he thought Tangpa's reason the nobler. It was braver to kill for a principle, a feeling about truth, than to kill for food. But he wished to be just to the Benguet.

"We shall know then," he said, "to watch for you as we watch for any enemy. We understand your reason. Your tribe will not accept you till you have taken a head. We shall prepare against your taking ours."

"I am not a bad man." The strange rough dignity was still Wigan's. "You are safe from me in my country. All Bontocs, I tell you now, are henceforth safe from me. If I kill, it will be a Kalinga or an Ifugao. I will not take the head of a Bontoc."

"That was the talk you made before," Tangpa cried. "And today——"

"To prove that I am your friend," Wigan said to Anangka, "I will tell you what I would not tell the insulting old man in your *ato*. I will tell you what you need to know about Don Pedro." He paused. "Don Pedro is already on his way to your village."

Anangka met the news with narrowed eyes. "Don Pedro follows his message," he said, "closely."

"He set out with it," said the Benguet. "He started from Pangasinan when I started with the message. But he came by the long horse-trails. And he stopped in other *pueblos* doing deeds of evil. But he will be in your *barrio* by three sunsets."

By three sunsets—the Bontocs inevitably looked at the sky. The clouds were gathering, as they had gathered every noon for a week, only to scatter again. Not even a soothsayer could promise rain by three more sunsets. Was Don Pedro to reach the canyon before the *boos-boos* could, by any possibility, fall?

"We bear a message," Anangka said, "to Don Pedro. A message of defiance,

M. C.—3

challenging him to come to our village."

The Benguet shrugged, his curious slouching shrug. "You can reach him," he said. "I will tell you trails that will take you to the *pueblo* where he slept last night. You can deliver your message and still return to your village in time to warn your people. Will you choose to spend your time before the third sunset in that way?"

It was a strange question. Anangka waited for an explanation. But the Benguet gave none.

"We shall certainly," Anangka said, "deliver the message."

"May we put down our shields?" Wigan waited Anangka's permission, but when it was given he lowered his shield without waiting for the action from Tangpa. "And after delivering your message," the Benguet said, with that queer insistence, "will you meet me here, at a place that I shall appoint, in my country?"

"But to what purpose——" Anangka objected, frowning.

"It is of that purpose," said Wigan, "that I will now speak to you."

4

OLD Itliong scrambled up the side of the mountain. Even with his twisted body and his feet turned so that his heels were almost where his toes should have been, he went up swiftly. He was one of those tortured, in years past, by Don Pedro. The screws had twisted his arms and thighs and neck, and had done injuries within that left him a prey to many diseases and strange attacks in the head. But as a compensation for his sufferings, Itliong, so the tribe believed, had been favored by Lu-ma-wig, dwelling in the sky. He had such skill as had no other man in reading from the omens the will of the gods. It was believed that he had the gift of prophecy. Inevitably he was the one to plant the witch-stick on the mountain to hold back the fall of the *boos-boos,* the avalanche.

His hand, that had grasped the witch-stick firmly when he started, as he scaled one turn after another in the trail began to twitch and tremble. He had been sure of the success of his mission. The gall of the chicken examined for the omen had been dark-colored as it should, favorable for the enterprise. Three nights Itliong had spent in incantations to give witch-power to the stick. Not a rite had been neglected; not a ceremonial slighted. The auspices were excellent. The witch-stick would most surely hold the *boos-boos* while the witch-stick stood upon the mountain.

But from the beginning of his climb, the morning had darkened to Itliong's sensitive apprehension. Warnings came to him. The snake, rustling in the high grass just above the terraces, said in the snake talk Itliong understood that evil was pending. The rat that scuttled into the crevice by the wash repeated the warning. Dirt slipped from Itliong's feet and crumbled where the witch-stick touched the ground. All these were solemn warnings to the soothsayer.

Yet he went on. The omens had directed him to plant the witch-stick on the top of the mountain. Whatever dangers beset his path, he must fulfil the will of Lu-ma-wig. Shaking but vigilant, the sacred stick held high in his free hand, he pulled himself with the other up the last steep pitch to the rounded knoll above.

There he made all preparations with care. He performed every rite necessary for sustaining the power of the witch-stick. He cannily surveyed each inch of the crack that ran from the top of one wash to the head of the other. He selected the exact spot where the earth had broken widest. There, firmly bedded in rocks and in earth scraped up in his poor mangled hands, he set up the witch-stick.

He worked intensely, his lips constantly moving, every nerve in his shrunken body on edge. When the task was at last done, he stood dazed, stretching himself from his concentration. But his habitual alertness made him, even before he had shaken off the cloud of the trance, quicken to what was happening about him. He was aware that a black bird, a crow, had circled three times about his head. Before its shadow floated from the hilltop, another sound pricked him. A bird flew close beside him, the wings actually brushed his shoulder, not a crow, but a small red-brown bird, the *i-chu,* the bird of omen. Itliong's old dim eyes, sharpened by anxiety, pierced the air to determine the direction of its flight. There was no mistaking it. The bird flew to the south end of the canyon, returned to Itliong, flew south again, returned again; it clearly pointed to the trail that led into the canyon. Danger was approaching on that trail. Itliong sped to the path that led down to the village. He must warn his people.

But he paused one moment on the highest point of the knoll and peered down searchingly to the mouth of the canyon. From this height, the trail lay visible for many kilometers as it wound among the mountains to the south. An observer from the knoll should have seen white and black spots upon that trail, and gleam of metal. But Itliong's poor eyes were dim with age and suffering and sleeplessness. What lay beyond the circle of his incantations was to him a haze. He realized his weakness. He knew that the best he could do was to swing like a spider down the mountain wall and bear the warning of he knew not what danger to the men of the village.

Small heed he gave to the path beneath his twisted feet. Those feet had carried him, for all their weakness and aching, where his will had told him they should go. But perhaps his will was too reckless a master today. Down a ravine he had many times scaled in safety, today his foot slipped wildly. He was thrown headlong. He snatched at cane and rocks and clung to a bit of ledge. But one leg was crushed beneath him. He pulled his feet to the path, struggled to get his weight on them. They crumpled under him. He fell again, this time with pain that blinded him. The daylight went black. His face fell into matted grass and stones.

After a while, clouds darkened the sunshine. The wind rose; rain fell. Up the trail below, Don Pedro marched with his soldiers. The mountain that was to crush him stood firm beneath the witch-stick planted by the soothsayer. Itliong, unable to remove the stick, powerless to release the *boos-boos*, lay crushed, senseless, on the mountainside.

5

OBTOGAN, the headman, in those days following Anangka's and Tangpa's departure, was full of action. If, as the days went on, no results came from his actions, it was not his fault.

The morning following the one when Anangka and Tangpa went down the trail, Obtogan called the warriors into the court of the *Fawi*. He chose ten picked men from their number. He instructed them to set forth from the village and scout the trails in all directions. He told them to return with tidings of what they found.

"Ten of our best warriors gone weakens the guard of the *barrio*," the old man, Simian, complained.

"Danger approaches the *barrio* only from the trails," Obtogan retorted promptly.

The old men did not argue with him. They knew well what was on the mind of Obtogan. His son had gone into the land of the Benguets. Anangka, who had long ago taken the head from a Benguet, would be a choice prize for a young Benguet warrior. Obtogan, his father, from his own old memories of Bontoc *cañaos*, could well picture the Benguets dancing about the head fire, could see the very features of the head they celebrated. In his deep hunger for news that this fate had not befallen his son, he was sending forth the warriors.

They went eagerly. Those detailed to remain in the village looked enviously on the ten as they slung their axes from their belted gee-strings. Their own feet chafed restlessly the ground of the court.

And more days of restless chafing were before them. The clouds that gathered in the afternoons were no darker than the uncertainty that hung over the village. Two mornings following the departure of the ten, the village again assembled in the court. The headman's face had deep creases in its leathery skin. His eyes were sharp with anxiety.

"Our warriors have not returned!"

He made no attempt at explanation of their absence. There was, as everybody knew, no explanation. A head-taking among the Benguets might account for Anangka's and Tangpa's continued absence. It could not account for ten able-bodied warriors who had set out from Tulok in ten different directions. The mystification in the village settled heavily into dread. There was but one power that could thrust into silence ten strong Bontoc warriors. Don Pedro was, they believed, at Pangasinan, many kilometers south. But some long arm of Don

Pedro must have reached into the mountains, an arm that held the fire weapon, the gun more powerful than the swiftest spear. Yet how could even many of those guns have stricken down ten Bontocs scattered on as many trails?

Or were the hills on all sides peopled by countless unseen enemies? Itliong had gone to plant the witch-stick on the mountain early that morning. If, from the mountain, he had seen danger approaching, he should have returned to report it. But he too had not returned. Had he seen what led him to stay on the mountain ready to release the *boos-boos?*

Obtogan did not attempt to answer his own questions. He looked out upon the murmuring old men, silent women, restless warriors and eager boys.

"We can spare no more warriors to disappear we know not where. The Bontoc warrior defends his own village. I will send no more of you out upon the trails."

The disappointment of the warriors was intense. One threw his head-ax angrily to the ground. Another struck a rebellious note on the ganza. Several lifted their feet in the war dance.

"Silence!" The old headman could still thunder forth his will. "Shame on the Bontoc warrior who asks for himself the task of a child! To scout a trail is the work of a boy. I send forth now six boys who shall report to me before sunset what they find in the surrounding hills."

A gleeful cry rose from the lads. Armed importantly with their first real spears, with less ceremony than swiftness, they skipped from the village.

"More waiting," growled the warriors, with rebellious glances at the clouds settling low on the hills.

"More youths who will never return," murmured the old men, as those clouds blackened and finally broke into rain.

But one youth did return. Up the trail from the south, just before sunset, there came running at full speed, soaked with rain, breathless, terrified, yet brandishing his spear, young Milas.

"The enemy!" he shouted. "One kilometer away. Just beyond the turn of the canyon. With horsemen—twenty horsemen with guns—on great white horses—Don Pedro of Pangasinan!"

6

SLOWLY the blackness cleared from the eyes of Itliong. He was conscious of cold first, of cold and clinging wetness. The scratching of the grass against his face and fierce throbs from his broken leg he did not feel keenly. Perhaps his poor old body had become immune to agony. For years he had thrust pain from his mind by the force of his one passion—fulfilment of the will of Lu-ma-wig.

That passion dragged him back now to consciousness. He twisted on the rocks till he could look below. He saw lights. He heard noises. His hand clutched the dirt beneath him. That noise—the war-gong! Warriors were dancing the war dance. His hands clasped his head, his face, his dripping thighs. Wet—wet with rain. The rain had come. The war dance could only mean that Don Pedro was close upon the village. The rain had come, sent from Lu-ma-wig. The mountain waited for the hand of Itliong to release the witch-stick that the *boos-boos* might fall on Don Pedro of Pangasinan.

So began the supreme struggle of the old man's life. He reached for the rock above him; he pulled himself to that rock. He got hold of a bamboo sprout that did not break, and hauled himself up a few more centimeters by that. His leg dragged under him. It had to be pulled along like a dead thing. But he pulled it along. He drew himself hand-breadth by hand-breadth up the trail that was hardly a trail, the path for some animal like a lizard.

At moments he grew faint and his muscles refused to make another effort. Yet after they were still a moment, they did move again. His blood throbbed and a ringing was in his ears. Presently he lost the sound of the war-gong. He lost the lights of the village, but he thought a turn of the ravine hid them from him. Spells of blackness came upon him, and he did not know how long they lasted. When he came out of them, he found himself still edging upward. He did not worry about lapse of time. Lu-ma-wig had decreed the moment for the *boos-boos* to fall. He had only to fulfil the will of Lu-ma-wig by releasing the stick. Finger by finger, he fought his way to that witch-stick.

Lu-ma-wig was with him throughout the struggle. It was Lu-ma-wig's voice, that rumbling beneath the ground, Lu-ma-wig urging him on. Lu-ma-wig loosened the earth and let stones rattle down that he might know just where the trail lay in the blackness. Twice he slipped and fell back many of the precious steps he had gained. But Lu-ma-wig set a ledge each time for his toes and hands to grasp. In full confidence in Lu-ma-wig, he dug his fingers into rock and earth and clung to grass and cane and bamboo, and so went on and on.

For many hours, as it seemed to him and as indeed it was, he climbed. But after that toil of hours, his hand reaching up felt not earth but air. He groped and found the steepness gone. The ground was smooth and almost flat. He was on top of the knoll.

Laboriously he crawled over the smooth grass. He knew to a clod where the witch-stick stood. He was a long time reaching it, but he did reach it. His lips

moved—moved in prayer, in incantation, in thanksgiving. For, with the last effort of his exhausted body, he pulled—he wrenched the stick from the ground. It dropped to his side as he fell, blackness closing in upon him.

Of the great blast, when it came, the thud as of a hundred carabaos thundering in one solid mass, the stupendous crack and roar and crash, Itliong knew nothing. His poor twisted body, writhing in a last curl of torture in his last effort for his people, was swept below with the avalanche.

7

THE women were sent out from the *barrio*. That was the first order of Obtogan after Milas' report of the coming of Don Pedro. Obtogan had full confidence that the *boos-boos*, released by Itliong above, was to fall at the will of Lu-ma-wig and crush Don Pedro and his party. But not even that confidence could change the unalterable law that, in time of war, women must be out of the village. In a swift silent line, looking in their grass raincoats like a moving file of haycocks, they scurried up the trail into the jungle beyond the head of the canyon.

The old men and the warriors left in the court tensely awaited the arrival of Don Pedro. One circle of the war dance Obtogan permitted. To the dull beat of bone on the ganza, the warriors slowly marched around the fire, knees lifted rhythmically to the alternate muffling and accentuating of the gong. But Obtogan would not allow them to rouse the spirit that had so often led them to frenzy of war. Theirs were not the hands to take the head of Don Pedro. Don Pedro was to be stricken down by Lu-ma-wig through the *boos-boos* from the mountain.

So the gongs were silenced, and the men assembled in a silent group before the sputtering fire of the rain-soaked court. Every eye was on the brooding paunch of the mountain. Champ of horses came from the trail below, and the warriors drew choking breaths, but did not lift a foot from the ground. Dull white showed down by the camote patch; voices came through the wet darkness, and the clang of metal. But the men by the fire stood motionless. Riders wound up the trail almost to the banana trees just beyond the *Fawi*, leaves crackled as the foremost horse brushed the trees— they were on the very toe of the mountain——

"Fall!" shouted Obtogan, his roar of triumph like the *boos-boos* he summoned.

But it did not fall. There was no *boos-boos*. The Bontocs stood in their tense prayer, their faces lifted in dazed anguish to the solid mountainside where the rain fell softly, uselessly. The Spaniards, on their tall white horses, rode unscathed along the mountain's foot and straight into the court of the *Fawi*.

"Ah! A welcome!" It was the smooth snarl of Don Pedro of Pangasinan. He rode so close up to Obtogan, the headman, that the foam from his horse's mouth smeared the tufted feathers of the old man's head-dress. "This is the greeting of the Bontocs to Don Pedro of Pangasinan! This is the defiance so arrogantly boasted of in your reply to his message! What! We expected warriors drawn in battle eager for our heads. We are greeted by a yell from an old man and meek silence from faint-hearted warriors. We are disappointed, men of Bontoc."

Those men of Bontoc stood in a silence too deep to be pierced by his taunts. The fire was at their back, their faces in shadow and darkened too by the rain. All their stunned wits were summoned to

keep Don Pedro from guessing what lay behind those darkened faces.

"We give you no welcome," Obtogan spoke coldly. "Don Pedro long ago forfeited all rights to courtesy from the Bontocs. If you ride into our *barrio*, Lu-ma-wig so wills it. You are in his hands."

The warriors felt that Obtogan's answer was shrewd because it told Don Pedro nothing. But Obtogan was not trying to be shrewd. He spoke almost without knowing what he said. A fiercer preoccupation beat in him than desire to save the face of the Bontocs. Don Pedro's words had told him that the Spaniard had met Anangka. Obtogan quivered to know the result of that meeting. But he knew well that he would never know it if Don Pedro guessed his eagerness. He spoke with but one thought, that of concealing his dread about Anangka.

But his words were, as the warriors recognized, wise. They baffled Don Pedro. He knew and cared nothing about the Bontoc gods. But he was aware of a veiled threat in the old man's speech. He raised a contemptuous laugh at that warning.

"So—no welcome is given from the Bontocs to Don Pedro of Pangasinan. That must distress us. Has not Don Pedro in years past shown the Bontocs he will take from them what he wishes, without benefit of *gift?*" His snarl toughened to a command. "Lead Don Pedro into the best of your houses! Provide food and shelter for his men and horses!"

But the headman stood unmoved. "You enter our houses by force, not by our invitation or guidance. We stand aside."

Don Pedro knew every warrior's hand could be at a flash on his spear. His own men could shoot down those warriors before a spear could fly. But Don Pedro had use for these Bontocs. He did not intend to deplete them again of men so that only boys and women were left to work for him. He wheeled his horse from the group.

"Many thanks! So be it, hospitable Bontocs! We ask no hospitality from wild pigs—we seize their sties at our will. Sanchez, open that door!"

It was the door into the *Fawi*, the sacred council-house, where no foot but a Bontoc's must step. The old men gave a choked cry; the warriors sprang forward. But Obtogan raised a trembling arm.

"The *Fawi*," he said, in a Bontoc dialect that only a Bontoc could understand, "lies in the path of the *boos-boos*."

That was true. The warriors stood back, looking with new hope but with misgiving too at the mountain. The *boos-boos* had failed them once; could they depend on it now? They had never expected the *boos-boos*, when it fell, to reach the *Fawi*. Yet Lu-ma-wig had willed that the *boos-boos* should crush the enemy. And what hope had they otherwise than in the *boos-boos*?

Haughtily they withdrew from the court. They left the *Fawi*, the *pabafunan*, the men's dormitory, even the *olag*, the women's quarters, to the Spaniards, and withdrew to the nipa shacks at the head of the canyon. If the *boos-boos* was to be mighty enough to cover the *Fawi*, it would be well to be far beyond that end of the village.

The Spaniards, all ignorant of the impending avalanche, turned the *Fawi* into a barrack. The treasured skulls and jawbones of its decoration they tossed into the court. They spread mats brought from the *pabafunan*, and ransacked the storage shacks of what rice the women had not carried over the hill in their baskets. The men growled at the shortness of food, and Don Pedro promised them full revenge on the morrow from the Bontocs.

They were all weary after their ride in the rain, and they slept, on the straw mats, hard and long.

In the nipa shacks above, the Bontocs slept not at all. Old men and warriors gathered in the darkness and waited. They waited for the *boos-boos*. It must surely come now, according to the omens given by Lu-ma-wig, for the destruction of the man more hated than the Evil Spirit himself, the man who had insolently entered and now slept in their sacred *Fawi*, Don Pedro of Pangasinan.

They waited till almost dawn. It came then—the crack, the roar, the crash. Every Bontoc stood with arms folded, lips moving in prayer, while the mountainside tore itself loose and thundered down, buried the terraces in its lap, smothered the banana trees at its foot, scattered rocks and dirt even over the court of the *Fawi*. But the *Fawi* itself stood unharmed.

8

THE Spaniards, half dressed but armed, leaped out from the *Fawi*. They stood in the dim wet dawn, their ears hardly able to attune themselves to the silence that followed the crashing echoes of the avalanche. Don Pedro's eyes flashed to the Bontocs at the nipa shacks. For a moment he would have turned his guns on them. But he was no fool to attribute to a handful of hillmen power to produce an avalanche. His full red lips curled in contempt of the thought. Then his teeth were bared in an uglier grin. No, the Bontocs had not produced the avalanche. But they had foreseen its coming. They had left for him the building they thought would lie in its path. They had permitted him, he now saw as the bafflement of last night suddenly cleared to him, to enter their village that he might be crushed by the avalanche.

The narrowness of his escape from that fate drove him to fury.

"Sanchez — Corranzo — Diaz!" His ringing command could not but reach the Bontocs by the nipa shacks. "Whip those pigs hither to prepare food for us."

The Bontocs came without whipping. To their minds there was nothing else to do but come. Lu-ma-wig, for reasons inscrutable, had again failed them. They knew well the power of the Spaniards' whips and guns. Anangka and their best young warriors had gone, apparently never to return. What was left but submission to Don Pedro?

They brought food, they served it to the Spaniards, they received in silence their curses and kicks. When Don Pedro had eaten, he ordered the Bontocs to assemble before him. He looked over the little band with scorn. It looked to him a smaller group than even that of the night before.

"A scurvy lot! These are the fine Bontocs who send a message of defiance to Don Pedro of Pangasinan. Where are the mighty warriors behind that challenge? Where"—his tone suddenly sharpened with suspicion—"is the young warrior who bore me that message?"

His keen eye caught the likeness to Anangka in the face of Obtogan, father of Anangka.

"Where," demanded Don Pedro, "is your son?"

The question relieved Obtogan of a mighty dread. He said, quietly, "I do not know."

"You do not know! Don Pedro accepts no such dodge. You know well where that proud young cock is hiding. Shall I put on the torture screws to draw from you where your son lies in ambush?"

"You may torture me," said Obtogan, from between his teeth, "and I will tell you nothing but the truth. A Bontoc does not lie. I do not know where my son is."

"You dare to tell me that he has not returned to your village since delivering that message?"

"He has not returned."

Don Pedro eyed him calculatingly. The old man, so far as he could see, had no purpose in lying. And his statement seemed likely to be true. The headman's son, Don Pedro reckoned, would naturally have chosen to return to the village to witness that dastardly scheme about the avalanche. But to return Anangka had to go through the land of the Benguets. Don Pedro had thought the Benguet country singularly free of warriors as he rode through it yesterday. Still, the Benguets would lie in wait for the son of the Tulok headman, their enemy of years.

"Your son, old man," he said, with another baring of his teeth, "probably adorns with his head the shack of a Benguet. You might send one of these pretty boys in exchange for your fine son's coconut."

He kicked a skull that lay at his foot. It rolled down the hummock of loose dirt, dislodging a stone above that rattled to the feet of Don Pedro. He stooped suddenly and picked up the stone.

"Gold!"

His fingers closed greedily about the piece. He would not release it, even into the hands of Sanchez and Diaz, who crowded near. They and he scrambled over the dirt hummocks that covered the court. They snatched up one piece after another. Their eyes went greedily to the mass at the foot of the mountain, to the mountain above laid bare. Their voices rose in a shout. "Gold—a ledge of it!"

The Bontocs followed their gaze. On the wall laid bare by the *boos-boos* ran a ledge of colored rock of such richness as neither Bontoc nor Spaniard had ever looked upon.

Don Pedro feasted his eyes on that ledge of gold. Then he threw back his head in a ringing laugh, and turned to the Bontocs.

"So! Mighty men of Tulok, this is your challenge! You would welcome us with an avalanche—you have indeed. Your avalanche has laid bare gold to fill the saddle-bags of Don Pedro. He is here, in response to your invitation, to receive it. Gather that gold for him!"

They moved haltingly to the rock piles. Don Pedro watched them closely. This was the moment, he gaged, when they would turn on the Spaniards, if ever. They would fight to the last drop of their blood to keep such gold. Don Pedro believed that the Bontocs had his own lust for gold. He suspected them of having hidden, in those past years, stores of gold beyond the hills. They should have no chance of secreting this gold. Under his very eyes they should sort every grain of those broken piles and deliver the precious sands to him. When the loose rock was sorted, he would set them picking at the ledge above. But he scowled at the scant score of men before him.

"Where are the rest of you? Where are your Bontoc men? I need men. Bring me workers."

"These are all the men in the *barrio*, *Señor*," said Obtogan.

Don Pedro cursed. "To be short-handed now—and with that gold!" he muttered. He flung his chin forward.

"Send for your women!"

The defiance, unkindled for the sake of gold, now blazed. Obtogan's shoulders stiffened; his eyes shot fire.

"You may take our gold. You may rob us as you have robbed us before. Our gold lies at your feet. Stuff your flabby stomachs with it. But you shall not have our women!"

"Shall not?" Don Pedro raised his sword and would have struck the old man across the face. But a spear whizzed through the air, was struck aside by another sword, rattled to the earth.

DON PEDRO ground his teeth. He loved blood for its own sake, but he loved one other thing more—gold. He would hold his hand from cruelty only at the drive of avarice. He would not kill a man who could dig gold for him. He would not chance the loss of one of his own men who could drive a man to dig gold. With stern hand he held back his soldiers. He waged the fight with his taunting tongue, not knowing that every taunt but added resistance in the men before him. Don Pedro, like many a better and wiser man after him, mistook utterly the nature of Luzon hillmen. He fitted living men to an old idea of the word "savage"; it never occurred to him to redefine that word to describe actual men. A life spent among these natives had never wakened him to the fact that they had brains as alert as his and feelings so sensitive as to make his own the reaction of an animal by comparison. Their feeling about their women was not for him to comprehend. He believed that their refusal lay in their resistance to his demand for gold.

So he applied the last screw of Spanish argument. He ordered youths brought forward. He seized young Milas, handed him over to two dark-faced Spaniards. Guns were held over the Bontocs. The two men dragged Milas into the *Fawi*. From within came presently the sound of scuffling feet, of choked groans.

"Young Milas," Don Pedro smiled at Obtogan, "will some day, no doubt, resemble your ancient soothsayer. If what they do to him in yonder shack is not sufficient to send you after your women, you will show us a young bamboo plant quickened by the rain. Aha, will not the prickling of the bamboo bring you to reason?"

The old men shook as with the chill sickness of the lowlands. They knew well the ghastly torture of the bamboo—when a man was bound above the plant, the growing shoots pierced his living flesh. Almost they hoped that Milas would die before he came out of the *Fawi.*

But Milas was strong—and brave. The warriors knew that, and they set their own jaws. Then a deathly silence within the *Fawi* was followed by a boy's scream of such agony that the warriors leaped upon the soldiers. A gun was fired. A Bontoc dropped to the earth.

"Stop!" There were two commands, one of triumph, one of despair. Don Pedro and Obtogan both gave the order. Both looked to the hill at the head of the canyon. Down the zigzag trail, heads bent forward, their long black hair falling low over the grass raincoats that covered their bodies above their skirts, came slowly but steadily the figures of the Bontoc women.

9

THE old men gazed on that silent procession with stolid eyes. Don Pedro chuckled at their silence under the renewal of their old ignominy—the ignominy of their women driven again beneath the whips of Don Pedro, insulted, subjected to the bidding of the Spaniards.

"They come willingly," Don Pedro jeered. "The yells of your young pig in the sty yonder could hardly have reached the head of the canyon. Your women did not wait for them. They come willingly. Ah, they have pleasant memories, perhaps, of former visits of our men to their *barrios.* See how readily they come!"

In his triumph on securing his end, he could not forbear merry gibing of the Bontocs. But the Bontocs seemed not to heed his words. Old men and warriors looked without one quiver of their features at the figures now passing one after another between the nipa shacks. On the mountain above, still more striped skirts came to view.

"*Dios!* A goodly number," Don Pedro exulted. "You are rich in women, old men of the Bontocs. Your warriors are poor stuff—hardly a head among them left to take. Never mind. These big fine sows shall breed you a new litter, now that the Spaniards——"

But the Bontoc men did not stir a muscle even under that insult. Nor did the women, trooping quietly forward in the rain, give a look at either Spaniards or Bontocs. With no need of direction, they went straight to the rock piles. They bent to the broken earth. With a rhythm that might have been remembered from old days under the whips of the Spaniards, they lifted a handful of earth, sifted it to the other hand, tossed the residue into their basket. Their speed at the sorting needed no Spanish taskmaster.

But the Spaniards could not resist pressing forward among the workers. Under the pretense of egging them on in the work, they pushed in among them, watching with greedy eyes every handful of rich ore tossed into the baskets. Their jokes and jeers at the women passed unheeded. Not a woman's voice was heard; not a glance came from behind the tangled black hair that fell on all sides of their bent heads. The Spaniards did not insist on answers or looks. They were too greedily intent on the jeweled rock scattered over the slope to give more than scoffing attention to the women. Even the rain that fell ever more steadily could not keep them from the open hillside where the workers gathered gold. Don Pedro's men forgot that they were soldiers; they became looters, pirates, frenzied fiends for gold.

One man flattered himself that he forgot nothing. Don Pedro stood before the *Fawi*, his sparkling eyes on the women that swarmed like ants in his service, but his hand was on the holster of his gun, his voice, smooth and liquid and gliding, played in taunts on the Bontoc men.

Those taunts recalled the first coming of the Spaniards to the land of the Bontocs; he jeered at the crude gifts and food fit for pigs offered by the hillmen; he recounted in honeyed tones the lessons taught these barbarous savages by their civilized masters, the Spaniards; he reminded them of discipline under whips and swords, of men bound and tortured, of women forced to submission. His tongue lashed in invective that these whipped natives had, for all their training in obedience, sent no gold in these last years to Don Pedro of Pangasinan.

"Even without his bidding, sons of pigs, you should crawl to his feet with gold from your ledges whenever there is enough for Don Pedro to trouble to cast his eye upon it. At his command, you are to bring him gold if you must tear open the mountain with your own claws. Another message like that one of defiance you sent him three days ago and your stomachs shall be ripped from your ribs."

Then his rage smoothed again into a snarl.

"Aha—that message! A proud message that! Let him try—let Don Pedro defy the avalanche—let him challenge the uncouth god that was to crush him under the sacred mountain. You pigs of Bontocs, Don Pedro accepts your challenge. He stands unscathed from the avalanche that has hurled your riches at his feet. Bontoc swine, Don Pedro challenges every savage god of brush and fires and incantations. Let the pig god of your mountain dare to lay a hand on Don Pedro of Pangasinan!"

He thrust both arms high above his head. They did not come down. From the mountain he had challenged came such a yell as had never filled that canyon. What happened on that slope of broken rock was over almost before it happened. A flash of a head-ax from a woman's skirt, that shout to heaven, and a Spaniard fell. A leap of warriors on Don Pedro, and his arms were lashed above his head. When Don Pedro's wits got clear of the fiendish yelling, of the earth ground into his skin where he was rolled in the dirt as his captors bound him, of the cut of those cords into his skin—when his eyes and brains were finally able to take in what was around him, he was hunched in the middle of the court facing the *Fawi*, under him the broken gold of the avalanche, before him the livid face of Obtogan, headman of Tulok.

"Our god," said Obtogan, "Lu-ma-wig, dwelling in the sky, has spoken. He has laid his hand on Don Pedro of Pangasinan."

10

SWIFT preparations were made for the ceremony to follow. Don Pedro's burning eyes watched them, the eyes that he kept staring open though that stare told him it was his last. The gag across his mouth shut in his screams. But he cursed inwardly, writhed in defiance and fury. He took defeat, as he had taken triumph, ungraciously.

A great fire was built in the center of the court. The rain had settled to a thin mist and the flames scattered that mist. Boys with grass brooms smoothed the dirt littered by the avalanche. The skulls and jaw-bones had disappeared from the court. But some strange round objects remained. They were placed in a long row in front of the fire, facing Don Pedro. He writhed up on his elbows, and looked into the faces of Sanchez and Diaz. Twenty heads of Spaniards were in that file before the fire.

War-gongs sounded, and warriors moved into the circle of the dance. It was a huge circle. Don Pedro's blood-shot eyes counted the warriors. There were three times the number that had come from the nipa shacks at dawn. And the men that crowded beyond the circle of the warriors ran into the hundreds. Not one woman was in that crowd. Don Pedro set his teeth. Yes, they had deceived him, these Bontocs who boasted that they did not lie. They had had warriors hidden beyond the village, warriors whose leader was that proud headman's son who now moved at the head of the dance. Don Pedro knew now that it was Anangka who had outwitted him. Anangka and those other warriors secreted beyond the village had come back in woman's dress. They had walked, hidden by their grass coats and their matted hair, straight into the band of armed Spaniards. At the appointed moment, they had snapped head-axes from those skirts and had laid low the proud soldiers of Don Pedro of Pangasinan. Don Pedro cursed by all the gods in whom he had no faith Anangka, son of Obtogan of the Bontocs.

The beat of the ganza went on and on. Boom—boom-boom—boom—boom-boom—boom. . . . The repetition of those syllables, over and over, tore Don Pedro's nerves. But it was a grave, a solemn dance. Anangka, at its head, held the circle from frenzy. There was to be no sudden orgy of triumph, Don Pedro saw, ending in the swift and merciful taking of his own head. He was to live yet for hours. Revenge on Don Pedro

was not to be a hurried matter. It was to be a thing of ceremony, of elaborate celebration.

And it was to be more than a local ceremony. Don Pedro's eyes fastened on that triple rank of men beyond the dancers. Those were not Bontoc men. That was not the Bontoc dress. He saw the brilliant gee-string, the beads of the Benguets. Benguets in the court of the Bontocs! This too was the work of Anangka. This was the reason for his absence from the village. He had united the strength of the Benguets with his own strength. That was how he had dared to come boldly into the camp of the Spaniards. He had the united warriors of Bontocs and Benguets behind him.

But the old men—with a fierce throb of hope, Don Pedro looked to Obtogan, the headman. If, even at this hour, he could set the old men against the Benguets, the Benguets against the Bontocs! . . .

THE dance ended. Anangka, master of ceremonies, led the warriors to the side of the fire, extended his arm to Obtogan.

"The headman speaks."

In the full glory of his striped robe, now thrown proudly over his shoulder, with the tufted feathers of his cap soaring above his head, Obtogan stepped before the fire. He stood with ten heads of Spanish soldiers to the right of him, ten to the left. His eyes seared the prostrate leader of those men. His address was to Don Pedro of Pangasinan.

It was the great moment of the old man's life. It was the recital of the wrongs of the Bontocs at the hands of Don Pedro, a saga shouted into the ears of the defeated Don Pedro, bound, gagged, at his feet. The old man's voice rose and fell, soared and thundered and pealed, poured out in invective, in triumph, in exaltation.

"Evil spirit of Don Pedro of Pangasinan!" The old man spoke as if the spirit he invoked were a visible thing, dark and slimy and venomous as the flame in Don Pedro's eyes. "It was not enough that you should rob our tribe, defile our homes, outrage our women. In your insolent defiance of the powers of good, you must defy the Great Spirit himself, you must hurl your challenge in the face of Lu-ma-wig, dwelling in the sky. Say, evil spirit that inhabits this man, has Lu-ma-wig answered that challenge?"

The gagged face yet managed a sneer. The head twisted in a negative.

Obtogan could not brook that defiance. He would force submission from the fallen one.

"Unbind his mouth!"

Anangka gave a quick frown as Milas took the gag from the bleeding mouth of the Spaniard.

Obtogan flung his question. "Are you not lying, bound and helpless, the heads of your followers at our feet, you and they crushed by the hand of Lu-ma-wig?"

The answer came through blood and foam, but in the snarl of the Spaniard. "Not by Lu-ma-wig. Nor by the Bontocs. Your Bontocs are babes. Weeping, they go for help to the Benguets. Heads you must take from strangers who have trusted to your hospitality because you lack courage to take them from the Benguets who have taken yours. You are afraid of the Benguets. They stand safe in the court of your *Fawi.*"

The murmur of the Bontoc warriors was just what he wanted, and the rage that whitened the old man's tough skin.

"Afraid of the Benguets!" His voice was hoarse. "This day will yet show whether we are afraid of the Benguets." His glance swept the Benguets with

scorn. "We deal with you first, Spaniard. Answer my question! What has happened in the land of the Bontocs today—the *boos-boos,* the gold, the return of our warriors, the death of your Spaniards, you, bound, soon to feel every torture you have worked in the years past on our people—say to me, is this that has happened or is it not the will of Lu-ma-wig?"

"It is," said a strong voice, "the will of Lu-ma-wig."

Anangka had stepped forward from the warriors. He strode to Obtogan and looked him squarely in the face. "I will answer for Don Pedro of Pangasinan." He turned to Milas. "Bind the Spaniard's mouth again."

Obtogan, in his hour of triumph, in the presence of his people and with the witness of his lifelong enemies, the Benguets, choked at such insult from his son.

"Stand aside," he demanded, harshly. "I speak with the Spaniard."

"You speak with me." Anangka addressed the old man with the gentleness of a Bontoc son to his father, but with determination. Behind him stood the warriors of the Bontocs, behind them the Benguets. Anangka reached out his arm and led Wigan, the Benguet boy, to his side.

"My father, we have a message to give to you more important than anything you could hear from the evil tongue of Don Pedro of Pangasinan. We, the warriors of the Bontocs and the warriors of the Benguets, came into the village this morning for two purposes. One was the taking of Don Pedro. That we have accomplished. The other purpose has not yet been spoken."

He paused. Obtogan said, "State your other purpose."

"The young men of the Bontocs and the young men of the Benguets," Anangka said, resolutely, "come today to announce to you, what we have already announced to the old men of the Benguets, that we war between ourselves no more. We are finished with taking of heads between our villages. The Bontoc heads formerly taken by the Benguets were burned two days ago in a peace fire in the court of Kubong. The heads that have lined our *Fawi* will be burned in our peace fire today. Every young man of our two villages pledges himself to peace between the villages henceforth."

"The young men!" shouted Obtogan. "Whose will is it, insolent one, that makes the law of the village? Will you dare to say it is not the will of the elders, the will of the headman?"

"It is the will," said Anangka, "of Lu-ma-wig."

He waited till the headman's trembling features worked to a calm.

"There is no denying it, my father," the young voice said, quietly. "Today's events have worked, not by the Spaniard's will to evil, not by your will to violence, but by the will to peace that Lu-ma-wig has set in the hearts of your young men. You have told the Spaniard that Lu-ma-wig is the spirit of good. We act according to that spirit."

Don Pedro, keenly attentive, was quick to the chance of what might lie for him in the words of this soft young man, Anangka. He twisted forward on the ground until he writhed at Anangka's feet. He got himself into an attitude of prayer there, his arms raised in supplication above his head. Anangka, so his attitude pleaded, would show him mercy.

Anangka looked down upon him with features sterner than the headman's.

"Our Lu-ma-wig," he said, "is the spirit of justice." He looked at Milas. The boy had swollen stains along his throat. He moved with limbs that were stiff and shaken. He was years older for those few moments in the Spanish torture chamber in the *Fawi*. "To Milas," said Anangka, "is the duty to carry Don Pedro to the bamboo plant."

In the hush that followed that departure, Anangka faced the headman again. "It should be known," he said, "that the will of Lu-ma-wig is expressed through strong men."

"Let it then be known!" The headman removed his head-dress. He stretched forth his war-spear. "Take my spear. Take my command. You are stronger than I. My day is past. I will follow you." But he turned again to the company. "One order I give—my last. Prepare food for the *cañao* in celebration of the peace between Bontocs and Benguets."

You know, my Friends, with what a brave Carouse
I made a Second Marriage in my house;
    Divorced old barren Reason from my Bed,
And took the Daughter of the Vine to Spouse.

For "Is" and "Is-NOT" though with Rule and Line,
And "UP-AND-DOWN" by Logic I define,
    Of all that one should care to fathom, I
Was never deep in anything but—Wine.
            —*Rubáiyát of Omar Khayyam.*

King's Assassins

By WARREN HASTINGS MILLER

A stirring tale of French Indo-China, intrigues, heroic deeds, and the picturesque monarch, Sisavang Vong, who must not be disturbed at his pleasures

"The king lay writhing and helpless under Arnold's spread legs."

THE explorer sat his horse and eyed a primitive scene even for Indo-China. Most mines in the Orient begin, cinema-fashion, with savages, and this one did. So had begun the great Hin Boun Tin Works, some distance farther south in the Laos jungle, for which Arnold was exploring mineralogist. His eyes swept over that green valley floor dotted with bamboo clumps and hemmed in by tall limestone cliffs. Native smelting-forges were scattered over it. Bellows of thick bamboo cylinders, with brawny Kha savages working their piston rods up and down; tuyères of baked clay led to the charcoal fire-pots, around which squatted elderly natives tending crucibles filled with black oxide of tin ore. They all scowled at the explorer on his horse and had no word of friendly greeting. Arnold was estimating roughly the extent and value of this newly discovered tin deposit up in the headwaters of the Sé Ma, when a voice came thinly at his horse's withers: "Master going to Luang Prabang?"

Arnold was nettled that the man had got so close unobserved. An explorer owes his life to his keen jungle awareness, at all times. This coolie was apparently some stray Tonkinese, but what he was doing here in the jungles of Laos was mystifying.

"I much-much fright, master. Bad mans!" The coolie pointed at the Kha forge men. "Coolie go 'long, master?"

"All right," Arnold agreed good-humoredly. He generally collected a band of stray waifs when he went anywhere. They valued the white man's protection against leopards, *hantus,* the casual bandits to be met on any trail.

The coolie was talkative and eager to display his French as they turned away from the valley and entered a jungle trail to the next *dak-bungalow* in the direction of Luang Prabang: "Master live in Luang Prabang? You want house-boy?" he gabbled.

"No, I'm just seeing the king there, coolie." Arnold laughed indulgently and wondered why he had gossiped that much. But he was full of it inwardly; an audience with His Majesty Sisavang Vong, that educated and progressive young ruler of Laos; a concession to develop this deposit along modern lines—good Lord, it was rich in ore, that pocket far up here in the headwaters of the Sé Ma that he had stumbled on!

"You seeing the king soon, master?" The coolie had pressed up close to the saddle in his excitement. Any one who knew the king would be useful in furthering obscure native grafts—a mere word or so for the humble servant whose cousin, let us say, had ambitions of becoming fifth assistant stable-boy.

"Tonight, I hope."

And then the fellow struck. His dagger flashed out and up for Arnold's stomach in a single swift lunge. But Arnold's fist had the instantaneous quickness of the trained boxer's. It smashed aside the dagger blade and kept on to crash the point of the jaw. The coolie went over in a heap.

Arnold jumped down to disarm him. The dagger was short, double-edged and had a double grip, a cross of metal in behind the hilt, such as are found on the old rapiers. The second and third fingers gripped over it. The palm was supported by a Tonkinese character-sign in cast bronze terminating the hilt. It was purely a thrusting-weapon.

"Explains why I knocked it aside so easily, my friend." Arnold chuckled a heavy and cheerful bass laugh. He was binding up a long gash from the razor edge of that knife. "Guess I'll tie you up for the Kha to find."

The dagger he proposed to keep as a souvenir. It was an awkward thing to stow anywhere. He thought of displacing his own hunting-knife with it, but it would not fit in the sheath. While tying the coolie with strips of his own turban he came across the scabbard. It went up the man's left forearm under the loose sleeve and was secured by a leather buckle to the lean wrist.

"Why not?" Arnold grinned and transferred it to his own wrist. "Complete outfit, while I'm about it."

The dagger rode there very well, with its character-sign hilt just touching his palm. A single snatch with his right hand drew it ready-gripped for the thrust. Might come handy in this lonely jungle where chance coolies attacked with no motive that *he* could puzzle out!

He reached the *dak-bungalow* about an hour later. The Annamese *chowkidar* led away his horse and Arnold ascended the ladder to the veranda and ordered dinner. The afternoon's ride would bring him into Luang Prabang and audience with the king.

ARNOLD was surprized at the feed the *chowkidar* presently set out. Served in the large airy living-room, redolent of dried thatch and vegetable scents, usually it was tough chicken, a doubtful fish, hard sago bread. There came on a salmi of duck, a pilaff of curried fowl and rice, French white bread, and a huge flagon of Hanoi wine. Arnold sat down to it with gusto.

"Why the fine spread, *chowkidar?*" he asked.

"Tiger-beat, master. *Dak* is in the king's hunting-grounds. Much-much people in this-here." He waved a silk-clad arm around the surrounding jungle.

"King hunting?" Arnold asked, disturbed. No audience till tomorrow in that case.

The *chowkidar* shook his head. "King he fright. Stay in him palace. Man-man say that Prince Hou Bac have hire assassins in Hanoi. Must be up in jungle by now, around Luang Prabang. Therefore court beat for tiger. Maybe catch'm assassin."

Interesting, if true. Arnold had never met His Majesty Sisavang Vong, but he had a friendly interest in him because of his encouragement of outside capital and its explorers. He downed the curry and duck, with libations from the flagon of wine, in an immense good humor. The king was in Luang Prabang, and the French Resident could easily arrange an audience with him that afternoon. . . .

A heavy step on the veranda caused him to look at the bungalow doorway. A large and rather handsome Laotian gentleman was entering. He wore European hunting-togs and carried a heavy double rifle.

M. C.—4

"*Pardon, Monsieur.*" He advanced with a polite smile of greeting.

"*Monsieur,*" returned Arnold, rising to bow cordially.

"The *chowki* has outdone himself, *hein?* Do you mind if I join you?" He spoke a precise Touraine French, evidently acquired at the Sorbonne.

"*À votre service,*" Arnold purred.

Relieved by the *chowkidar* of his topee, the stranger wiped the perspiration from his broad ivory-white brow and remarked: "I got lost in the tiger-beat and came here for a bath and a *répas*. Monsieur Tou Giaou is my name. And yours, *Monsieur?*"

"Arnold. I'm explorer for the Hin Boun Tin Mines Corporation. This is a mighty good wine, *Monsieur.*"

"Excellent. Burgundy? — *Bah!* We have as good native vintages. The king keeps his *dak-bungalows* well stocked."

"He is not hunting, I hear," said Arnold and related the *chowki's* gossip about assassins being at large.

Monsieur Tou Giaou laughed. "They are always trying for the throne, these princes. Jealousy. Intrigue. Uprisings. The French support His Majesty Sisavang Vong because he is educated and progressive. But he is a younger son, you comprehend, *Monsieur*. The elder princes do not like. Some have been banished by the French; no matter, there is always the assassin's dagger. But I fancy the King can take care of himself."

Monsieur's face set sternly with that. Arnold had no doubt of his loyalty and proceeded to make a friend at court of him. "I'm seeking an audience with His Majesty this evening," he said. "We might ride in to Luang Prabang together, if you have nothing better to do." He spoke of his discovery of that tin ore basin up in the Sé Ma valley.

Monsieur nodded pleasantly. "His Majesty welcomes new developments, new capital. You will have no difficulty about the concession, *Monsieur*. Look you, she is backward, my poor Laos. But we have built the Trans-Ninh highway in from the coast, and now a railroad is pushing in over the Annam Range from Vinh to Thakhek. A spur up from there to your new tin deposits——"

He stopped with a sharp catch of his breath. Arnold saw his almond eyes narrow to mere slits. An expression of suspicion and awakening hostility frowned on his face. Arnold followed his glance. He had been leaning his chin on his left hand, with his elbow resting on the chair-arm. The peculiar character-sign hilt of that dagger was in full view above the linen cuff of his jacket.

"Oh, that!" Arnold laughed. "A coolie tried to stab me with it back yonder on the jungle trail——"

"You will excuse *me, Monsieur!*" said Tou Giaou with force. "I—I think I had better get back to the tiger-beat at once. This must be known! A coolie, you say?"

"Tonkinese, by the look of him. He joined me for protection. When I told him I was visiting the king tonight, dashed if he didn't lunge at me with this thing."

"Precisely. . . . *Adieu, Monsieur.* . . . Pardon." Tou Giaou laid a twenty-piaster note on the table abruptly and called for his horse.

"Sorry. Not riding in with me, *Monsieur?*" Arnold grinned at his discomposure.

"*Je suis desolé.* It is impossible. Regrets, *Monsieur!*"

He was gone in quick strides. Arnold heard him mount and gallop off.

He looked at the dagger curiously. Tong-mark of some clan of assassins was that character-sign. He decided to keep on wearing it. There was no telling what

adventures it would get him into; but it might be the means of his saving the king's life. The *chowkidar's* gossip seemed true enough. A group of assassins was at large in the jungles around Luang Prabang. He had encountered one of them, purely by chance. And the fellow had stabbed on learning that he was to have audience with the king this night. . . . Why? Because he was a white man and would be much in the way, Arnold concluded. There was a plot set for the king, and they could not have it spoiled by this audience occupying him with official business where they could not get at him. The king received Europeans, not in the throne room, but in a modern office with a desk in it and chairs and a fireplace, all copied from the French idea of a business office—a place where you could talk over things with a man in privacy and comfort as your guest. It would be too well guarded. . . . No; for the plot to succeed they must catch His Majesty out on some of his nightly pleasures. Arnold had heard that he was a sad dog with the dancing-girls of Luang Prabang.

ARNOLD was thinking it out that far as he rode down the trail through the dense Laotian jungle. It debouched on a dirt road. Presently thatch houses on piles, long-horned buffalos driven by small boys, and natives afoot told him he was in the outskirts of the capital of Laos. Its monuments of the ancient civilization that once populated all this region were to be glimpsed, ruined pagodas, Buddha shrines, stupas with tall plaster roofs, *beeloas*, those fabulous monsters in stone, credulously believed to frighten off evil spirits. The yellow-robed priests of the present were going from house to house with their begging-bowls. Then he was stopped by a guard of native soldiery in conical straw hats and blue uniforms. They were armed with the French Lébel rifles.

"Your passports, *Monsieur*. This way, please."

Arnold dismounted and went into the small Bureau de Place. A mandarin official sat there behind the desk.

"Pardon. All the roads are closed, *Monsieur*," he informed Arnold. "There is a plot against the life of the king. You will not be annoyed at an examination?"

Arnold laughed. "You'll find my papers all in order, sir. I've come for an audience with the king."

Just then one of the soldiers hissed sharply. He held up Arnold's left arm. The mandarin's eyes fastened on that dagger hilt. He rose slowly, steadily out of his chair. His eyes rounded to two brown circlets around the profound blackness of the pupils, two steely rings that gave the impression of an extremely efficient weapon—like a pair of machine-gun muzzles staring from a tank cupola. He waved the soldier off as he advanced from behind the desk.

"*Du courage, Monsieur!*" he whispered; then in a harsh swirl of Tonkinese: "Seize this man!"

Arnold was astounded. That *"Du courage, Monsieur!"* could mean but one thing. This mandarin was in the plot. He had taken Arnold for one of Prince Hou Bac's paid assassins, though a white man. There were plenty of renegade adventurers in Indo-China who could be hired to run an affair of this sort. His arrest was a blind, for the benefit of these soldiers.

Chuckling inwardly with pleased excitement, Arnold suffered them to lead him, closely guarded, through a rear door of the yamen. It gave on a typical courtyard, barracks, a small jail, masonry walls all around. Over them he could see the crowded jumble of Luang Prabang's city buildings, its pagoda spires and intricately carved monastery gables, its tile roofs of noblemen's dwellings. The many-horned ridges of the palace roof rose some distance away. Its gilt gables shone in the afternoon sun. Masses of tropical greenery, palm fronds, banyan foliage, teak, and bamboo buried the stone and thatch of Luang Prabang in a setting of emerald.

THE soldiers unlocked the jail door and thrust Arnold within. He found two other prisoners in that bare room. They were hard-visaged Tonkinese, in the flat black turbans and long black gowns of anywhere in Hanoi or Haiphong. They eyed him sullenly and with suspicion. But Arnold had decided to play it boldly. He raised his left arm in a commanding gesture. They saw at once that bronze tong character on the hilt jutting up above his sleeve. There was a moment of glum perplexity; then one of them kotowed, followed by the other. This white man, too, had been hired. He bore authority. The white man always did. They were to look to him for further orders. Hadn't he been given the weapon of the tong for a sign to them?

"Be of good cheer," Arnold said. "This mandarin is for the prince."

"That we were told, master," said the elder coolie. "Yet he thrusts us in this place. The king visits the gardens of Ma Mé tonight. They are near by—but we might as well have stayed in Hanoi." He looked sourly at the bare prison walls.

"We'll be let out," Arnold said confidently.

The Tonkinese shook his head. "I trust him not. The Prince Hou Bac has been betrayed here before. These mandarins fear the French more than him.

Also there is merit in arresting us all. The king will reward him! *Hoah!*"

He grinned sardonically. "But look you, master, we wait not on him." He motioned to the other coolie, who at once moved over to the wall. "I name Han Lé. Look; I show you!"

Out came a knife from his belt, similar to Arnold's. With it in his teeth he climbed the other's shoulders. Mortar already loosened came out in two places at the pick of the knife. With his toes in the pockets Han Lé went up that wall like a lizard and hung with one arm over the wall top. A lift of his hand on the tile above let daylight in through the cracks that gaped around it.

"Tonight. Have we done well, master?"

Arnold laughed. "One way. Perhaps I have a better. I, the white man, have audience with the king tonight. It is about some tin mines." He winked.

Han Lé let himself down. He was turning that over in his mind with perplexity. "The king *not* coming to Ma Mé's gardens?" he demanded suspiciously.

"The mandarin is arranging me an audience. More better." Arnold tapped the hilt of his dagger significantly.

"Does the prince know about this change, white man?" Han Lé asked still more suspiciously. "He and Dien Phi are to meet us outside the gardens. They came over through the Sé Ma valley."

Arnold kept a poker face over that information. He was getting the threads of this plot pretty well in hand. That was Dien Phi's dagger that he was carrying at that moment.

"How *could* the prince know?" he asked. "The mandarin thought of this audience when I came to the gates, and he saw—this." He indicated the dagger hilt. "He will let the prince know."

Han Lé looked unconvinced. He was no ordinary man. He was taking no chances on this assassination. And he had arranged one sure way—out through the roof tiles and a stealthy entrance into Ma Mé's garden. Jealousy smoldered in his eyes over this other plan. This white man would come into the presence of the king, but the reward would have to be split no matter what part he took in that. And the white man might be lying; a friend of the king, who had somehow got possession of that dagger. Subtly he put that to the test.

"Swear it on the knife, master, that you will take Chien Lou and me to the palace with you; that you will divide the reward equally. Five thousand piasters has the prince promised."

Arnold had no suspicion of what he was driving at. Readily he drew his as their daggers came out. There seemed to be a kind of tong ceremony in it. The points were touched in a circle of three blades, hands were laid on them, the oath taken. Arnold wished he hadn't, a moment later! There was a character-sign engraved on the steel of his blade. And Han Lé's eyes had been on it. It might be Dien Phi's private mark for all Arnold knew. He could learn nothing from Han Lé's inscrutable eyes.

They sheathed, and there was a silence. "You'll share, men!" Arnold broke it by declaring with assurance. "Or"—he indicated the pockets in the wall—"we have two strings to our bow."

They remained impassive, dumb. "Confound these Orientals!" Arnold fumed inwardly. You could not tell what they knew, or did not know! Han Lé was probably biding his time now, after trapping him into displaying that knife. He would have to be keenly on his guard, for minutes, hours, in here. The sooner he could reach Ma Mé's gardens himself now, the better.

Night was falling and the room growing dim. Han Lé would act if the mandarin did not come soon. And, if he did come, he would denounce this white man with Dien Phi's dagger on his arm. . . .

They seemed to avoid him from then on. The natives squatted, eyes on the floor, in that attitude of interminable patience characteristic of them. Arnold leaned against the opposite wall, waiting. There were two ways of escape open to him; up those pockets and out in a sudden leap—but that would mean first shooting them both down with his revolver. Repugnant, unless they started something themselves. . . . The other way was a quick break out when the mandarin came to unlock the jail door. Some fast fist work would do it. . . .

After a time he noted that they both seemed unaccountably nearer to him. Not so much as a mutter had he heard them exchange, but with a creeping movement of their toes they had managed to inch over toward him, still squatting. He whipped out his revolver as the better defense.

"No nearer, Han Lé! Master forbids!"

No reply. They were content to wait. Complete darkness would render his revolver powerless against a combined attack. The minutes increased in tensity. Arnold was locked up with those two; he had to shoot, in cold blood, while there was yet light, or——

He couldn't do it! Get into an adventure like this, with a gay zest, in behalf of a native king whom he had never seen, yes; but to kill these two wretches, as cold reason told him he must or die himself. . . . Yet their plan was perfectly simple. Lunge for him in the dark, from both sides; then out through the roof and make their way to Ma Mé's gardens to strike down the king. Two lives,

Sisavang Vong's and his own, at stake. . . .

Shuffling sandals approached the jail door; there was the click of a key in the lock. Arnold jumped to it. His gun covered the two tong men. "Don't move or I'll shoot!" he grated. The door opened a crack behind him.

"Hurry! Hs chair has just passed the yamen!" The hoarse whisper of that mandarin was announcing that their time to act had come.

Arnold shoved the door in a foot, jumped through and slammed it behind him. "Hands up, you!" he growled menacingly.

Astounded, the whites of his eyes staring, the mandarin raised his sleeves. He swore hoarsely as the bore of Arnold's revolver threatened him. Arnold had to work fast before those two could reach him from behind.

"Back!" Arnold's free hand reached behind him to find and turn the key on them. "That will do. Stand there. Keep 'em up!"

Quickly he turned the key again and flung wide the door. The room gaped empty and cavernous within. There was a scrape of sandals high up in the rafters and the dim apparition of a lean leg drawing up through the roof tiles like the vanishing tail of a snake. The assassins had made the most of their brief moment to escape.

Arnold had no time to lose. He was in this now, up to the hilt, for the king's sake. He jumped toward the mandarin. "Turn around. Move! On the run!" he ordered. "Ma Mé's gardens!"

The mandarin exploded a squall of Tonkinese. He did not understand this at all, and cried out injuredly, bewilderedly: "Why gun on me, master? I come to take you there! You make mistake."

Arnold choked back a laugh over the

value of that misunderstanding—to him —and said, wrathfully: "How do *we* know who come? You lock us up. My men have cut a ladder of holes up your wall. They are gone out through the roof tiles to the gardens. Hurry!"

"Come!" said the mandarin. He crossed the courtyard to a small gate. There were still soldiers on duty in the yamen, he explained. They came out into a native alley. Up ahead Arnold could see a sedan-chair like a small golden shrine, having a seven-roofed spire of intricately carved and gilded teak. The shoulders of a double line of bearers carried it above the swarming crowds in the street.

Through the jostling natives Arnold shoved his way with a grip on the mandarin's arm. The chair stopped at a gay gateway illuminated with paper lanterns under a sweeping roof of glazed tiles. A figure in tropic whites and an European sun-helmet got out of the chair and entered the gate. It reminded Arnold of Monsieur Tou Giaou of the *dak-bungalow* and he cursed with chagrin. All this for that courtier who had fled at the mere sight of his assassin dagger-hilt! However, the chair was undoubtedly the royal one, though Arnold had noticed that the crowd had not squatted abjectly, as they always did when the king passed. He hurried on faster. The king must be already with Ma Mé, and perhaps *Monsieur* had come in haste to warn him. At the gate they were stopped by an ugly and glowering Moï eunuch, a giant of a man whose foot blocked the stout teak door.

"Open in haste, slave!" squalled the mandarin. "This white man must see the king at once."

"No man disturbs His Majesty at his pleasures, Your Highness," the Moï growled. "It is an order."

He made to slam to the door in their faces, but Arnold's boot was in the jamb,

and none too soon. "It's urgent, eunuch. Open, I say, or the king will be much displeased," Arnold insisted.

THE fellow hesitated, his weight against the door. Arnold nudged the mandarin with his elbow. Their combined shove swung in the gate against the grunting eunuch. Arnold sprang through to land a fierce uppercut on the man's chin. The fellow went over like a log. They hurried past him through a small court of greenery and gold-fish pools lit up with huge globes of color from Chinese lanterns. A saucy little house, all colored tile and ornament, centered gardens that were an oasis of beauty surrounded by the compound walls. Music —mellow gongs and twanging stringed instruments—tinkled a dance rhythm within. Arnold, with the mandarin gripped fast in his clutch, strode hastily to the doorway, his revolver drawn.

A flurry of girlish shrieks greeted that apparition of the two strange men on the threshold of Ma Mé's establishment. It was a scene of utterly feminine charm, beauties in silks and jewels, color in cushions and hangings everywhere, the soft glow of lanterns, the sheen of light on polished musical instruments and lacquered furniture. A raving little beauty, gorgeous in gay silks and with an overpowering head-dress of pearls crowning her intense blue-black hair, reclined with her arms about—Monsieur Tou Giaou! Again Arnold swore. Damn it, he had come to rescue the king, not this chap! But at sight of him *Monsieur* jumped to his feet in a single leap, at the same time drawing a stubby blue-steel automatic.

"Ha!" he barked. *"You!"* The pistol swung up on Arnold in a blue arc of reflected light.

"Don't shoot, you damned fool!" Arnold interposed his hasty shout. "Where's the king? He's in the utmost danger here — hold up, you ass! — *Don't!*" he yelped as *Monsieur's* stern face eyed him over the sights of that pistol bore and he seemed about to pull trigger. "This is one of those assassins I've got with me; the rest are all about the gardens———"

"*Hoah!*" That furious exclamation came from the mandarin. It was accompanied by a violent wrench that tore him free of Arnold's grip. He knew instantly that he had gambled on the mandarin's not knowing much French—and had lost. The fellow snatched for the dagger on Arnold's left arm—and with it he lunged in one headlong leap for *Monsieur* almost before Arnold could swing on him. At the same time the hoarse shouts:— "*Kill! Kill!*" sounded on all sides. In through windows and the door they came —Han Lé, his mate, two others, and a tall and gaunt coolie wearing a mandarin cap with the red button of the prince of the first rank on it.

Monsieur's pistol barked and stretched Arnold's mandarin sprawling at his feet. Arnold fired hastily at Han Lé and jumped to *Monsieur's* side. They were instantly hemmed in by that murderous ring that had closed in, quick and active as tigers. The guns spurted flame at close range, chopped and warded desperately, with no time to pull trigger. The daggers thrust in at them in a typical Oriental attack, reckless of life—anything and everything that *one* blade might get home!

Arnold heard *Monsieur* gasp: "*Ha!* You would, brother?"—*Whang!* the stunning explosion of his automatic roared over Arnold's shoulder. Then came a gasp and a groan from *Monsieur.*

The *king* was falling! Arnold knew that, now, as he stood over him at bay. There seemed to be no end of that assassin tong that Prince Hou Bac had brought up here to Laos. They kept on pouring in through the windows and leaping to the attack. He heard Ma Mé's shrieks outside: "Help! Help!—The king!— *Au secours!*" Immediately the angry roar of the crowd in the street, the slam of the gate flung open, shouts of military command. Hard pressed, Arnold fired his last cartridge and stooped to snatch up the king's automatic. Thrilled, he knew that it was indeed His Majesty Sisavang Vong that he was defending. That gaunt coolie whom the king had shot down with the bitter taunt:—"You would, brother?" was none other than Prince Hou Bac. The king lay writhing and helpless under Arnold's spread legs, but—just a few minutes more. . . .

Bang! The last cartridge spat from the automatic, followed by a sickening click. Arnold warded the dagger thrusts in desperation, with no more than a chunk of steel in either hand. He was gashed and bleeding, gasping out hoarsely the last reserves of his strength. They crouched on all sides as he whirled and struck—then a bristle of long steel bayonets drove in through the doorway and there were yells, shrieks, stabs, and whirl and stamp of muscular uniformed bodies; then a profound silence.

The room reeked with sulfurous smoke, with the smell of warm blood, with the hard breathing of soldiers. Gay butterflies of girls wept and gibbered where they were hiding in corners, under smashed furniture and behind dishevelled hangings of silk. An officer stood kotowing at Arnold, who was kneeling with the king in his arms.

"Get busy with your first-aid, man!" Arnold barked up at him. "Here!"

He indicated the red gash he had found in the king's side. The officer seemed afraid to so much as put a hand on His Majesty's sacred person—but Ma Mé was not. She came darting in at this juncture and snatched the first-aid packet from the officer's fist. With it she and Arnold got a compress glued on with surgical tape. She was an efficient little body, for all her frivolous beauty, and there was no doubt that she loved him, devotedly.

"There, beloved!" she cried. "He's all a man, *Monsieur!*—What a man! What dagger could kill Sisavang Vong! Thou too, who did fight by his side, art all a man!" Her eyes were gorgeous with admiration on Arnold.

THE king opened his eyes. A gleam of merriment came into them as he recognized Arnold. "So I'm a fool and an ass, *hein?*" he said.

"I was speaking, then, to Monsieur Tou Giaou, not to Laos, sire," Arnold reminded him.

"So you were coming to see me about that tin after all?"

"With an adventure or two thrown in!" Arnold laughed. "That dagger that disturbed you so at the *dak* looked interesting. So I decided to keep on wearing it and see what happened."

"*Ah bah!* But you are a man after my own heart, *Monsieur!*" His Majesty declared. "Most concessionaires would have thrown away the so-intriguing dagger and kept out of trouble. . . . I, too, should have kept out of trouble. . . ."

He roused up and put an arm around Ma Mé's slender waist. "*Bah!* Better be happy with you, my beauty, than cower in the palace because some assassins of my esteemed brother happen to be in Luang Prabang, eh? . . . Eh, what say you, *Monsieur?*"

He laughed jovially, did Sisavang Vong, in spite of his wound.

"After danger, revelry—for men of spirit! We shall not spoil their fun, shall we?"

To the officer: "Clean up this carrion. . . . And pass the word through the city that the king is not to be disturbed at his pleasures."

"Your Majesty, hadn't we better send for a competent surgeon?" Arnold suggested respectfully.

"*Bah!* It is nothing. Tomorrow we will attend to business, your tin, *Monsieur.* But tonight you are my guest. Strike up, girls! Bring the wine, Ma Mé. Come, *Monsieur,*—the world is not all *les affaires!*"

He reminded Arnold of the brave days of rapiers and gallants and kings who went about incognito, to risk their thrones at the call of beauty! Sisavang Vong was a man after his own heart. It was good to know there still existed such a king, in these humdrum days of mines and industrial concessions! The brown-eyed Laotian butterflies had done with bandaging Arnold's gashes. One of them held a glass of cordial to his lips. It was fragrant, aromatic, pungent—like Laos itself. Arnold raised it to the king:

"May you live for ever, Majesty!"

"*Pouff!*" said Sisavang Vong. "It's enough to be alive *now*—thanks to you, *Monsieur!*"

The Tiger's Cubs

By SEABURY QUINN

Carlos the Tiger and Black Hassan plunge into startling adventures, with plenty of thrilling fighting and abundant spilling of blood

1. How We Met the Lady in Scarlet

THE horns of the crescent moon were silver-sharp against the purple of the evening sky as I and good Black Hassan, my doughty squire, rode down the hills of Portugal. For hours we had journeyed on in silence while the heavy sun dragged down the sky and twilight covered its retreat, and each of us had been companioned by his thoughts, for I dreamt open-eyed of her whom I had rescued from the Hounds of God in the good city of Granada, and into whose white hands I had given my heart, while only Allah the Compassionate knew on what great schemes of blood and plunder Black Hassan's fancies dwelt. Now evening was come, and with it a

441

great emptiness in our bellies and no friendly inn whereat we might find respite from our travail.

"*Wallah*, Protector of the Fatherless," great Hassan's booming voice cut through the silence of my thought, "yonder stands a roof amid the trees; methinks we eat and drink and sleep upon a bed this night, after all."

I looked where his black finger pointed and saw a red-tiled roof rising from the bowered greenery of a grove, and at the sight the craving in my middle became so great I could scarce restrain myself from setting spurs into the sparsely padded sides of my poor, tired nag. "Go to," I told him; "let us hasten ere they eat what store of food they have, and turn us supperless away."

We shook our bridle reins, urging our spent horses to something like a trot, and headed for the distant house, but at the turning of the trail I drew my steed in sharply, for I was like to have ridden down a woman kneeling at the roadside.

Unmindful of our approach she knelt before a wayside shrine and lifted her hands in supplication to the graven image of a woman in a crimson cloak, and as she prayed tears coursed down her cheeks and stained the gold-hemmed collar of the scarlet mantle wherewith she was enshrouded. "*O Magdalena, santissima!*" she cried, striking her breast with the clenched knuckles of her hands; "you, too, have suffered; you, too, knew what it was to give yourself for love—have pity on me, and grant that by the mortification of my suffering I may find favor and have my sin forgiven. *O, Santa Maria Magdalena*——" Great sobs smothered her petition and again she smote her breast, then bowed her fair head into the wayside dust and gasped all chokingly, "*Me miserable!*"

"Now, by the fruit of Allah's tree,"

Black Hassan sware, "meseemeth this woman hath a case against this idol of the Infidels. Surely the painted thing hath done her wrong. Shall I dismount and hack it in pieces with my sword, Sustainer of the Famishing?"

"Let be," I ordered testily, for Hassan was ever more ready with tongue or sword than with helpful thought. "Do you hold the horses while I bespeak her, and if she suffers wrong mayhap we can correct it."

Therewith I slipped from out the saddle, right glad to exercise my legs, and approached the suppliant maiden. "Madonna," I made bold to say, "we could not help but hear your prayer, and whilst the holy saints in heaven are doubtless moved by your sweet fervor, methinks a mortal man or two can be of even greater aid. If it be so, here stand two to do your bidding, for we have great skill in swordcraft and not a little subtlety, and if any have affronted you——"

But further I said naught, for she lifted up her head and looked on me, and with her glance my heart beat faster in my bosom, for she was very fair. Her long and loosely braided hair was smooth and bright as hammered copper and her eyes glowed golden-brown like great twin topazes in the ivory of her face. At sight of her I was more determined than ever to proffer help, but:

"I thank you kindly, sir," she answered, "but I alone may bear my cross. Alas, there is no Simon of Cyrene to help me with it, and even if there were, at the end of the road there still stands Calvary."

"Nay, by Al—by St. Christopher," I returned. "Behold, I, too, have been beaten by an unkind fate, yet live to cast defiance in its teeth: Bereft of mine inheritance and cast a wanderer upon the world, I yet have lived, and lived **right** well, and put mine enemies beneath my feet at every turn; come, tell me of your troubles, and I will surely aid you if so be I can but find a plate of food to give me strength for the encounter."

She put her hand in mine and rose from off her knees, and on her face there came a smile so kind and sad that I was like to weep at sight of it. "Myself I can not help," she answered me, "but you I can and will give service to. Yonder in the valley is my house. If you and your good squire will come to it with me you shall have food and lodging for the night, and be right welcome, too."

The lady had no steed, and as the way was passing rough I sat her on the saddle of my weary horse and walked along beside her till we were come unto her house in the wooded vale between the sleeping hills.

It was a pleasant place. Built in the Moorish manner, the house stood bowered in a grove of olive trees, surrounded by a shady garden traced by sanded paths with here and there a deep, still pool where golden carp played roguishly amid the roots of star-shaped water lilies. Rose trees shook their blossoms out like banners in the still, cool evening air, and matched their perfume with the scent of trailing jessamine. Within the house was a wide patio where a marble fountain played and lemon and orange trees stood in tall green tubs of painted wood. Here we were made to sit upon a white stone bench while swarthy serving-men ran to fetch our horses to the stables and bring us refreshment.

The lady's amber eyes went round with wonder when we disdained the blood-red wine her servants brought, but methinks she had still greater cause for marvelling as she beheld what quantities of eggs and roasted fowl and fine white wheaten bread we stowed beneath our girdles and

what prodigious drafts of chocolate and sweetened lemon-water we used to wash the victuals down.

At length, when we were full to heaviness and rose to wash our hands, I thought me of our beasts and turned me toward the stable where we had seen them led. A sudden chilling of the air sent a tremor through me, and at my sigh Black Hassan took my tiger cloak from out the silken bag wherein he carried it and laid it on my shoulders.

"If so be you will excuse our absence," I began, bowing full courteously to the lady, "I shall see to the stabling of our mounts, for though they be but sorry nags——" but further I said naught, for at first sight of my striped coat the lady blenched ashen-pale and signed herself all fearfully with the cross while she shrank from me as though I bore the plague upon my garments.

"*Aie*, and art thou truly he?" she cried with frightful voice. "Art thou that monster who has come to bring foretaste of hell to earth? *Aie*, that it should be I who gave you food and shelter! O Holy, Blessed Trinity, grant that the viands he ate may turn to poison in his stomach and slay him in the midst of torment! May the meat turn bane within him and the sweet white sugar become gall to rise into his throat and choke his breath away!"

Now at this sudden change in her I was taken much aback, for I had entreated her most courteously, and she had welcomed me into her house, so:

"By the Prophet his beard, Madonna," I exclaimed, "what means this sudden change of front? Have you or yours suffered at my hands? Did not my faithful one and I bespeak you fairly in the road and offer to redress your wrongs? How comes it that you shrink from us and call a curse upon the food you gave us willingly a moment since?"

"The Prophet?" she asked doubtfully. "Sware ye by the Prophet?"

"Why not?" I answered, for, though I realized my slip of tongue had branded me no Christian, and therefore made me liable to seizure as a Moresco spy, I was not minded to make matters worse by some lame explanation.

"Then ye do not come from Italy?" she asked.

"Not we. Our homeland is not this, nor yet is it Spain, but in Italy we have never been, although we purpose going there some time."

What seemed a doubtful gleam of hope brightened in her face. "Are ye not called 'Charles of Torture'?" she asked half timidly.

Thereat I burst into a laugh, and Hassan joined his laugh to mine. "Nay, Mistress," I informed her, "the one of whom you speak, the Florentine torturer, we met with at an inn in Spain, but his boastings liked me not, and so I slew him, and because his black clothes and tiger's cloak had caught my eye, I took them for mine own, for a dead man hath small need of raiment, especially in the place to which that one is gone."

Now when she heard this the lady laughed till she could scarce support herself, and seeing my puzzlement she laughed the more. At last, when she somewhat regained her gravity, she bade us sit and listen to the reason for her mirth:

"Wot ye of the history of this unhappy land?" she asked, and when we shook our heads continued:

"Eight and twenty years ago Don Enrique the Cardinal died and Spanish Philip claimed the throne of Portugal. Our loyal nobles would have said him nay, but with a mighty force under Alva he crushed our army at Alcántara, and since that day my country bows beneath the Spanish yoke, even as the Jews of old were subject unto Babylon.

"Now I and all the house of Meneses are patriots and hate the Spaniards as only subject people know the hate of cruel masters, and all our peasantry are likewise loyal to the hope of independence. The Spanish governor of the district, Don Miguel de Cortez y Palma, has ruled with fire and iron these ten years gone, and whoso dares to dream of freedom is good as dead if his secret thoughts come unto the tyrant's ears.

"A year ago my father died and I was left to minister his estates. The Spaniard has wrung much wealth from his position, but he is one whose longing is but whetted by what he has; therefore he would wed me and hold my lands in fief. A dozen times I've said him nay, and with each refusal his will to take me—and my property—to wife has grown the stronger. A month gone he made pretense to seize some fifty of my faithful tenants upon a charge of treason and holds them captive in his castle.

"By every saint in the calendar he swears unless I give myself to him he'll put my people to death with torments such as no man ever saw before, and in furtherance of his threat he sent to Italy for its most famous torturer—e'en now the monster's coming has been bruited about, and, rather than allow those who trusted me to suffer at his fiendish hands I had resolved to give myself to Don Miguel in hateful wedlock. Indeed, good sir, I was praying to the blessed Magdalene for strength to carry out my resolution when you found me yonder in the hills.

"Of the Italian torturer's appearance I knew naught save that men say he is well-favored and struts like any cockerel and wears a cloak of tiger's skin in token of his ruthlessness and lack of pity. Behold, then, how I trembled when I beheld your tiger cloak and thought I had unwittingly given entertainment to the human fiend who comes to force me to this loathsome marriage!"

Now even as the lady voiced her plaint a plan took form within my thoughts, and from the sudden brightening of his eyes I knew Black Hassan's thought kept pace with mine.

"*Wallah*, Giver of Bread to the Hungry, is not this fruit ripe for our plucking?" he asked me with a laugh.

"Is it so written?" I answered.

"Yea, by the eggs of Allah's hen and by the crow of Allah's cock, it is graven in the books of destiny!" he returned. "As Allah and the Prophet (on whom be peace!) live, it is kismet. *Wah,* can a man escape his fate or a dog outrun his tail? Surely, the Lord of Paradise has put this Infidel within our fingers' grasp, Protector of the Helpless!"

"By the Prophet his beard, thou hast said it!" I agreed, and on it we clasped hands.

2. How We Fared Through the Forest

DARK lowered the night and full ghastlily keened the wind among the branches as Hassan and I picked our way toward the gloomy abode of Don Miguel de Cortez y Palma, Governor of the district and representative of his Most Catholic Majesty of Spain in seaward Portugal.

"By the tail of Allah's mare, Master, I think we ride through the country of the afrits," Hassan declared, gazing over his shoulder with more fear in his glance than I had ever seen him show before.

"Be silent, O monstrous uncouthness!" I ordered him, for though I was fain to deny it even to myself, the memories of stories learned in the harem of my child-hood came crowding round me like direful shapes seen in an evil dream, so that I should have been right glad of a sight of open country and clean, revealing moonlight. "Be silent, O offspring of a nearly noseless mother; wot ye not that afrits and djinn live only in the terror-tales of women to fright their little ones from naughtiness?"

"Not so," he answered sullenly. "It is most certain they exist. Are not the old books filled with stories of 'that people'? Do not they dwell in tombs and gloomy forests such as this, and seek to lure the wayfarer to his doom by wailing like a woman in distress, what time they build their fires to roast their victims' flesh? Yea, by the horns of Allah's goat, it is true. Have not I heard——"

"*Wallah*, ye have heard much, but what do ye know?" I asked, for his chatter of djinn and devils was working on my nerves till I was ready to see a monstrous form in every changing shadow cast by the wind-blown trees. "If ye can give me proof of what ye say, say on; if not, then in God's name hold thy peace, for——"

"*Ya Allah!* In His glorious name I take refuge from the darts of Satan!" the black one screamed. "Behold, my lord, the proof for which thou asked!"

And as if to lend full color to his fancy, the sudden wailing of a woman in extremity rang through the wood, and through the black-boled trees there flashed the flickering reflection of a newly lighted fire.

My jaded horse proved restive, as though he started at the sight of something invisible to me, and Hassan's ebon skin was gray with terror; natheless, for very shame, I dared not show my fright, but loosening my good sword in its sheath I headed toward the uproar in the woods.

"On, follow on, in God and the Prophet's name!" I cried to Hassan as I spurred between the trees.

The firelight showed a little clearing in the wood, a little patch of cultivated land where grapes grew scantily on a crudely made arbor and a little patch of corn was slowly ripening toward the harvest. Amid this scene of humble husbandry there stood the low-thatched hut which even now blazed crackling toward the sky. Upon the doorstep, clad in a scanty night-rail, lay a little, curly-headed child, not sleeping, but very still, while in the full glare of the flamelight a heavy-bodied man in ragged dress and peasant's rope-soled sandals fought like any fiend with five tall ruffians in cuirass and morion, matching his turning fork against their long swords with the valor of hopelessness and the strength of madness. At the limit of the clearing, where darkness and firelight strove for mastery, crouched a woman in torn and blood-stained night-shift, and in her long, unloosened hair another caitiff wound his fist whilst over her he flourished his spadroon.

"By Allah's choicest camel, the wine-swilling swine are at their work, it seems," Black Hassan muttered; then, enraged at what he saw, and shamed at the superstitious fears he had displayed, he raised his voice in battle-cry and charged upon the rapscallions duelling with the husbandman.

"*Din, ed-din!*" he shrieked, and at the fearful Moorish war-cry one of the rascals turned round to see from whence it came, and seeing, saw no more, for great Black Hassan's blade went through his throat as if it had been cheese, so that the fellow's blood and soul and foul Nazarene curses came pouring from his mouth at once.

Even as I reached him the villain who held the woman by the hair brandished his great brand aloft, then lowered it and passed it through her body from back to breast and shook her from the sword-blade as a cook may free his skewer of a roasted frog, then faced me with a mighty oath. "Now by the bones of San Antonio," he roared, "what have we here to offer let unto the servants of his Excellency, the Governor?" And saying thus he aimed a slash at my good horse's legs, cutting through flesh and splint and cannon and making the poor beast to rear screaming, then topple to the earth like any tree beneath the woodsmen's axes.

E'en as the wounded beast fell thrashing to the ground I kicked my feet from out the stirrups and leaped aside, for that trick had been taught me in my boyhood; so, instead of sprawling helpless underneath his sword-stroke, I faced the evil Spaniard foot to foot and matched my keen Damascus blade with his Toledo rapier.

"By Satan and his family of imps, I'll learn ye to meddle with the Governor's business!" he promised and drove his point straight at my face.

But I had been well tutored in the armory of Nicolaides, the Greek, who taught the fence without the use of masks; therefore I fought with head well back, and his steel fell short of its mark, throwing him nearly off his balance and leaving an opening for my simitar, which gashed him on the neck above the gorget and let the red blood trickle down his breastplate of damascened black iron.

"Ha, a swordsman, eh?" he muttered jeeringly as he regained his poise and locked his blade with mine. "Say, then, sir fencing-wright, canst rede me this trick?" and with sudden twisting motion he latched his point against my hilt and would have wrenched the weapon from my hand had my sword been fashioned like a Christian blade. But the old craftsman who hammered out my hilt had set no pas-d'âne beneath the quillons, wherefore his guile outreached itself, for not only did his blade fail to hold my hilt, but it slipped along the brass gerfalcon's head whereof the cross-guard was formed, caught beneath the curving nib of the bird's brazen beak and snapped short off as though it had been glass.

Now at this the bravo would have given ground before me, but I followed hard upon him, striking with my dagger and driving the curved blade through the scye of his cuirass so that it sank a hand's length into his armpit and let a spilth of blood from out his veins.

He cried me mercy, but sooner would I have shown favor to a scorpion than to such as he; therefore I bent above him as he gasped upon the ground and cut and hacked at his face with sword and dagger till no semblance of a human countenance was left. Thereafter I turned to see how Hassan and the husbandman fared in their encounter with the other murderers; but nought remained for me to do but watch them in their game, for even as I ran to aid them it was finished.

Black Hassan fought like forty fiends and the stout franklin gave good reckoning of himself, so that between them they had disposed of three adversaries; and as I joined them great Hassan let forth the soul from out the one remaining with a mighty sweep of his saber which hewed head and half a span of bearded neck from off the varlet's shoulders.

"*Wallah*, 'tis pleasant work, this killing of the Roumi," declared Hassan as he wiped his bloody blade upon the dead man's cloak. Then: "Tell me, good comrade of the fight," he asked the husbandman, "are there no more cross-kissing knaves to slay, or must we seek them elsewhere?"

"Have done, O son of a she-goat!" I ordered sternly. "We kill them not as Christians, but rather as vile murderers and warrers upon babes and women." Then of the doughty peasant I inquired:

"Who were these bloody dogs, and wherefore did they slay the child and woman yonder?"

"They serve El Tiburón—'the Shark' —as the Governor is called," he answered. "Mercilessly he piles oppression on oppression, because he seeks our lady, Donna Leonora da Meneses, in marriage, and well he knows the sufferings of her faithful peasants are torture to her gentle heart and will sooner break her spirit of resistance to his wooing than any other pressure he can bring to bear. This very moment in his cursed castle there are half a hundred of our comrades awaiting the coming of a torturer from Italy, that they may die in direct torment, and, to add to their unhappy number, the tyrant sends his bravos through the country heaping injury and insult on us and arresting all who dare resist them.

"A short time since, these wretches came and ordered food and wine. We gave them what we had, though it was little, for our crops are not yet fully ripe, and they straightway fell to cursing us, then turned their beasts to pasture in our corn, and when we dared protest they fell on me and beat me, whereon my little Pablo—my first-born son—the good God rest his baby soul!—raised up his little hands in my defense, and there, upon the very threshold of our home, before his mother's eyes and mine, they slew our little one.

"Then on my wife they would have worked their evil will, but she fled from them to the forest and I at last found courage to defy them. Why not? My son was dead, my wife was hunted like a beast to serve their lust; what more had I to live for, save the long chance of sending one of them to hell before they took my life?"

Now when he heard these things great Hassan's breast was like to burst with rage. "May Allah send an earthquake to devour them!" he swore, kicking at the corpses of our vanquished foes as though to provoke them to rise and fight again. "Meanwhile," he added, "let us fling their unclean carcasses in the fire, that they be utterly consumed," and as he spoke he seized the nearest body by the feet and dragged it toward the flaming house.

THE husbandman assisted us, and soon the soldiers' bodies were roasting in the blazing hut, even as their souls were being grilled in Satan's everlasting fires. My own sore-wounded horse we killed, that it might suffer no longer, then set about the digging of a grave for the mother and her child.

Clasped in each other's arms we laid them in the earth, and while the weeping franklin whispered Christian prayers above their tomb Black Hassan and I stood to repeat the *Fatahah* in chorus:

In the name of Allah, the Merciful, the Compassionate,
Lord of Angels, Djinn and Men,
Praise be to Allah, Lord of all Worlds,
Who giveth Mercy,
The King of the Day of Faith. . . .

When this was done we turned again to questioning the husbandman. "How art thou called?" I asked.

"Nuno Cabral," he answered.

"And what would you do now, O ruler of a desolated house?"

"What can I do?" he answered, sobbing. "All I hold dear is couched in earth before us, and though my heart burns for revenge like fire among the grass in autumn, it needs must burn itself in hopelessness, for how can I make war upon the Governor? Even

though I roused the countryside, we are foredoomed to failure; for can a peasant band cope with men-at-arms, or forks and scythe-blades prevail against muskets and halberds? Alas, no!"

"Would you attempt it, if there were one chance in many thousand of success?" I asked.

"Aye, by St. Andrew's wounds, though I knew my own death were ordained, if I could but pay the Spanish tyrant blood for blood, I'd go to death as a bridegroom hastens to his bride—but we waste time, we three; such things are hopeless."

"Nay, by the Prophet's beard, naught is hopeless while we remember the wisdom of God and the foolishness of man," I answered. "The first we know; the second we go now to prove. We be seafaring men, my Hassan and I; I doubt not we shall find a way to strike our gaff into the gills of this tyrant whom you call 'the Shark', though he lurk in twenty moated castles and have a thousand times ten thousand knaves like these to do his will. Do you go out amongst your neighbors and tell the tale of what was done to you and yours tonight. One week from now await us here with what force you can muster. The rest is in our hands—and in the hands of Allah."

And so we sent him on his way while we resumed our journey to the stronghold of the Governor, my own poor mount replaced by the best horse ridden by the troopers we had slain.

3. How We Met With El Tiburón

THE old *fortaleza* where Don Miguel made his lair was reared ere the beautifying influence of Araby had come to the Peninsula. Built on three levels, it was made up of donjon, courtyard and three sustaining towers. It rose upon a rocky headland which split a deep but narrow river in twain, thus being guarded by swift water on two of its three sides, while a fourteen-foot moat, spanned by a single narrow drawbridge, connected the two arms of the stream at its lower side. Thus its walls were safe against surprize attack, but had small virtue otherwise, since no palisades defended their base and no outworks protected the Y-fork of the stream. Loopholes in the masonry were the only source of light, for beauty and comfort alike had been sacrificed to surety in the days when its gray stones were laid.

Before the moat Black Hassan and I came to halt and sounded a challenge on the bugle-horn to let the warder know we waited.

"Who are you?" called the sentry at the gate, and:

"One from Italy, whose coming is waited at the castle of his Excellency Don Miguel de Cortez y Palma," I returned, "and one who lacks for food and sleep as well. Wilt open to me, or must I stand for ever here like a beggar at your gates?"

Now when I spake thus haughtily to them there was a great commotion in the castle. A dozen soldiers let the drawbridge down and hoisted the portecollys, while at the warder's hail the guard turned out and ranged themselves in order in the courtyard so that we rode between twin files of swarthy halberdiers in gleaming iron caps and breastplates who came to the salute as we passed by as though we had been royalty.

Within the chiefest chamber of the keep the Governor made us welcome, and I was bound to say that for a man of his repute his looks belied him hugely. As tall as I, and thin as almost fleshless bones could make him, he stood arrayed in satin finery of deathly black, the white lace at his throat and wrists no whiter than the smooth skin of his hands and bloodless, narrow face. A beard of black

M. C.—**5**

adorned his chin, and black mustachios were upon his lip. He spoke us fairly in his courtly Spanish way, and though I saw he was amazed by my forked beard and weather-colored cheeks, he made no comment, but bade us welcome cordially, nor would he suffer anything to be discussed till we had laid our baggage by and I had sat me down to table with Black Hassan at my back, his hungry eyes fixed greedily upon the leg of roasted mutton which a servant set before me.

"How now, Don Carlos, drink'st no wine?" he asked amazed when thrice the lackey offered me the cup and thrice I put it from me.

"Nay," answered I. "I am a sinful man, your Grace, and as a penance for my sins am under vow to touch no wine till thrice three candlemasses have gone by." Whereat the rat-faced chaplain who hovered ever at his Excellency's elbow grinned approvingly, and spoke to me in quick Italian, of which I understood less than a dozen words.

"Nay, good my father," I protested as he paused expectantly for answer, "my Spanish still does trip and stumble like a lame man, and I would practise it at all times, therefore let us speak Don Miguel's speech. 'Twere better so." But:

"Have no regard for me on that score," laughed his Excellency. "I spent ten summers at our embassy in Rome, and I should be right glad to practise my Italian while you stay, Don Carlos." And thereupon the priest smiled once again and whispered something in the Governor's ear behind his upraised hand.

Now great Black Hassan bent across my shoulder, as though to serve me more completely, and as his lips brushed past my ear he whispered, "By Allah's falcon's beak, my master, I think this shaveling Nazarene has long outlived his usefulness to us!" And soberly I nodded my assent, for to be suspected in the Governor's house while yet I sat at meat was adding to my peril more than I could like.

And so to turn their thoughts to other channels, I pushed my plate aside as though I had done eating, though Allah the Compassionate was witness that my shrunken belly still cried out for food, and turning to the Governor, "Where are these fifty rebel varlets you would have me flatter with my art?" I asked.

"San Salvador!" his Excellency cried, while he and the priest exchanged a startled glance. "Who told you they were fifty? For that matter, who told you there were any rebels here?" Their glances bore upon us, and there was little friendship in their eyes.

"Why, can a man come through this rebel-ridden place and fail to hear the gossip of the countryside?" I answered with some show of anger. "On every side it was: 'There goes the torturer from Italy —there rides the tormenter and his Indian slave; he goes to make our fifty comrades die a thousand deaths before death grants them glad release!' Sâo Francisco! Had it not been for the terror of my gentle calling and the dread inspired by your Excellency's name, our gullets had been slit a dozen times while we rode through the last score miles unto your castle!"

Somewhat assured by my reply, yet not entirely satisfied, his Excellency led the way down to the dungeons where the wretched captives lay.

A MISERABLE, louse-bitten crew it was that huddled in the windowless oubliettes sunk twenty feet below the castle moat. The hopeless flashing of their rolling eyes amid the filthy tangle of their rank-grown beards struck horror to my heart as I looked down into the well-like hole in which they were confined while a man-at-arms flashed a torch through the one small hole in the vaulted roof which was the prison's only opening, and the noisome fetor which rose from their unwashed bodies was like to have turned my belly inside out like an off-drawn glove when it assailed my nostrils.

"We lack the finish of your fine Italian hand in Portugal," his Excellency laughed, and for the first time I saw resemblance in his narrow face to Christian pictures of the devil, "but we have done the best we could by them. For upward of two months they've lingered there, and only two of them have died. You'll find rare sport practising your skill on them, Don Carlos."

I teased the point of my mustachios between my thumb and finger as I affected to be deep in thought. "How are they fed?" I asked.

"Once every other day they're given salted fish," he answered, "and on the days between we lower a skin of water to them—three gallons for the pack. 'Tis sport to hear them at each other's throats for just a single extra sip of liquid, and when occasionally we give them salted water—by Satan's horns, the jest is infinitely rare!"

I smiled a slow and patient smile as one who hears a child repeat an ancient tale. "Torture is like good wine, to be tasted delicately, not gulped down at a single draft," I told him. "Your sense of pleasantry is most keen, but like to prove embarrassing to me; for men denied strong food and air for any length of time are like to die before we've fairly started our festivities—it is the strongest bull which holds the dogs at bay the longest and furnishes greatest sport for those who watch. Therefore I would most earnestly request that you withdraw them from the dungeons and hold them safely in a strong room in the keep where light and air are plentiful, and have them richly fed on meat and bread and not less than a pint of red wine thrice a day. Meantime I'll watch their health most carefully, and when they are restored sufficiently I shall be ready to officiate. San Raphael, 'twere insult to my art to give me such poor crow-bait to work on! They'd die before I'd stripped a foot of skin from off their shrunken carcasses, and I have promised me a pair of boots and gloves to match, and covers for a score or more of sacred books, all made from these debased insurgents' hides!"

Now when I first began to speak the Governor was wroth, for feeding meat and wine to rebels liked him not, and that they be allowed to see the sun again was little less than treason in his ears; but when he heard I purposed flaying them alive as fishermen may skin an eel, his pale face brightened and he gave orders that my bidding be carried out forthwith.

But it was otherwise with Frey Tomás, his silent-footed chaplain. The diet of salt fish with water every other day had been that Christian gentleman's idea, and that I overruled him thus in nowise pleased him. He looked at me with no friendly glance as we returned to the main hall, and when we bid his Excellency good-night and mounted to our chamber there was small charity in the blessing he bestowed on us.

Midnight had sounded on the tower gong when the chaplain came soft-stepping to our chamber door and tapped upon the panels. *"Benedicite,* fair sons," he greeted as we arose and louted low before him, but there was only venom in his eyes, for all the sweetness of his words.

Then he launched forth a flood of Italian, and when I answered him in Spanish he smiled more sourly than ever.

"I was in Florence two years back," he told me in Castilian, speaking slowly, as to a foreigner to whose ears the words were strange, "and there I saw you work judgment on one condemned for treason. Your work was deft, and greatly I admired it. Surely, you have not forgot we dined together at Messer Giovanni Stitta's table?" He stopped and gave me a look half questioning, half playful, and when I muttered an assent he smiled still wider, saying: "And at that time, good Messer Carlos, I noted that *your eyes were brown,* and you seemed older than at present, and that great scar was nowhere on your face. Also, you spoke to me in Spanish with the accent of Italy, while now, unless I do mistake much, you have a trace of Moorish bur upon your tongue. How comes it? Has the sunlight bleached your brown eyes blue, by any chance, or——"

"A thought comes to me, holy father," great Hassan interrupted, moving toward the friar with raised hands joined piously before his breast as though in great humility.

"Indeed, and what is that, sirrah?" the chaplain answered haughtily, for, like most of his breed, he assumed meekness before quality but treated those of meaner station with overbearing pride.

"By Allah's turban, it is that you have lived too long!" the black one answered with a roaring laugh and darted forth his great black hands like twin black snakes, seizing the friar's thin throat between his crushing fingers and snapping his neckbone as though it had been but a sundried reed.

"Wah, Master of my Life," he chuckled as he laid the dead man's body on the floor, " 'twas not for nothing that they named me 'Strangler,' I ween. And it is well. A knife-thrust might have missed the mark or failed to stop the clacking of his endless tongue, and we had

been undone if he had given but a single dying scream. Besides, the blood would have been hard for us to hide, and——"

"O great and uncouth cockroach, O mentally defective descendant of a hundred crazy monkeys," I scolded him, "dost prate of the embarrassment of concealing blood while here we have the carcass of a murdered man to hide?"

"Why, as for that," he laughed, "it is a matter quickly mended. Let us thrust him through the loophole yonder. The stream flows swift below, and will bear him far away ere morning comes. Meantime, let us strip him of his raiment—it may come handy to our purpose at some other time."

We stripped the dead man's habit from him and forced his thin form through the narrow loophole, but so strait was the opening that we had much ado to pass him through, and not till we had sweated half an hour did he slip from our hands and splash into the rushing stream some twenty yards beneath us.

Next morning all was stir and bustle in the castle. The good Frey Tomás had been lost, and nowhere could a trace of him be found. They searched from dungeon to turret-top, and then sent parties out into the woods, but these returned anon with no news of their quest. Only a man-at-arms declared he had espied the chaplain entering the castle chapel before the hour of twelve, and from that time his trail led nowhere.

4. How We Left El Tiburón

Now for the next week time passed lazily within the fortress. At my command Hassan played the dummy and returned a silly grin and wagging head to all they said to him, so that the men-at-arms soon came to think him but a harmless zany and spoke without restraint

before him. In this wise we picked up much information we should otherwise not have had, for I was soon to learn the seed of suspicion planted in his Excellency's breast by the vanished chaplain was bearing fruit, and though he treated me most courteously the Governor told me nothing that I wished to learn, and everywhere I went a full-armed soldier dogged my steps.

The prisoners in the keep fared well and soon began to show such signs of fast-returning health that I knew I could not long put off action, for the Governor's mistrust grew apace, and more than once he hinted that he would be glad to have me finish torturing the prisoners and be upon my way.

Our observations showed us that the castle mustered some six score men-at-arms and half as many more retainers of lesser station. The armory was richly stocked with gear and weapons, and a magazine of powder held ample ammunition for the barbettes on the walls. For half the soldiers there were mounts of fair breeding, and more than enough pieces to furnish forth a company of musketeers. In a wooden barn built in the courtyard was stored a goodly stock of hay, and grain sufficient to make bread for all through an entire season lay in the storehouse. Against a well-armed force of soldiers with suitable artillery the castle would have stood but little chance, but it was safe as an eagle in his eyrie against any force the peasants could enlist.

For four succeeding days and nights I planned and planned, but nowhere could I find a way to throw the castle open to Nuno Cabral's foresters, whom I planned to lead in an attack. But meanwhile Hassan was not idle.

Upon the second day of our sojourn I noticed furtive glances cast in my direction as I passed through the courtyard, and more than once a soldier crossed himself as I went by, or thrust his first and little finger toward me in token of defense against the evil eye. The next day the restlessness was more pronounced, and on the fourth the Governor called me to his cabinet and asked me bluntly when I thought the prisoners would be ripe for torture, "For," he said, "my men like not your presence, and there are ugly rumors of a ghost that walks by night, and whether they be true or not I do not know, but six of my best soldiers, including the captain of the guard, have deserted since you came, and the temper of the garrison grows short."

That night I lay upon my bed, thinking over what his Excellency had said, when the soft and swishing rustling of one walking in the dark aroused me. "Who's there?" I challenged, rising from my couch and laying hold upon my sword, and meantime my heart beat quick within me, for though I barred the door when I lay down, the unseen person was within the room and less than an arm's length from me.

"Another of the Infidels has gone to reap his everlasting torment, Master," Black Hassan answered and laughed like any schoolboy who plays a prank successfully behind his teacher's back.

"What mean ye?" answered I as I laid down my sword and sighed in some relief to know the visitant was not a secret assassin.

"Why, only this—behold," he made reply, and striking steel to flint and flint to tinder, set the candle going and showed himself arrayed in the dead friar's robes, the cowl pulled upward to conceal his face. "Each night, when midnight sounds from yonder tower, I 'tire me in these clothes and go all silently throughout the castle. If any sees me he gives me

room, for I am taken for a ghost. And when I find a sentry drowsing on the walls——" He paused and laughed again, and thrust his great black fingers forward, making dumb show of twisting a man's neck and throwing his body from the battlements. "The score was six this morning," he continued, "but since the sun went down I've 'counted for a seventh. If we but stay here long enough, there will be none to say us nay when we decide to leave."

But though the garrison dwindled beneath the black one's hands, and every soldier in the place had come to start and cross himself at any passing shadow, I knew our time drew short, and we must make our plans with Nuno Cabral if we would take the castle. Therefore next morning I craved his Excellency's pardon for making the request, but told him I would fain ride into the forest to perfect my plans for torturing the prisoners, and, to avert suspicion that I meant to run away, I asked a guard to go with us and shield us from the peasants' wrath.

Accordingly four stalwart ruffians were told off to guard us, their heads being forfeit if we came not again by sunset, and off we set into the woods.

WHEN we came near the spot where Nuno Cabral would meet us, I signaled a halt and slipped down from my horse. "Your master's plans for death and torture like me not," I told the captain of the troop. " 'Twould be more knightly if he hanged the rebels from the castle walls, or put them to the sword, and if you can but help me to convince him to this view——"

"How now, Sir Torturer," he laughed, "hast turned white-livered at the thought of torment? By San Antonio his bones, I knew thee for a craven when first I laid my eyes on thee. Now, comrades, hear what the Governor's tormenter proposes —that we should hang the rebels! And after he has had us feed them like honored guests! What say ye, shall we take him to the castle and say, 'Here is thy torturer from Italy, your Grace, turned womanish and pleading for the rebels' comfort'?"

With that he struck me full upon the face with his gauntlet and dared me take the challenge.

I answered quicker than he thought, for scarcely had he handed me the blow when I had fleshed my dagger in his breast.

Then up and at the three remaining knaves we sprang, and metal rang on metal and curses mixed with curse as we fought back and forth across the clearing. The memory of insults borne in silence was like salt in a raw wound to Hassan, and he laid round him with his saber till two tall Spaniards fell beneath his blade and kicked their lives away upon the forest grass, and of the one remaining I made little work; for though he fought right fiercely, his swordsmanship was awkward, and his thrusts went wildly past me while mine were aimed so truly that at my second pass I spitted him upon my blade and laid him low. Thereafter we hid their bodies in the brush, then sat and waited Nuno Cabral's coming.

The day had gone and night was come ere Nuno Cabral came, but with him came a hundred hearty varlets, and in the woods beyond, he said, were twice a hundred more, all ready for the fight.

I praised him for his work and called his fellows round while I revealed the scheme I'd hatched for storming Don Miguel's stronghold. When all was understood we left them to instruct the others and rode again unto the castle, striking spurs to our mounts and covering the last half-mile at greatest speed and

clamoring at the drawbridge as though ten thousand fiends pursued us.

Within the castle courtyard we spun a yarn of having been beset by armed men of the forest who slew our guard and would have taken us alive, but that a brazen-haired young woman who served as their commander had been thrown from her horse and so drawn interest from us long enough for us to flee.

"A woman, quotha?" his Excellency cried. "What seemed she like?—how looked she?"

And thereon I described the Lady Leonora as closely as I could and even swore I heard her name called by the peasants as we struggled.

"Now by my soul's salvation, good Don Carlos, this news ye bring is more than compensation for my soldiers' loss!" he sware. "For upward of a year I've wooed this haughty slut of a da Meneses and she has laughed my suit to scorn. Me, Miguel de Cortez y Palma, grandee of Spain, she dared to flout. Now, by the tombstone of San Pedro, I'll not go seeking her as suppliant wooer, but as an officer of her king and mine with plenary authority to arrest and try her for high treason! *Por Dios,* we'll see whose laugh is last this time, Madonna Leonora! Thy goods and lands are forfeit to the Crown —which means his Majesty's Governor— and all are mine without the need for marriage! This very night I'll send my men to take her, Don Carlos, and may I burn in hell like any heretic if she is not given into your skilled hands for torment before we are a sennight older."

And so within the hour a hundred men-at-arms rode forth to take the Donna Leonora.

Low twelve was sounding solemnly upon the castle gong the midnight following when from the moat there rose the sound of horsemen riding furiously, and into view there came the remnant of Don Miguel's troopers. I had foreseen the action which the Governor would take, and at my command half Nuno Cabral's followers had waited them where the forest trail was dark and narrow, and as they galloped by had fallen on them with fork and scythe-blade pike and set on them so hotly that half their number went down beneath the first assault, and those remaining, taken by surprise and unable to form for a charge, had been mowed down until a tithe or less of those who rode away came seeking shelter at the castle gate once more.

The soldiers in the guard room ran to let the drawbridge down, and Don Miguel himself stalked into the courtyard to see what the commotion was about, and as they sallied forth from out the keep we fell upon the warden of the cells and struck him down, then snatched away his keys and barred the inner door against those in the court. A moment later we had loosed the prisoners, and while Black Hassan led them to the armory at a run I lighted me a torch of pitch-soaked tow and flung it through a loophole into the wooden hut wherein the horses' hay was stored, and up there shot against the midnight sky a great red flame which shone forth ruddily and drenched the castle in a blaze of light.

And now there sounded cries and curses of alarm, for those we had locked out were largely without weapons, save their sidearms, and those who rushed across the bridge were already half benumbed with fright and weakness from their flight, and when the prisoners, bearing each a musketoon, came flocking to the loopholes and fired their pieces pointblank into the crowded mass of men within the courtyard the place became a shambles.

"Treachery!" screamed Don Miguel, rallying his men as best he could and snatching forth his sword. "Out, out, and face them in the open. Form ranks! A horse—give me a horse that I may ride before ye in the battle!"

And sooth to say, although he was a monster of inhuman cruelty, the man they called El Tiburón was brave as that sea-monster whose dread name he bore, and though he was beset and taken by surprise his courage did not falter for a moment.

But now from out the wood there came the cries of running men, and upward of a hundred peasants charged in ragged ranks. And as they burst against the armored horsemen as waves crash on a rocky headland, there came another yell from up the stream, and Nuno Cabral and his men came floating down the river on wide, stout rafts of timber, and beached their craft upon the shore, then leaned their scaling-ladders to the walls and swarmed above the parapets. For this had been my strategy, that half the band pursue the troopers and harry them about the gate while we released the prisoners within and Nuno Cabral and the others of his band float down the river and assault the castle walls while those from out the woods held the garrison in play about the drawbridge.

And well the plan succeeded, for when Cabral came swarming over the walls with twice a hundred blood-mad men behind him, the Spaniards' valor melted like the morning dew before the rising sun, and they would fain have cast aside their arms and yielded them, but there was no one to receive surrender, for not as foeman unto foe, but as wronged men who must wash out the memory of their wrongs in their oppressors' blood the frenzied peasants came. And so there was no quarter asked or given.

Maugre their discipline and armor the soldiers were sadly disadvantaged, for the yokels far outnumbered them and bore them down by very weight of bulk, and as most of them had nothing but their swords — their firearms and halberds being locked within the guard room—the peasants' eight-foot pikes and pitchforks outreached them and made the issue of the fight but a matter of time.

Natheless, El Tiburón, the Governor, fought right manfully, and I could have found it in my heart to plead for him had not the memory of Nuno Cabral's murdered babe and wife stood before my eyes and the echo of his threats against the Donna Leonora warned me that her only safety lay in his death.

At last a long pike smashed down upon his sword and snapped the weapon short within his grasp, and like a messenger of Allah's righteous judgment the thick-set Nuno Cabral bore down on him, and clipped him in his mighty arms. Swearing and fighting like a wildcat in the trapper's snare, the Governor was borne across the drawbridge and dragged through the courtyard. For a moment he wrestled loose from his captor and turned defiantly to sell his life as dearly as might be, though a slender poniard was his only weapon, but half a dozen ready hands laid hold on him, and as he shrieked a final malediction, hurled him writhing into the fiery ruin of the blazing hay-barn.

Thus we took leave of Don Miguel de Cortez y Palma, surnamed El Tiburón, his Catholic Majesty's representative in seaward Portugal, and thus El Tiburón took leave of earth.

As with the leader, so was it with the men. The cries of battle lulled and gave way to moanings of the wounded, and these in turn were drowned out by the savage shout of victory the husbandmen set up when the last Spaniard ceased to breathe.

So was the plan Black Hassan and I had formed in the hacienda of Donna Leonora concluded, and thus our vow to help her was redeemed, albeit we were yet to do her one more service.

5. How the Tiger's Cubs Were Whelped

Now for a month or more we busied ourselves mightily within the castle. All those who needed grain were welcome to come to the storehouse and help themselves, and such of those who had suffered injury in body or estate through the Governor's tyranny were repaid as far as money could repair their hurts, for in the castle strongroom we found a mighty hoard of gold wrung from the suffering peasantry, and this we disbursed freely to the needy of the district.

Meantime, on talking with the peasants, we found the number widowed and bereft of family by the slaughtered soldiers was greater than threescore, and these, all ties to homeland broken, were all for seeking service in the wars or forming a guerrilla band to harry the king's officers; but when I heard this talk a further thought came to me.

"You fight like gallant men," I told them, "but you lack leadership and training. If you fare forth as bandits the end must be the same, whether you succeed for one month or a score. In time gone past the Governor's soldiers have put ye to rout; and the greater your success as bandits, the greater force of trained men will be sent against you, and four feet of rope and the burial of an ass is all life holds in promise.

"Join me, then; become my men, and I will lead ye where Spanish blood may yet be spilled in warfare and where rich spoil awaits the victory as well." And when they pressed me for an explanation of this promise, I broached my plan.

We were to form a band of mercenary soldiers, equipped and drilled to compete with the best, and sell our swords to whoso bid the highest, provided that his principles and ours agreed. And so we struck a bargain.

I was to be supremest in command, and no appeal lay from my orders. Black Hassan was my chief of staff and personal lieutenant, while Nuno Cabral was made second in command.

Bound by a solemn oath, six and fifty of the stoutest fellows enlisted under me, and straightway we began their training. Within the castle armory was a goodly store of weapons, and of the best of these we made our choice. Each fourth man—fourteen in all—was furnished with a finely wrought and tempered halberd which served at will as pike or poleax, and in addition he wore slung between his shoulders in the Scottish fashion a four-foot double-handed sword with which he could do yeoman service if his halberd broke or was discarded in the mêlée. A shortsword and a dirk also were strapped upon his belt, and thus armed cap-a-pie these fourteen took command each of a squad of four.

The soldiers of the file I furnished with good muskets, each having one of the new French weapons called bayonets to fit within its muzzle, and to fit them better for close conflict I added a two-foot cutlas and a dirk to every man's equipment, and to top it off a sixteen-inch-helved ax to carry in his girdle. From the stores of gear we took a stock of high boots, leathern breeches and stout buff jerkins to furnish every man two changes of apparel, and for each one a cuirass and gorget of black polished iron. In lieu of morions, which topple off when most their wearers need them,

we took supply of close-fitting Moorish steel caps which we found stored away, and on each helmet-front and on the breastplate of each man an artificer we found within our ranks cut the design of a tiger's head with wicked ears laid back and glaring eyes and open, snarling mouth.

For myself I chose a suit of plain black stuff and tall, soft-leather boots to match and a suit of fine black body-armor and a dead-black wide-brimmed hat with sable plume, and over this, when on parade, I draped my cloak of tigerskin lined with red satin.

Black Hassan, to his infinite delight, came on a suit of Arabic chain-mail of finest workmanship, and when he donned this and had wound a turban of black silk about his pointed steel cap, he seemed the very devil's self, for face and hands and armor all were black as night, and only flashing teeth and eyes showed any contrast.

Thus fitted forth we entered on our army's training, and both I and Hassan worked ourselves like slaves to teach the unschooled countrymen the soldier's craft. Time after time we feared our arms would drop from out their sockets ere we could beat into their stupid heads the elements of swordsmanship, and many were the thumping wallops I received while struggling with the petty officers to teach them proper handling of their halberds.

With musketry we fared much better, for the men seemed naturally to take to marksmanship, and soon they proved ability to strike a target contrived of clothing stuffed with straw in likeness of a man and hung loosely in the wind from a tree bough a hundred paces distant at almost every shot.

To speed our fire I devised a cartridge in the form of a small sack which was suspended by a cord from holes pierced in the men's baldrics. When the order came to load, the musketeer jerked the cartridge loose with a smart tug, thereby tearing off the end made fast unto his baldric, and thus possessing himself of a load all ready to be rammed down the muzzle of his piece without having to stop to bite the cartridge-end. By use of this contrivance we were enabled to fire as many as a half-dozen volleys in a single minute.

When all was done and I at last was satisfied with the training of my men, we set a clever needlewoman to the task of broidering us a flag, and proudly flung out to the breeze our standard of the tiger-head device. Then, with my tiger-cloak upon my back and with the tiger banner flying o'er me, I swung into my saddle and with Black Hassan at my side reviewed my little army as it filed by. 'Twas good to note the soldierly appearance of the men, to see the ordered rows of slanting musket barrels and the gleaming halberds lowered in salute and know that this band of well-trained fighters was a thing that I had shapen with my own two hands. When I raised high my sword to answer to their hail I felt myself a very king, albeit my kingdom was a small one.

Then to that castle of unhappy memories we laid the torch, and as its red flames mounted in the sky we sounded a farewell upon the trumpet and turned our backs on it for ever.

I LAID a line of march toward Donna Leonora's house, for I desired to tell her how our pledge of help had been redeemed, and everywhere we went the country folk flocked to see us pass and hailed us as deliverers.

Upon the third day of our march one came to us in mighty haste and told us of banditti which swept the countryside and ate the people's substance. Their leader, I was told, was one who had forsworn both Spanish king and Portuguese allegiance, and swore he was a Spaniard when he plundered Portuguese and Portuguese when he fell in with Spaniards. Even then, the messenger panted, he did besiege a company of travelers within an inn three miles or so away, and swore he'd have their life-blood for that they resisted him.

Now when they heard these things my men were hot for battle, and so I ordered an advance and soon we came in sight of the beleaguered inn and heard the popping of the fighters' guns and saw the flashing of their weapons.

The travelers were handling themselves right manfully, though from the way in which their firing lagged I knew their ammunition must be running low and it would be but a little while before the circling robbers set on them and took their stronghold by assault.

Like ordered oars thrust out from any galley's sides my musketeers went through the exercise when I shouted, "Load!" and swiftly they rammed home their cartridges in the barrels of their guns.

"At trial!"

Their heavy muskets swinging in right hands, gun-rests all ready at the left, with matches smoking ready at their belts, my good men stood while I rode on the right and Nuno Cabral flanked the left to order them.

We formed into a crescent-shape, and at my word hurried down the field until we halted fifty yards or so from the dooryard of the inn; then:

"Take aim!" I called, and every man set up his musket-fork and rested his piece therein.

"Blow matches!" And the red fire glowed upon each fuse as my good followers breathed upon their cords.

"Give fire!" And from the ordered rank there burst a thunder-cloud and flames, and through the air there roared the crashing volley, while from the musket mouths there sped a rain of four-ounce bullets, and each ball went so truly to its mark that two-and-forty robber knaves fell prostrate in the dust.

Then: "Halberds! — Bayonets! — Charge!" I shouted, and down upon the startled foe we swept like wild bulls in stampede.

"*Din, din; ed-din!*" Black Hassan roared as round his head he whirled a spiked mace and crushed a caitiff's skull with every swing; but, "*Carlos! Carlos el Tigre*—Carlos the Tiger!" cried the rest, smiting with sword and halberd and reeking bayonet wherever they could find a foe to stand and fight.

All taken by surprise, fully half their number slain by our first volley, the enemy gave ground before our onslaught, and scarce was there a one of them who did not fight with many a backward glance, seeking an avenue of escape while yet he swung his sword or clubbed his musketoon.

I found myself opposed to a great ruffian in cloak of tattered scarlet whom I took to be the leader of the robbers, and though he measured almost twice my bulk and swung a broadsword which would have furnished metal for a pair of blades like mine, he scarce had brought his heavy-footed horse into position ere I saw I need but withstand his blows a little while in order to best him in the fight. He aimed a mighty thrust at me, and I did not try to dodge it, but let his point strike full against my black-steel body-armor, and as his blade bent beneath the impact I brought my simitar down upon his arm and clave it nigh in twain so that he dropped his brand and would have turned to fly had not a pair of my

stout fellows seized him and dragged him from his mount.

The fighting was now done. All but a dozen of the enemy had fled, and those remaining were our prisoners. The giant varlet I had bested and his principal lieutenant were ours, and his other fellow-leader would never more slit a throat or cut a purse, for great Black Hassan had disposed of him and mashed his head as soft as any pudding with a single down-stroke of his mace.

Forth from the inn the beset travelers came to make their charge against our captives. They were a band of twenty men-at-arms, not soft-fleshed swaggerers like the Governor's troops, but lean, flat-bellied veterans of the wars, and at their head there strode a tall, spare man in somber black attire without one single spot of color on his person. At his side there hung a long straight sword of finest temper, but with a carved steel hilt as somber as his clothes.

As he removed his hat and greeted me full courteously I saw his head was shaved upon the crown, and recognized him for a priest.

"How now, good my father," quoth I, "it gives me greatest pleasure to have serviced you, but I would ask, if ask I may, how comes it that you travel in this guise and head a troop of men-at-arms."

He smiled a cold, austere smile and answered in his turn, "Whom have I the great honor of addressing? Perchance ye're from the household of his Excellency the Governor?"

"Aye, we come from that direction," I replied, "but service with his Excellency I can not rightly claim, since he and I were scarcely friends, and——"

"Know ye of one called Frey Tomás, who resides with the Governor?" he asked quickly.

"Why, now, methinks I've seen him,"

I responded. "A member of the order of St. Dominic, he is, I think? Let's see—he was a spare man of a most unpleasant habit, and——"

"He'll wear a habit even less pleasant when I have come upon him," the priest again broke in. "I hold the Bishop's warrant for his apprehension, and an order of the greater excommunication against the one who harbors him or dares withstand the execution of my warrant. The fellow is a rogue, a cheat—an unfrocked priest named Caraccioli who masquerades as a Dominican, and for purposes which bode no good resides within the Governor's castle. We were content to let him pose as though he still possessed his holy orders, but the rascal has grown bold through overmuch of favor and it is said that much of the oppression beneath which the people groan is formulated by him, for he has great influence with Don Miguel; and none of it is good. I go to hail him before a court spiritual, and none may say me nay, for though I have but a small force, behind me stands a power greater than the might of Spain or——"

"Marry, good Father, it is a power you'll not need to use," I broke in with a laugh, "for know you that this Frey Tomás, or Caraccioli, has been food for worms this month or more, and I was present at his death."

"How, now, didst see him die?"

"I did, in very truth; and right unwillingly he quit the earth, albeit he did it suddenly."

A smile of understanding crossed the warrant officer's face. "I think we need not ask more questions," stated he. Then, with the inconsistency of priests: "And the Governor, what of him?"

"Gone, alas," I answered mournfully. "Gone to a better world—I hope."

"Your hope bespeaks your charity—or optimism," he answered with a laugh. "If all I've heard about His Excellency be true, whatever world he's gone to will be small improvement on the one he quit. Howbeit, I am not concerned with him. My duty is to verify your report, and if I find this Caraccioli really dead, why, then, my work is done."

"Why not take back his habit for a proof of what you tell?" I asked, and from the bag wherein we stored our gear I took the false priest's vestments and gave them to him.

Now when this business had been done, we held a court-martial and heard the evidence against our prisoners. They offered no defense, but stood by sullenly while the priest and his entourage accused them, and at the end I gave my judgment that they should die forthwith.

Then, when the prosecutor had turned confessor and heard the doomed men's prayers and granted absolution, we tossed some lengths of rope across a beam and hanged them by their necks. This done, we wished the priest a safe and happy journey and once again resumed our march.

6. How I Waged Battle for the Donna Leonora

THE day succeeding our encounter with the bandits, as we marched through the wood I heard a plaintive wailing from a roadside thicket, and when I slipped from out my saddle and made search I saw upon the sward a little lad, not more than thirteen summers old, who wept as though his heart were split in twain.

"Now tell me, boy," I asked, "wherefore weep you thus? Hast been deserted by thy fellows, or has a bird's nest which ye fain would rifle been visited before ye came there?"

"Nay, good my master, 'tis nothing

small," he answered, the while his childish shoulders shook with renewed sobbing. "I weep that I am all alone, with none to call me kin, and that I too am soon to die most horribly in torment."

"Who says so?" I demanded, and even as I spoke the little chit threw back his fair young head like any wild thing harried by the dogs, and bade me listen.

"Canst hear them, now, my lord?" he asked. "They come, they come; O, master, save me; do but make them spare my life, and I will be thy docile slave for ever!"

"What foolish talk is this?" I asked, but even as I spoke the baying of a hound belled through the woods, and crashing through the undergrowth I did espy a dozen burly louts in leathern garments, a brace of dogs upon a leash held by a hangman-faced varlet at their head.

"Ha, hast seized him, friend?" the fellow called. "Good. By St. Andrew's bones, thou art a noble fellow and I'll see thou art rewarded fittingly!"

"What say ye, sirrah?" I answered haughtily, whereat he noted for the first time my fine raiment, and took a more respectful tone.

" 'Tis the witch-woman's brat, Luiz Castro, which ye hold, good sir," he answered me, "and we are come to take him. 'Twas but a pair of days ago his dam was executed for the working of a witch's spells, and this young imp of Satan is her brat, and well she schooled him in her infamy, for not only does he say she was no witch; he shouted out in public that her sentence was unjust, and that we did work a grievous wrong when we did execute her. So give the brat to us, good sir, for he is also under sentence and would have suffered death ere now had not he schemed by Satan's help to slip from out the prison yesternight and fly through these accursed woods. He

would have got away, methinks, had we not traced him with the hounds."

"He lies, good master!" cried the little lad, wringing his pale, thin hands together, but regarding the stern huntsman with burning, angry eyes. "By all the holy saints in heaven, he lies in his throat! My mother was no witch, nor did she ever work a wrong to any one. 'Twas Dom Diniz da Cunhz who swore away her life because she would have none of him — by God's own throne I swear it! We were tenants on his land, and when he saw my pretty mother he desired her and caused my father to be sent afar into the woods where he was gored to death by a wild boar; then when my mother said him nay, he took her to his castle by main force, and she defended her honor with her bodkin till he was wounded in the face, and so he let her go, but vowed he would have vengeance. So he preferred charges of witchcraft against her to the Holy Office, and though they tortured her by fire and water, she did maintain her innocence till they declared they'd send for me, and torment me in her sight unless she did confess. Then she gave in and agreed she was a witch most vile, the paramour of Satan, and when they heard her make admission to the charge they turned her over to the civil arm, and she was sentenced to be worried at a stake by dogs, then burned to ashes.

"These things she told me her last night on earth, for a kindly jailer let me visit her in prison for one little hour, and when I heard how they had made her utter falsehood of herself, I would have stood forth and denounced it, but that she begged me hold my peace, for she was sorely crippled by the torture-engines and could not flee, and Dom Diniz would surely not forego his vengeance; but I might run away, she said, and live to be the man she'd hoped to see me grow to. Natheless, I could not leave her thus, and as they bore her to the stake—for she could not walk upon her poor, burned feet—I ran to her, and then they did lay hold on me and make me watch her death. Thereafter, when I cried out against them, they said I, too, was servant of the Devil, and clapped me into prison, but yesternight I slipped between the bars and fled. O, good my master, do not let them take me back to torture and to death!"

Now when I heard this sorry tale I was exceeding wroth and turned upon the leader of the party with hot anger. "Get gone from out my sight, ye knave," I bade, "or by the Prophet's beard, I'll give ye cause for grief!"

And when he heard me speak thus he laughed right heartily and summoned on his rogues to overawe me, saying: "By Judas' body, methinks there will be two to face the dogs instead of one, for know ye, good Sir Coxcomb, 'tis death to hinder me in the pursuit of my duties. I be the Dom's chief justicer, and——"

"And know ye it is death to speak with disrespect to Carlos who is surnamed the Tiger," I cried back at him, and blew upon my silver whistle, whereat Black Hassan and Nuno Cabral and all my fellows came flocking through the woods.

"Tie me yonder jackanapes," I ordered, "and take from off their feet their shoon; then let them taste the ramrod on their naked soles until they learn what it portends to offer insult to any of our band."

Then, nothing loth to have a bit of sport, my men performed my bidding, nor did they leave off beating of the captives' feet till one and all had swooned away and little else but bloody meat was left of their tough soles.

We dashed a horn of water in their faces, and when they had recovered consciousness, I bade them: "Go back to him who sent ye, and show what I have done, and tell him, 'Thus saith the Tiger, he who leads the Tiger's Cubs: "If ever it comes to my ears that ye have offered hurt unto another little child, I'll drag ye from your house and serve ye as I've served your men." ' "

Then of the lad I asked: "Where wouldst thou go?" For I was minded to send him where he willed, and fill his pockets well with gold ere he had gone. But he kneeled down upon his knees before me and took my hand in his and kissed it and swore that he would for ever follow me, though death and soul's damnation were his portion.

And so I took him for my orderly, and after some small search we found an outfit for him, complete from tall boots to peaked steel cap, and I and great Black Hassan swore that he should be our little brother and we would deal with whoso offered him affront.

THE days passed swiftly as we marched, and we were nearing Donna Leonora's house when we espied a throng of country folk all hastening in the same direction. "Whither go all the crowd, brother?" I asked a yokel trudging down the road, whereat the fellow grinned all foolishly and answered:

"We go into the town to see the Lady Leonora defend her lands and goods, although God wot, she'll have some trouble doing it, for never will she find a champion."

"Why, how is that?" I asked, and he replied:

"Her father died a year ago, and she was left with his estates, but now there comes one from the North who bears a deed of writing whereby it seems her lands and goods were mortgaged by her sire, and so her property is forfeit to the bond, and he who holds the pledge stands on his ancient rights and swears that if she challenges his claim it must be by ordeal of battle. But challenge him she will not, for where is any champion to battle for her, and if she found one, of what avail were it? Surely there is none in all the land who can withstand the skill and fury of Dom Diniz's sword."

"How is he called, this man who seeks to take a maid's inheritance?" I asked.

"Dom Diniz da Cunhz, the mightiest swordsman in the land."

"A mighty fighter is he, quotha?" I returned. "By God and by the Prophet, methinks he'll fight his final fight the morrow!"

Then to my little orderly I bade: "Ride hard and fast to Donna Leonora's house, and when you come there, tell her thus: 'My master, Carlos, whom you will recollect by reason of his tiger's cloak, bids me come to you and say to be of cheer, for Don Miguel, the Governor, is no more, and even his wicked castle is in ruins, and on the morrow, when this false oath-bearer stands forth to prove his claim, accept his proffer of ordeal by battle, and a champion will surely come to you."

N EXT morning when the sun was barely up, a great concourse of folk were gathered in the plaza of the town to witness Donna Leonora's discomfiture, but forasmuch as she had ever been a kindly mistress to them, they looked with saddened faces on the coming trial, for well they knew she could not find a sword to stand in her defense against the great Dom Diniz, and they knew, moreover, that her foeman came with a great might of armed retainers at his back, that he might overawe the court and force them to false judgment, whatever the true rights of the case might be.

Now when all had been made ready and the justices were sat, Donna Leonora stood herself at their right hand, and on their left there stood a great, wide-shouldered fellow with hair and bristling beard of fiery red, and from the chiefest of the justices they took their oath . . . "to tell the truth and only all the truth, without mental reservation or equivocation of mind, and so God take my life if I hereby bear false witness in this, the cause which is now called for trial. Amen."

Then forth stood Dom Diniz and spake thus: "Your worships of the *consejo*, I be the holder of a certain writing poll in which and by the terms whereof the late Dom Fernandes Alvares da Meneses did make over unto me all and sundry his lands, tenements and hereditaments, and all his property, both of lands and goods, as surety for a certain loan of fifty thousand pesos which I at that time did advance him. Now this money has remained unpaid until this day, and I stand here to ask fulfilment of my bond."

Then stood the Lady Leonora forward, and looking once upon the deed denounced it as a forgery, saying: "My lords and countrymen, ye all do know me and my family, and well ye know we would not take a wrongful penny or wrongfully withhold a debt, though it were but a farthing, for our family motto is *Death Rather than Dishonor*. Yet this I say on my honor as a Meneses and as I one day shall answer for my sins before the foot of God his Throne—this writing is a forgery. My sainted sire (God rest his soul!) had no need to borrow, for we had enough, and more of lands and goods and money than our need required; so much so that we oft forgave our tenants' rent in bad years when the crops were scanty; yet never did we suffer for the lack of anything."

And when they heard this saying all the people nodded in assent, and many were the murmurs which confirmed what Donna Leonora spake, but still she did continue her defense:

"Again, I say that if my sire had borrowed aught of any one he would have surely told me and charged me to acquit the debt, and on my sacred honor, I'd have done so, or else sought out the creditor and deeded freely all my property to him, for rather would I beg my bread than live in luxury on wealth which is the purchase price of honor.

"And finally, I say again this deed of mortgage is a forgery, for well I know my father's signature, and though the seal upon the deed be his, the writing is another's."

And now the people murmured all the more, and even the justices nodded gravely in agreement, for there was plainly truth in what the lady said, and well they knew the faith and honor of her family. But:

"Have done with this!" Dom Diniz shouted out. "The deed is mine, and well and truly was it signed, and who says otherwise is a foul and stinking liar. And here I stand and demand my ancient and inalienable right to make my claim good by wager of battle. Who says I prosecute a false cause, I'll write the judgment of high heaven on his body with my sword, and thus I make my challenge!" And so saying he drew off his gauntlet and hurled it in the dust full at the Lady Leonora's feet, and cried, "Now take it up who lists!"

"Go quickly to the troop," I ordered little Luiz, who stood beside my elbow, "and big good Nuno Cabral hold the men in readiness according to our plan." Then to Black Hassan I whispered, "Come!" and clambered over the rail which held the mean folk back from out the square.

And when I stood before the court I took Dom Diniz's glove from the dust where Donna Leonora had left it lying, and hurled it full into the caitiff's face, the while I shouted loud for all to hear:

"I take thy challenge, despoiler of the poor, lying bearer of false witness and persecutor of the widow and the orphan. As God Himself sits judge upon the heavens and the earth, I'll champion this maiden's cause, and also, by the Grace of God, write judgment on thy body for what ye did unto the Widow Castro and what ye would have done unto her little son!"

Now when he heard my answer to his challenge and my accusation of the shameful way he had entreated poor Luiz's mother, and felt the sting of leather in his face, Dom Diniz waxed exceeding wroth and ground his teeth in rage, and turning quickly unto a varlet at his side, he whispered something, whereat the fellow slunk off through the crowd, and in a moment more he heard the tramp of marching men, and forth into the plaza came three-score pikemen, who took up their station opposite the court.

"What means this show of force before our court?" the president demanded angrily, and then Dom Diniz smiled an evil smile and answered, "I think we well may call it check, your Worship, for what I have I hold, and what I wish I take. First I will slay this coxcomb upstart who challenges my deed, and then I'll take your judgment in the matter, and if ye should refuse it, I've men enow to make ye change your mind; for by St. Stephen's wounds, nor ye, nor any other of your company shall leave this spot until I'm given judgment."

"Mark out the course and sound the bugle," I demanded; "I'm sick of war with words, and would come to the fighting while there yet is light to see."

And so the herald blew a blast upon his trumpet, although the poor knave's knees did strike together as he blew, and scarce could he force enough of breath between his chattering teeth to make the bugle sound at all.

But sound it did, and ere the echo of its blast had died away, there came the ordered tramp of marching feet, and down into the square there strode my musketeers, the sunlight glinting on their polished harness and every man with stern-set face and glowing gun-match held between his teeth.

"Now by the Devil's blood, what meaneth this?" Dom Diniz cried, and some of his assurance had gone from him, for my men set their gun-rests in position and brought the muzzles of their pieces into line against his pikemen.

"By Allah and by Allah, thou Infidel dog, it means that to your check I've cried checkmate," I returned. "Let but a single foot be stirred among that hang-dog crew of yours, and we will blow them all to hell. Now draw and fight you for your life, for naught of mercy will you find, that much I promise ye, and as the Prophet lives, I'll hew thy evil head from off its neck and toss it in the dust at Donna Leonora's feet where once your foul gauntlet lay." And as I spoke I drew my sword and slapped him with the flat of it across the cheek.

And now we fought like rival cockerels in the ring. His sword was longer by a hand than mine, for his straight blade had greater reach, and to his steel's extent his long and ape-like arm gave added length, so that he struck his point against my breastplate many times while my blows fell a hand's width short of him.

And he could fight. The Prophet knows it! Again and yet again I tried my

M. C.—6

subtlest tricks, but for each trick of mine he had another one more cunning, and more than once I all but lost my weapon, and more than once I felt the sting of steel against my face. And always did he jeer at me and ask me if I still was minded to write judgment on his body.

What might have been the outcome Allah knows, for I was breathing hot and fast, and in my wrist there was the pain of coming weakness; but he was not content to fight me honorably, and needs must stoop to treachery. So, from his girdle he did pluck his poniard and hurled it at my face, and as I dodged to let it pass me, I stumbled on the pavement, and fell sprawling to my knees. But as I fell my sword point jerked upward, and straight against the inside of his thigh the razor-sharp steel struck, so that the great artery of his leg was severed and the purple gore gushed forth like wine from out a riven wine-skin.

The end was swift. Before a leech could come to him and cut away his clothes, this evil man who yet was a great fighter had bled his life away.

And thereupon the court gave judgment in the Donna Leonora's favor, and underneath the muzzles of my musketeers Dom Diniz's henchmen were unable to prevent it.

Then I struck off his head and laid it at the Donna Leonora's feet, and she did give me her sweet hand to kiss, and spoke me as her good, true knight, and all the people shouted loudly when they saw us thus.

So I waged battle for the Donna Leonora.

"AND what shall we do next, Protector of the Poor?" Black Hassan asked. "There be some towns I think would be the better for a sacking, or we may take the open road and levy tribute on such caravans as pass, but what we do we must do quickly, for the gold we took from out the Governor's castle will not last for long, and we have six-and-fifty hungry mouths to feed, and by the horns of Allah's bull, the fellows' bellies are as bottomless as any sea!"

"Nay, as soldiers we were banded and as soldiers we shall serve," I answered. "The Portuguese are in rebellion at the Spanish yoke, and to assist themselves they carry on a secret trading with the Dutch, who also fight the Dons. Tomor-row night, I'm told, a Dutch ship will put in to yonder cove, and it is strange if they'll not give us passage to the Low Countries where every extra sword against the Spaniard is a welcome guest. What say ye, shall we ship?"

"Aye," answered Nuno Cabral, who was spokesman for the troop. "Let us away to Holland and try our fortunes in the war. I doubt not work and payment worthy of that work await us there."

And so the evening following we set sail for Holland.

Death in My House

By PAUL ERNST

Thrice in one night fabulous wealth was offered to old Nakabi, keeper of the jade shop, and twice he refused—a tale of Japan

THE rain came down as though all the moisture in the Orient had concentrated to soak this portion of Japan. It gathered on the dwarfed pine in the tea-house garden, dripping from the tips of the lower boughs, to fall tinkling into puddles of its own making.

Under one bough, however, the rain drops did not fall with a bell-like note. They ended their downward career with a flat, splattering noise. Spat, spat, spat. With a space of perhaps two seconds between drops, the chill water trickled over an object which showed only as a whitish blur in the dusk.

The whitish blur was a man's face. But though the drops were falling square-ly into one glaring eye, the body belonging to the face never moved. For the man was dead.

Under the stunted pine the body lay, a darker outline in the darkness, with a distant street-light seeming to hide more than to reveal it. One arm was doubled under it. The other was outflung; and in the hand was a small leather pouch.

There was a sound of voices from the doorway of the near building, followed by a swish of footsteps as some one came through the garden.

The footsteps faltered, changed direc-tion. A shadowy figure stopped beside the dead man. There was a hiss of in-drawn breath. Then a hand reached down for the leather pouch held in the dead fingers.

It was a withered, ancient hand, yel-low as antique ivory. On its third finger gleamed an oval jade ring. Like a claw it gripped the leather pouch in talon fin-gers, and pulled the drawstring. Into the withered yellow palm tumbled some-thing that looked, in the faint reflection of the distant light, not unlike a symmetrically cut fragment of rose-colored glass—save that the glass seemed to glint with internal fire.

Again came the hiss of indrawn breath. The claw-like hand clenched over the thing. Then, slowly, the hand opened, to slide the glittering crystal back into the pouch and replace it in the dead fingers. The swishing of footsteps was resumed as the shadowy figure took up its course toward the street.

From the deepest shadow behind the pine came a sigh. The sound had nothing to do with the wind that now and again rattled the rain-drops with increased harshness. It came from human lips.

A MAN stepped forward and bent swiftly over the body, as if taking up again a task in which he had been interrupted. He was big, this man, with a florid face and coarse red hair and a nose that had been twisted to the left in some past fight. Though he was dressed in civilian clothes, he was obviously a man of the sea.

Once more the little leather pouch was drawn from limp fingers and opened. Once more the rose-colored crystal glittered in a man's palm—a broad, calloused palm this time.

"God!" whispered the man. "God! And the blinkin' fool—whoever he was —didn't take it. I suppose he thought it was phony."

Swiftly the broad shoulders straightened. The red-thatched head jerked this way and that as hard blue eyes attempted to pierce the darkness.

"Did he see me? Was that why he dropped it? But he couldn't have seen me through the branches, with the light behind him. Never mind. His ignorance saved me from goin' to hell with his life, too, on my hands."

He started. Again voices sounded from the door, outlined in yellow light twenty yards away. He crouched and slid through the gloom of the garden to the street.

Behind him a mask-faced man in a dark kimono materialized in the rain-laden night and bent over the body. The man's slit eyes gleamed as they fell on the empty, outflung hand. He searched the body in a few seconds, stared savagely at the empty hand again; then, head forward like a dog on the scent, he raced noiselessly to the street in time to see the red-headed man walking quickly toward the business section of the city of Kobe.

The man in the dark kimono slowed and trailed the other, almond eyes glinting with cold calculation at a spot in the center of the broad back.

The red-headed man looked behind twice, but saw no one. Meanwhile he muttered aloud as he walked, and reeled now and then as if drunk. And drunk he was, though not with liquor.

"Me—Bill Swayne—getting my hands on the Rose Queen! Think of that, now! Worth a hundred thousand dollars—two hundred—whatever a millionaire's willing to pay for it. And me—I got it!"

His hard eyes narrowed. His hand closed over the leather pouch in his pocket.

"Every crook in Japan would be after me if they knew I had this. But nobody knows. Nobody——"

A quick step sounded behind him— one telltale slip on the part of the trailing shadow that had drawn near enough to strike.

Bill Swayne turned with panther swiftness. His right hand caught a wrist in time to keep a knife from plunging into his breast. His left doubled and smashed into a mask-like yellow face.

The Jap grunted with pain, but his fingers clung to the knife. His foot shot out. Swayne tripped and fell backward, with the killer on top of him. For a moment the knife-point lowered grimly near Swayne's throat; then he arched his knees and threw the smaller man off him.

Cat-like, Swayne sprang on him. Right and left his fists tore into the distorted face. The Jap went down. Swayne drew back his foot for a murderous kick at the man's head; but now he heard some one coming up the street. Following the same sweep of movement, he leaped backward, whirled, and ran.

In a moment he judged he was safe. He slowed, and began to walk at a normal pace lest he drew curious looks; for now the street was beginning to show more signs of life in spite of the inclemency of the night.

"So somebody did know!" he snarled to himself. "Though how——" He wiped his fists on his trousers leg. "Anyway, I corked his slit mouth for him, the ——!"

He hurried on, ignorant of the fact that close behind still trailed a kimono-clad figure. The kimono was draggled, and the face above it was bruised; but from the bloodied features peered eyes as coldly calculating, as determined as before.

Swayne knew Motachi, as Kobe's shopping-center is called, very well. Ahead a short distance was a certain jade shop he wanted to enter. He knew the proprietor, an old fellow named Nakabi, by repute if not by actual acquaintance. A discreet old boy, and one who could keep his affairs to himself.

Swayne was about to do something that made him curse bitterly as he reflected on it. He was going to sell the Rose Queen locally and at once, instead of trying to hang onto it till he could find a real market for it. It would be good business to take it to New York or Paris; but he couldn't do that. He hadn't enough money to take it to either place.

He must have money; he'd get it from Nakabi. It was late, but the old man was probably still behind his counter. A boat was in, and the shops were taking no chances of missing out on belated tourist trade.

"He can give me twenty thousand for it. He's worth that much, all right. Twenty thousand ain't a lot, but I won't be a hog." His thick lips twisted virtuously. "And besides——"

A thought uncoiled for a moment in the back of his mind.

Besides—after he had the money, he might get the Rose Queen back again. You never could tell. Nakabi was an old man. Swayne could break his neck with one hand, if he had the chance. Then he could travel leisurely to a real market and get a real price for his treasure.

T HE jade shop stood next door to a booth whose long sign, bellying in the wind, declared that curios were to be bought within. Swayne passed under the sign and entered the jade store—and knew not that now, from across the street, two men instead of one watched him.

One of the two was the man in the dark kimono, his features washed of blood by the rain but showing puffed and discolored. The other was lighter in hue; and his eyes, hazel though slanting, proclaimed him a Eurasian.

Like a wrinkled ivory idol, Nakabi sat behind his counter, surrounded by his jades. His left hand went up to comb at his long, gray beard as his eyes, methodically, unhurriedly, roamed over the figure of the big man who had stepped in out of the night. Without comment he noticed the slight smears of mud still clinging to the soaked, European clothing in which the man was dressed; without comment he scrutinized the florid, hard face with its twisted nose.

"You are Nakabi?" Swayne put it more as a statement than as a question.

The old man nodded.

"Well, I'm Bill Swayne. Maybe you've heard of me."

"I have," replied Nakabi, in meticulous English. The tone of his voice intimated that he had heard much, and none of it good.

"I'm down on my luck right now," Swayne said. "I even had to sell my gun, day before yesterday, to get something to eat. But I've got what it takes to put me back on top again. I've got—this."

His hairy hand went out, with the leather pouch lying in the palm. Nakabi took the pouch, opened it, and glanced at the thing it held. No expression came to his face, nor words from his lips.

"Well?" said Swayne at last.

"Very beautiful."

"Is that all you got to say? Don't you know what it is? It's a diamond. One of the biggest that ever got into Japan——"

"I know," Nakabi interrupted, nodding like a mechanical toy. "I know. It is the Rose Queen."

"And all you can say is that it's beautiful!" sneered Swayne.

He changed his tone. This man must be placated; he must buy the Queen. "I want to sell it, Nakabi. See? How much will you give me for it?"

Nakabi passed it back across the counter.

"Nothing," he said.

"Eh?"

Swayne scowled in bewilderment.

"I said, I will give you nothing. I do not want it."

"Don't want it——" Swayne stopped, and laughed harshly. This was bargaining, that was all. The old fox was simply paving the way for a low offer. "I won't

stick you, Nakabi. All I want is twenty thousand American dollars for it. Twenty thousand! I bet you could sell it for five or six times that."

"At least," nodded Nakabi.

"Then——"

"But I would have to keep it for awhile before I could find a buyer. And that, my friend, would be keeping death in my house. These big stones bring murder with them. I, who am old, know this. And I do not want to be murdered."

Swayne stared. "I must say you ain't very ambitious. Who'd know you had the Rose Queen? Nobody saw me come here."

Nakabi forbore the retort that Swayne himself would know, if no one else did; and that Swayne's reputation was not one to inspire trust. Instead, he merely said:

"The air itself seems to have ears and eyes in such matters. I do not want it."

"But you stand to make a hundred thousand cold on the proposition," argued Swayne. This was beyond his comprehension. Not buy the diamond at the price asked? Only a fool would refuse such a bargain. And Nakabi was no fool. He was known as a wise man. "Come on, give me my twenty thousand—and here is the stone."

Steadily Nakabi shook his head.

"I am old, but life is still sweet. I will not touch it."

"Listen," Swayne snarled, suddenly leaning across the counter, "come across with the money or I'll take it and keep the Queen besides."

Nakabi smiled placidly and fondled his beard. "You would not try that, my friend."

"Oh, I wouldn't, eh? I could break you like this." Swayne's big hands clenched and twisted as though he were snapping a twig. "What's to stop me?"

"The Rose Queen," said Nakabi. "You

would not dare risk a disturbance with that in your pocket."

Swayne blinked. It was the first time the perfectly obvious thought had occurred to him.

"You won't buy it?" he grated, eyes furious, baffled.

"No. I shall keep poor—but alive."

Two American women came in, and Nakabi fearlessly turned his back to Swayne to wait on them. Swayne's fists doubled, but he turned and walked toward the doorway. There was nothing else to do.

In the doorway he halted, undecided where to go next. Nakabi's refusal to have anything to do with the Queen was a complication that had never entered his mind. It left him rudderless; he knew of no other shop-owner feeble enough and discreet enough to be trusted with the knowledge of the great diamond's present ownership.

Presently he walked down the street toward a small tea-house well out of the Motachi and not much patronized. He would have to think this thing out over a bowl of saki.

Across the street the two lurking watchers stirred. The Eurasian's hand went to his knife.

"Nakabi!" he whispered. "We shall kill him as soon as the two women leave the store—before he has time to put it in his safe."

He started toward the jade shop; but the other man stopped him. Through the dim doorway his hawk eyes had seen what the Eurasian had missed: the leather pouch being repassed across the counter, back to the hairy fist of the man with the red hair.

"Nakabi has not the stone. The other has it yet. After him."

The eyes of murder lifted from the shop of old Nakabi, who was wise, and fastened once more on the broad back of Bill Swayne.

Swayne was very cautious as he walked toward the tea-house. He kept glancing back to make sure he was not being followed; and at every twisting street entrance his eyes darted right and left on the lookout for suspicious shadows.

In a dim way he thought for a moment of the gem in his pocket in other terms than those of cash. He was packing a lot of trouble around with that innocent-looking lump of carbon. How had Nakabi put it? He did not want to keep death in his house.

These huge jewels! A big fortune in a small parcel—a fortune belonging to whoever could most deftly slit a throat and make away with it.

"They'll have a job getting it away from me, though," Swayne mumbled aloud. His jaw squared truculently. And, "The old fool! A hundred thousand in his hand—and afraid to take the chance."

Behind him, patient, soundless, slid the two trackers. The red-headed one was vigilant. But vigilance can not be maintained for ever. There would come a moment when he relaxed his watch.

They fingered their knives and waited.

Swayne plunged along a darker street, and reached his destination. For two hours he hovered over a feeble lump of glowing charcoal in a private room, trying to untangle the problem old Nakabi's unlooked-for stubbornness had set him. Nakabi was the only man in Kobe he dared try to sell the diamond to; and Nakabi had refused to deal with him. What next?

At length he decided to go to Yokohama and attempt to dispose of the gem there.

He paid his bill and left the place, to go to the unsavory hotel where he was staying. And as he left, two pairs of eyes noted grimly that he did not walk with quite the steadiness and sureness he had possessed when he went in.

THE trackers crept closer to the quarry. Closer. It looked very much as though the moment they had been waiting for was at hand.

As though intuition had warned him, Swayne hurried a little. His fingers tightened over the gorgeous stone in his pocket as he walked. His hotel was only a quarter of a mile away, but he wished that quarter of a mile were behind instead of ahead of him. He would feel safer indoors than out in the dark street.

"But I'm safe enough," he argued. "That blasted Jap that tried to knife me is the only one in Kobe to know I got the Queen. And I lost him, all right."

Just the same he wished he were in the hotel, in a lighted room. He increased his pace still more—and forgot, in his uneasy eagerness, to look behind him.

Once more a slight scrape of feet, a small telltale rustle, made him whip around. And once more light gleamed on steel intended for his back but flashing now toward his chest. However, this time two knives instead of one were lunging at him.

A sweep of his arm deflected one blade, but the other bit deep into his shoulder. Even as the icy sweep of it numbed him, he kicked out and felt his toe smash against a knee-cap. That ought to fix the fellow for awhile!

But Swayne's face was paler than the knife-thrust warranted. Two! He couldn't fight off two. He gathered air in his lungs for a shout for help. But the cry never came out.

The Rose Queen. With that in his pocket it wouldn't do for him to go yelling for the police.

Viciously he crashed his fist first into the already battered face of the Jap. A knife raked along his arm. He turned, snarling, to face the Eurasian again. Death in my house. Death in my pocket. But he'd keep the diamond in spite of hell!

The Eurasian bore in, disregarding the pain of his knee-cap in his maniacal greed. Swayne caught his right arm in both hands and twisted. The Eurasian moaned, and dropped the knife. Swayne stooped to pick it up. . . .

There was a sudden weight on his back and again he felt the ice-cold stream of a deep cut.

"Help——"

The shout was strangled by a hand that clapped over his mouth.

With the second murderous slash Swayne knew that he was fighting for life—and no longer for the Rose Queen. Of a sudden he would have given his soul to call for help. But now it was too late. With those savage fingers clamped over his mouth he could make no sound.

He bit down, felt his teeth go through flesh to the bone. But though he heard a gasp from the man on his back, the gagging hand merely changed position so that the flat of the palm was pressed over his mouth instead of the more vulnerable fingers.

Swayne reached up to stab at the hand with the knife he had taken from the Eurasian, on whose writhing body he now knelt. The man beneath him caught his wrist.

Maddened, Swayne turned his attention entirely from the burden on his back, and pressed the knife-point toward the Eurasian's throat.

The hand at his wrist fought desperately to stay the descent. But steadily, inexorably, Swayne forced the blade down. He was very weak; but with all his weight and failing muscle he pressed the knife toward the naked throat beneath him.

The Eurasian jerked and went motionless under Swayne's knees as the blade bit through. But even as the man's life bubbled out, the killer on Swayne's back struck a third time. Swayne straightened convulsively, and dropped his knife.

"He's got me," he said. He thought he said it aloud; for now he could no longer feel the hand tearing at his mouth. "He's got me——"

The Rose Queen. He'd never spend the fortune it represented now.

"But by God neither will you," he whispered into the bloody fingers.

He twisted under the murderer's weight to get his hand into his pocket. He drew out the leather pouch containing the rose-colored diamond. But before he could flirt his wrist to send the pouch off into the darkness, the knife ripped into his back once more. This time he did not feel it at all. The blade had gone squarely home at last.

ALMOST with the blow, the sound of footsteps rang out. Quick as thought the killer leaped to his feet and slunk back in the dripping shadows.

An indistinct figure appeared—halted abruptly as it came to the two bodies lying in the mud of the gutter. A hand went down to clutch at the small leather pouch held in the dead fingers of the larger man.

It was a withered claw, this hand, yellow as antique ivory, with an oval jade ring on its third finger. It clenched spasmodically over the pouch and the hard lump it contained.

"Again!" breathed Nakabi. "Three times in the space of an evening fate has offered me the Rose Queen. Can it be that I am meant to have it?"

There were two bodies here, attacker and attacked. Swayne had been followed, set upon—and both had died, leaving no one aware of where the diamond was. Surely, surely this time it was safe to take it.

But reluctantly the claw-like hand opened, and dropped the pouch beside the dead man.

"I have enough to last out my life in comfort," sighed old Nakabi. "I were wise to remain poor—but alive."

Two steps his feet carried him away. But then they brought him back again, as if obeying the command of some other person.

"Enough! There is such a thing as being too wise. Wealth beyond my dreams —offered me a third time by fate."

The man with the battered face moved soundlessly near from the shadows behind the old man. The knife, which had been lowered in a relaxed hand as Nakabi started off without the leather pouch, raised tensely again.

"This time," said old Nakabi, stooping low, "I shall keep——"

The knife flashed down.

With trembling fingers the murderer in the dark kimono caught up the little leather pouch, and slunk off into the night. And Nakabi, who had been wise but not quite wise enough, stared after him with wide, sightless eyes.

The Snake-Men of Kaldar

By EDMOND HAMILTON

*Another mighty tale of Kaldar, world of Antares
—a tale of red warfare against a race of monsters
on a distant planet*

*"They were fighting on the
swaying deck of the air-
boat."*

1. Back to Kaldar

"ALMOST midnight, Merrick. In minutes you'll be on Kaldar again!"

Stuart Merrick nodded. Tall and lean and browned, he stood on a square metal platform-apparatus at the center of the long laboratory. A strange figure he made, garbed in a flexible black metal tunic that reached from shoulders to knees, a red disk blazoned on its breast. At his belt there hung on one side a long sheathed sword and on the other a stubby, odd-looking gun.

In the soft-lit laboratory were more than a half-dozen men standing ready at the humming, crackling electrical apparatus that almost filled the room. All were elderly, with the faces of scholars and scientists, the oldest of them standing at a wall-switchboard beside which was a chronometer whose hands pointed almost to midnight. The laboratory's roof was open, and in the night sky overhead

473

sparkled a multitude of stars. Among them burned the fiery red light-point of Antares, toward which Merrick was gazing.

"Out there on Kaldar again in minutes," he repeated. "Kaldar, world of Antares—you're sure it will all work just as before?"

"Just as before," the man at the switchboard told him. "The projector's set has not been changed and it will hurl you out to the same spot on Kaldar where you found yourself the first time."

"And if I want to return?" Merrick asked.

"One week from now the projector will be turned on again at exactly midnight, with reversed power," the other answered, "and if you're on that same spot on Kaldar you'll be drawn back to earth in the same way as in your first venture."

Merrick's thoughts, as he stood waiting on the flat projector, were going back to that first venture. He had answered an advertisement of these nine scientists and had been amazed when they had told him that, working in secret, they had devised a method of projecting a living man out to any distant star and drawing him back again, by breaking down his body into its composite electrons and flashing them out across the void or drawing them back again almost instantaneously. To test the method, they had proposed to project Merrick out to a world of the distant star Antares, and to draw him back at an agreed time a few days later.

Merrick, accepting, had been hurled out across the void and had waked to find himself on Kaldar, world of the huge red sun Antares. He had found himself among a race of ruddy-skinned humans there, the Corlans, who were at that moment choosing a new Chan or ruler, and Merrick's sudden appearance among them on the dais of the Chan had made them choose him as their fate-sent ruler. Thus he had become Chan of Corla, making quick friends with Narna, daughter of the last ruler, and by that incurring the hate of Jhalan, a Corlan noble who had aspired to the rulership and to Narna's hand.

Jhalan had proved a traitor to Corla, plotting with its ancient enemies the Cosps, great intelligent spider-men who had long oppressed the humans. But Merrick, with the aid of Holk and Jural, two great Corlan fighters, and of Murnal, an old noble, had defeated Jhalan's plots, saving Narna from him and shattering the Cosp power for ever. Hardly had he done this when by his agreement, which he had forgotten, he was drawn back against his will to earth. In the weeks since, while the projector's condensers had been charging to send him forth again, Merrick had been chafing to return to the distant world of weird adventure where he was ruler of a race.

Merrick roused suddenly from his thoughts as he saw the chronometer's hands creeping over the last divisions toward the hour of midnight.

About him the nine scientists were waiting silently, some gazing toward the chronometer, some toward the projector on which Merrick stood, others up toward Antares' crimson spark among the stars. As Merrick turned his own gaze he saw the hands coming together at last to mark midnight, and turned to look toward the man at the switchboard. But as he did so the latter threw over four switches in quick succession. Merrick felt awful forces thundering through and about him, and then consciousness went from him in a flash as he was hurled out into bellowing blackness. . . .

OUT of that momentary black uncon-
sciousness Merrick emerged with a
clicking shock that jarred his frame
through and through. He was aware
that he was swaying on his knees, a fierce
heat beating suddenly upon him, and
then as he heard from about him a chorus
of wild shouts, he staggered up to his
feet and opened his eyes.

He was standing once more on Kaldar,
world of Antares!

His first glance upward told him that,
for in the heavens overhead there flamed
not the familiar yellow sun of earth, but
a huge crimson sun whose stupendous
circle filled a third of the heavens and
whose fiery brilliance was all but blinding to his eyes as he saw it thus again.
Antares, sun of Kaldar! Merrick turned
his dazzled eyes downward from it.

He stood on a round dais of black
metal at the center of a great plaza.
Around the plaza rose the numberless,
sky-looming black pyramids of the city
of Corla, their terraces and the streets between them swarming with black-tunicked
Corlans. Over the city there drove
thronging air-boats, long, slender craft
humming to and fro. And on the plaza
around the dais were other Corlans who
were pointing up toward Merrick and
madly shouting.

Merrick, still dazed by the tremendous
transition from world to world across the
deeps of space, saw that those in the
plaza were running toward him as he
reeled down from the dais. He was
aware of them gripping his arms, of wild
shouts of "Chan! Chan!" spreading out
over the city, and dimly knew that they
were half leading and half carrying him
through the swift-gathering, excited
crowds toward the great pyramid of the
Chan at the plaza's edge.

Passing into the dim coolness of the
pyramid's mighy halls, Merrick had

misty knowledge of black-garbed servants
rushing forward, of the red sun-disk of
the Chan blazing everywhere on the walls
as it blazed on his own breast, of whirling upward in a great lift-chamber.
Then, emerging into the great chambers
at the pyramid's tip whose broad windows looked out over Corla's far-flung
pyramids, Merrick was aware of other excited voices about him, and finally as
something fiery-tasting was given him to
drink, his brain cleared of the whirling
mists and he looked about him.

Three men were with him, one a great
weather-beaten warrior with huge shoulders, another a slender, quiet counterpart
of the first, and the third a white-haired,
fine-faced oldster. The biggest of them
was gripping his shoulders.

"Chan Merrick! Chan Merrick! You've
come back!" the three were crying.

"Holk! Jurul! And you too, Murnal!" Merrick exclaimed, recognizing
them.

"Chan Merrick, where in the sun's
name have you been?" cried the great
Holk.

"Why did you go, O Chan?" asked the
white-haired Murnal. "Why did you disappear from among us like that?"

"It was not of my own will that I
went," Merrick answered. "You know that
when first I came among you I told you
that it was from a far-distant star and
world I came. It is back to that star and
world I have been, drawn back against
my will and unable until now to return."

Uncomprehending awe was on their
faces.

"Truly when you vanished there on the
dais of the Chan it seemed that you had
gone back into the unknown from which
you came," said big Holk. "Never had
we had a Chan like to you, who had shattered the Cosps, and some said that never
would we see you again."

"Yes, many said that," Murnal added, "but Narna said always that some time you would return."

"Narna—where is she?" Merrick asked eagerly.

An embarrassment seemed to descend on the three at his question, a something in their faces that brought a quick throb of fear to Merrick. He gripped Holk's arm fiercely. "Narna!" he exclaimed. "What's happened to her?"

It was Murnal who answered him. "Chan Merrick, I will tell you all," said the old noble, "and wish well that it were not to tell.

"You know how you, Chan Merrick, with Holk and Jurul here, saved Narna from Jhalan and shattered the power of the Cosps for ever, and how you then disappeared from our sight so strangely on the dais of the Chan. Some said you would never return, but Narna was certain that some time you would come back. So we awaited your return, I still ruling Corla in your name.

"But a week ago came an unexpected event. Jhalan, whom we all thought dead, reappeared here in Corla by night with a half-dozen traitor Corlan followers. He seized Narna, and before any could reach them was gone with her in his air-boat. He sped north, and his last boasting word was that he was going where none dared follow, to the legended city of the great Gurs or snake-men!

"This city of the Gurs is supposed to lie in the far north, and it was northward Jhalan's craft headed. Holk and Jurul and I learned of his carrying away of Narna only today when we returned to Corla after a week's absence. We were discussing what to do when you reappeared out there on the dais of the Chan. But you have reappeared too late, Chan Merrick, for Jhalan again has Narna in his grasp."

Merrick, when Murnal finished, was silent for moments, gazing out over Corla's black pyramids beneath the crimson sunlight.

"So Jhalan lives still and works evil still — but not for long!" His voice lashed out, his hand twitched on his light-sword's hilt.

He spun around. "Holk! Jurul! Assemble five air-boats in the plaza as swiftly as possible. Full light-gun armament and ten-man crews for each. We start north after Jhalan and Narna as soon as they are gathered!"

Holk and Jurul raced wordlessly from the room. Murnal's face was grave.

"Chan Merrick, you go on a more perilous quest this time than before," he said. "Our legends say that these Gurs or snake-men are mighty, and it is said even that there is a barrier of death around their city that no living thing can pass."

"The Cosps were mighty too, yet I reached Jhalan and Narna among them," Merrick answered grimly. "I have a reckoning with Jhalan that is long overdue."

Holk and Jurul reappeared, breathless. "The air-boats are ready, Chan Merrick," they reported.

Merrick turned. "Murnal, you rule still in my name until I return with Narna. We start at once."

Minutes later the five swift air-boats soared up from Corla's central plaza, Merrick and Holk and Jurul crouched on the low-railed deck of the foremost. At the sides and stern of each craft gleamed the grim muzzles of their light-guns.

The air-boats rose over the great city's black pyramids and crimson gardens and then with Merrick's craft at their head shot northward. They passed over the city and the ring of huge black mountains around it. Then before them to the horizon stretched a sea of thick crimson jungle, and over this they flew on into the unexplored mysteries of the north.

2. *The Wall of Glowing Death*

CROUCHING in the air-boat's sheltered prow next to Jurul, Merrick peered ahead. For hours they had been flying northward and Antares' huge crimson circle had sunk half beneath the horizon to their left. Ahead and beneath stretched the same tangled crimson jungles that he knew covered vast stretches of Kaldar's surface.

The other four air-boats flew close behind, their crews of black-garbed Corlan warriors lying at length on their decks, one in each watching over the air-boat's compact propulsion-mechanism at the stern.

Merrick turned to Holk and Jurul. "How long do you think it will take us to reach this city of the Gurs?" he asked.

"According to all accounts, the legended city of the Gurs is more than two days flight northward," Holk answered.

"The Gurs—snake-men," mused Merrick. "It seems almost impossible that there should be such a race. Is anything authentic known of them?"

Holk shook his head. "No, for no people on Kaldar ever ventures far from its own land. Even we Corlans know almost nothing of the country beyond our mountain-ring, save that the Cosps who raided us came from the south. But we have heard rumors many times of other strange races even more weird and unhuman than the Cosps, and among these of a terrible race of snake-men called the Gurs, living in an inaccessible city far to the north."

"Jhalan must have heard the rumors," Jurul added, "and so has fled north to these Gurs to be safe from us."

Merrick nodded somberly. "Well, let us hope that he has reached them; for though it may be almost impossible for us to find him among the Gurs, it would be utterly impossible to find him if we had no idea of where he has gone."

"We'll find him," Holk reassurred. "Even if he's reached your cursed snake-men it ought to be easy—simply smash through them with all our light-guns going, kill Jhalan and get Narna before they understand what's happening, and smash our way out again."

Jurul nodded approvingly. "An ingenious plan, Holk, but don't you think it's a little too subtle, too intricate and tortuous?"

Holk scratched his head. "Why, it may be——" he began, and then as he saw Merrick and Jurul laughing aimed a bear-like blow at Jurul that the nimbler Corlan easily avoided.

Steadily they hummed northward, with Antares' blazing disk disappearing in the west and darkness rushing after it over the world of Kaldar. The five moons of Kaldar, four crimson and the fifth green, rose one by one to light their way. Merrick and Holk and Jurul relieved each other in turn at the air-boat's controls through the night, and when dawn came they were flying still over the same crimson jungles.

Through all that day the five Corlan craft flew north over unbroken red jungles, the only sign of life in them being some featherless flying-things that rose now and then to fly around their air-boats. As the next night passed a chill of apprehension grew in Merrick. Did the Gurs exist in legend only? Had Jhalan and Narna perished somewhere in these wild regions, and were they destined to search fruitlessly for them in these red jungles that might stretch to Kaldar's northern pole?

When the second dawn disclosed only

crimson vegetation ahead, their apprehension grew greater.

Holk was shaking his head doubtfully as he gazed ahead. "By the sun," he exclaimed, "I think the only intelligent life in these regions is ourselves. If your snake-men exist we must have passed them."

"But we can't have passed the city of the Gurs," Merrick said. "The great barrier that encircles it—we couldn't have missed that!"

"Two days and nights we've flown north," the big Corlan answered, "and that should have brought us to the city of the Gurs if the tales they tell are true. I'm beginning to think that they're legends only."

Jurul quietly shook his head. "Jhalan wouldn't have fled this way with Narna if he hadn't known something of where he was going."

"Well, it's more than we know," Holk growled. "If you ask me——"

"Look!" Merrick cried suddenly, pointing ahead. "That glowing across the horizon—what can it be?"

They stared, Holk exclaiming in surprize. For at the skyline far ahead it was as though a wall of glowing light stretched from east to west for miles across their path. They watched with intense interest as their five craft sped in the direction of the strange phenomenon, paying no heed for the moment to a group of the featherless flying-things that had risen from the jungle and were racing below and ahead of their air-boats.

And as they flew on Merrick and Holk and Jurul realized swiftly the stupendousness and strangeness of what lay ahead. It was a mighty wall of glowing light that sprang upward from the ground, which was not jungle at its base but bare rock. From this rock the stupendous glowing barrier rose almost as high as the eye

could reach, into the sun's glare. And the wall stretched from east to west for miles ahead of them, hiding from sight all that might lie beyond.

"A wall of glowing light!" Holk exclaimed, as they swept nearer it. "What causes it, in the sun's name?"

"I can't guess," Merrick answered, "but we'll soon be through it, and then——"

Jurul cried out suddenly. "Look at that!"

He was pointing to one of the featherless flying-things which they had not heeded until then, and which was winging on a little ahead of their five air-boats. It had flown into the great wall of light, a few hundred feet ahead, and the instant it entered the glowing light-wall it collapsed, crumpled, and fell down limp and lifeless. And the creature's body seemed to crumble and disintegrate as it fell in the glowing light, vanishing before it reached the ground!

Merrick's face went gray and his hands flashed to the controls. "Back!" he cried. "That wall of light isn't light but radioactive force that disintegrates anything in it! It's a wall of death!"

It was Merrick's action and not his order that saved them. For before Jurul or Holk had realized the nature of the astounding menace ahead, Merrick had whirled the air-boat up and back in a wild curve, the four other air-boats instinctively following and almost grazing the glowing barrier. They shot back, came to a halt together in midair.

"Radio-active force!" Merrick exclaimed. "If that flying-thing hadn't been just ahead and warned us we'd have been gone in a moment!"

Holk, his jaw dropping, was staring at the glowing light-wall. "But where does the force come from?"

Merrick shook his head, still trembling from the narrowness of their escape. "That rock underneath must contain radio-active minerals in terrific quantities and strength. The greater part of its radiations would be upward through the free air, and so form this wall of disintegrating radio-active force through which nothing in existence could pass."

"Then this must be the rumored impassable wall around the city of the Gurs!" Jurul exclaimed. "It is said to surround their great city completely."

"How are we going to get inside, then?" Holk demanded.

"We'll see first whether or not there is any break in the wall," Merrick answered. "We'll follow around its circle and if there's even a small break in it we may be able to get through."

They turned the air-boats and headed westward, following the stupendous death-wall but keeping a few hundred feet outside it. They found that the wall formed a vast inclosing circle, but there was no break in it and they had no slightest glimpse of what might lie inside.

At last, in late afternoon, the five air-boats came again to the spot where they had started their circuit. They had gone completely around the death-wall's circle, which was scores of miles in diameter, without finding the slightest opening in the glowing, deadly force.

They halted again in midair. "Truly the wall of the Gurs is an impassable one," Holk said. "There's no way through it."

"There must be some way through," Merrick insisted. "Jhalan must have got through to reach the Gurs."

Jurul's eyes met his. "Perhaps he never reached them," the other said. "Perhaps he and all with him blundered into the wall as we almost did, and met death."

Merrick's heart sank, but he shook his head. "I can't believe it," he said. "Jhalan must have known about this wall of glowing death and must have had some plan for getting through it, or——"

His eyes lit suddenly. "Or over it!" he finished. "That's it — Jhalan must have climbed as high as possible with his air-boat, to a height where the upward-radiated force would be far weaker, and then gone through!"

"Then that's our own way," Holk declared instantly. "Whatever Jhalan can do we certainly can."

"Wait!" Jurul said. "How do we know but that Jhalan and his boat weren't destroyed trying to get over the wall?"

"We don't know," Merrick said grimly, "but we will before long. We're going to try it now ourselves—order the other air-boats to climb with us, Holk."

WITH Merrick's air-boat leading, the five craft began to ascend in a close spiral, keeping well out from the glowing wall of death. Rapidly the crimson jungles outside the wall receded below them, and the air grew colder. But the glowing radiation of the wall was still too intense to dare.

Up and up in their endless spiral went the five air-boats, and when almost three miles above the surface the craft experienced difficulty in gaining greater height. Merrick and Holk and Jurul watched their progress with anxious eyes, for though by then the glowing radiation of the wall seemed somewhat weaker, it was not enough so for a dash through.

As they labored higher the air became freezing about them, and in their brief metal tunics they felt all its coldness. Holk's teeth chattered and Merrick saw that his own arms and legs were blue. At four miles it became evident that the air-boats could go no higher. At that height the glowing radiation of the wall was much weaker than at the ground, but still menacing in appearance.

Could they risk a dash through it, Merrick asked himself? Had Jhalan—and Narna—got through it or had it crumbled their craft and themselves into fragments? Merrick knew he must decide quickly, for only by strong effort were the air-boats maintaining that height. He made sudden decision, shouted an order. The five air-boats drew back a little farther from the glowing wall, then turned and dashed at top speed toward it.

Instinctively Merrick and Holk and Jurul crouched together at their air-boat's stern as they rushed to the glowing barrier. They struck it, and as they shot into the glowing radiations, even at that height, Merrick and the others felt tremendous, tingling forces sweeping up through them like hurricanes of invisible force that shook the atoms of their bodies.

The air-boats reeled on through the radiations, and as such sickening forces shook the men on them, the metal of the air-boats themselves began swiftly to glow. Merrick saw, knew that a few moments more in the radiations would disintegrate the air-boats and then themselves. The thickness of the glowing wall meant life or death now—but suddenly they shot out of the radiations into clear air again. They were through, were inside the death-wall!

Merrick and the Corlans clung dizzily to the air-boats' decks. It was not until moments had passed that they felt enough themselves to look ahead and beneath.

Before them stretched the huge circle of country enclosed by the circular wall of shining death. It was swathed in thick crimson jungles like those outside the death-wall. That deadly barrier towered in glowing magnificence around this immense circle, shutting out from view all that lay outside.

Merrick stared across the vast circle of red jungle for some sign of the strange civilization of the Gurs or snake-men rumored to exist here. He could see nothing of the sort at first; then he thought he made out a black mass of some sort far in at the circle's center, half hidden by the surrounding vegetation. But his attention was turned from it by a sudden cry from Holk.

The big Corlan had been staring downward as the air-boats gradually descended to lower levels, and now was pointing excitedly.

"Humans!" he cried. "Look—down in that clearing—and they're fighting!"

"By the sun, Holk's right!" Jurul exclaimed. "See them, Chan Merrick?"

Merrick had seen. A long, irregular-shaped clear space broke the crimson jungles a little ahead of the descending air-boats. At its edge he could see a score of red-skinned men garbed in black tunics like the Corlans. They were battling a larger number of black serpent-shaped creatures, both sides using glowing rays of short range.

"Those are snake-men they're fighting —Gurs!" Holk cried.

"And the men can only be Jhalan and his followers!" Merrick exclaimed. "Head down toward them—we're going to get into this!"

3. The Land of the Gurs

AT MERRICK'S order the five air-boats dipped and rushed down as one toward the distant combat in the clearing, their crews springing to the light-guns mounted on swivels along the deck.

"Why not let Jhalan and his men fight their own battle with the snake-men, Chan Merrick?" shouted Jurul to Merrick over the roar of wind.

"Because if that's Jhalan and his men

Narna will be somewhere near!" Merrick yelled back.

"What's the matter with you, Jurul?" cried Holk. "Don't you know when you see a fight the thing to do is to jump in and find reasons afterward?"

The battle at the clearing's edge seemed rushing up clearer and closer to Merrick's eyes as the air-boats dived toward it. He saw now that there were fully a half-hundred of the hideous black snake-shapes, the Gurs, and that they had almost surrounded the score of red-skinned men.

The Gurs held Merrick's momentary attention. These snake-men of the north were, as the legends of Kaldar told, each like a giant black-scaled snake in body but with a human-shaped head that had two close-set black eyes and a white lipless mouth. The monstrous things moved by writhing in snake-like fashion, but below their heads two short tentacle-arms branched from their bodies.

In these arms the Gurs held dark stone instruments like a bull's-eye lantern in shape, from which they released narrow glowing rays upon the humans they were attacking. These rays seemed of the same glowing force as in the great death-wall, since Merrick saw that the humans struck by them crumbled and disintegrated. The effective range of these rays of the Gurs was apparently not more than six feet.

The attacked humans were replying to the snake-men with rays of the same sort. Also the humans were provided with circular shields of dark stone like that of the ray-instruments, which appeared invulnerable to the glowing force and with which they warded off the rays of the Gurs. It was patent, though, that the snake-men were overcoming them.

But now the appearance from above of the five Corlan air-boats changed affairs abruptly. As the five boats swooped, Merrick and Holk and Jurul crouching at

M. C.—7

the prow of the foremost, their Corlan crews worked the light-guns and sent a hail of shining charges raining down upon the snake-men. These charges wrought terrible destruction.

Astounded as they were by this sudden new element in the combat, the snake-men quickly replied with a dozen glowing rays directed at the down-swooping air-boats. Most fell short, but two of the rays struck and disintegrated the third of the air-boats. But in the next moment the four remaining ones had landed, and the Corlans, with Merrick and Holk and Jurul at their head, were pouring out to attack the Gurs with their light-swords, except for a few remaining on each boat to work the light-guns.

Merrick found himself with hideous black snake-bodies all around him, stabbed swiftly with his shining light-sword and blasted Gur after Gur with its touch before they could bring their rays into action. Holk was fighting a little to his left, the big Corlan bellowing his fury as he laid about him with his weapon. Close on Merrick's other side Jurul, whose light-sword flashed and flickered among the crowding snake-men like a dancing lightning-brand, was laughing silently, as was his wont when the fighting became fierce. Flanking these three on either side the Corlans pressed forward.

The Gurs, though they had destroyed a half-dozen Corlans with their rays, gave back before the light-swords of their attackers and the charges still pouring into them from the light-guns of the four air-boats on the ground. They sought to flee, but the snake-men found retreat cut off by the humans whom they had been attacking moments before, who were coming fiercely at them with rays. Caught between these and the Corlans, the Gurs were speedily wiped out.

MERRICK and his Corlans looked across the heap of blasted snaky bodies at the men they had succored. Merrick's eyes searched among them for Jhalan or Narna, but neither was among the dozen men facing him. And now Merrick saw that though these men were red-skinned and dressed in black metal tunics like Corlans, they were not Corlans.

"Who are you?" he asked one who seemed their leader, in the tongue common to all races on Kaldar. "You're not of Corla?"

"Corla?" repeated the other. "We know it not. We are Dortas, as surely you too must be."

"Dortas?" said Holk to Merrick. "We Corlans have always thought we were the only humans on Kaldar, but it seems there must be others."

"I am Arlak," the Dorta leader was telling Merrick, "and I and my men thank you for saving us from the Gurs."

"Why were the snake-men attacking you?" Merrick asked.

Arlak looked blankly at him. "Why, a party of them stumbled on us out here and knew of course that we had escaped from the Gur city. Surely you must be Dortas escaped from there also, though your weapons and your flying-ships are strange."

Merrick shook his head. "We never saw Gurs or Dortas until now," he said. "We came in from outside the wall."

A buzz of astonishment ran through the Dortas, and they talked excitedly, eyeing the Corlans.

"You can not mean you came from outside," Arlak protested. "Why, nothing can pass through the glowing wall of death!"

"We did not pass through it but over it in our air-boats," Merrick told him. "But you said you Dortas had escaped from the Gur city. You mean you were prisoners there?"

"We were slaves there, like all the Dortas," Arlak answered. "We Dortas have always lived inside this wall of death. There are legends which say that long ago we were a free race and had here our own villages and cities, and that then the Gurs or snake-men appeared, coming up through crevices from some great space in the interior of Kaldar, and that the Gurs then first enslaved the Dorta people.

"Be that as it may, for ages the Gurs have dwelt in their city at the center of this land and have held there as slaves the whole Dorta race. Now and then slaves escape from the city into these jungles around it. We are such escaped slaves, and there are others. The Gurs send out parties occasionally to look for escaped slaves, and it was such a party that stumbled on us and would have destroyed us had you not appeared."

"By the sun!" swore Holk. "A race of humans enslaved by these snaky monsters!"

"It seems we did not make a mistake in mixing in this fight," said Jurul with quiet emphasis.

"Tell me," said Merrick to Arlak, "have none of you seen or heard of an air-boat like these with men like us coming here from outside the death-wall?"

Arlak shook his head, spoke briefly to the other Dortas, who made signs of negation also. "None of us has heard of such," he told Merrick. "Was it in search of such a one that you came?"

"It was," Merrick answered. "The air-boat we are hunting held an enemy of mine and also a girl, my friend, whom he and his men carried off. This enemy, this Jhalan, boasted that he was going to ally himself to the Gurs, the snake-men of the north."

Again Arlak shook his head. "He must have known little of the Gurs to think that they would receive him as a friend. But none of us has heard of such arriving at the Gur city, and some of us escaped from there but three weeks ago.

"There are some at our camp, though," he added, "who escaped from the Gur city less than a week ago, and they may know something of it if your enemy actually reached the Gur city."

"Your camp?" said Merrick quickly. "There are more of you, then?"

The Dorta nodded. "About a hundred of us in all—we have a camp in the jungle close to the death-wall."

"We'll go there with you, then," Merrick decided quickly. "The air-boats will hold us all and you can guide us there."

QUICKLY he issued orders, and the Dortas, not without some evidences of distrust, distributed themselves among the four Corlan air-boats. Arlak took place with Merrick and Holk and Jurul in the first boat and marvelled as the four rose smoothly from the ground and hummed low over the red jungles toward the glowing barrier.

Arlak guided their flight, the other three air-boats following the first. As they proceeded, Jurul, who had been examining curiously the stone ray-weapons and shields of the Dortas, obtained from Arlak a description of their nature.

The ray-weapons, Arlak explained, were merely containers in which was held a quantity of the intensely radio-active rock that caused the death-wall around the Gur country. The lantern-like containers were worked from a rare stone invulnerable to the crumbling radio-active force, and the force was released in a narrow ray from inside them by opening a small aperture much like the slide of a bull's-eye lantern.

Arlak added that the Gurs had originally devised these weapons for control of the Dortas, but that he and other escaped Dortas had been able to make them for themselves. Also they had made thin circular shields of the same invulnerable stone which protected them more or less from the rays of the Gurs. His band of escaped Dortas, he told them, had made some hundreds of the ray-weapons.

The talk broke off as Arlak indicated they were nearing the camp of the escaped Dortas. It was cunningly hidden in the thick crimson vegetation close inside the towering death-wall, but when the four air-boats slanted down to it, scores of Dortas swarmed forth to repel them.

At sight of Arlak on the foremost air-boat they held back their rays, and soon the four craft had landed and were surrounded by the hundred or more Dortas. Quickly Arlak explained to them the providential advent of the air-boats and the help Merrick and the Corlans had given them against the Gurs. Then Arlak singled out two of the Dortas.

"Hann, you and Shala escaped from the Gur city but days ago," he said. "Heard you of any strangers like these reaching it?"

Hann shook his head, but Shala nodded excitedly. "Such arrived there the day before I escaped—but six days ago!" he said. "A flying-like craft like these with a half-dozen men and one girl!"

Merrick's heart leapt. "What of that girl?" he said quickly. "What happened to her and to the men?"

"Why, the Gurs seized them, of course," said Shala. "We Dortas could not understand why they should come into the Gur city to be slaves. The leader of the men did not expect that, and they fought, but the Gurs overpowered them."

"So much for Jhalan's boast," Holk commented grimly. "He thought the Gurs would accept them as allies, and not make slaves of them."

"But what did the snake-men do to them?" Merrick pressed. "To the girl?"

"They must have been put with the rest of the Dortas in the slave-circle," Shala said. "But I did not see that."

Merrick turned to Arlak. "The slave-circle? What does he mean?"

Arlak explained. "The Gur city is one of four concentric circular walls, dividing the city into a central circular space and two ring-shaped or circular spaces around it.

"In the central circle the Gurs have their living-quarters and only the Dortas who are personal servants of the snake-men are admitted into that circle. In the next circle are the places and mechanisms where the Dortas work under supervision of the Gurs. In the outer circle are the quarters of the Dortas, while on the wall around it, the outermost wall of the city, Gurs are posted to prevent possible escapes."

"And Jhalan—and Narna—are somewhere among the slaves there," Merrick said. He looked to meet the eyes of Holk and Jurul.

"Well, now that we know where they are, we can break in to get them!" the big Holk said cheerfully. "To get Narna, that is—Jhalan can remain a slave of the Gurs several lifetimes without hurting my feelings."

"I've remarked before that your strategy is somewhat elementary, Holk," said Jurul dryly. "We can't go into that Gur city and walk around as though in Corla."

"As I see it," Merrick said thoughtfully, "our best chance would be to wait until night and go through that outer slave-circle. We could get over the guarded outer wall easily enough with our air-boats and might be able to find Narna and get out without the Gurs becoming aware."

Arlak interrupted, his expression excited. "You can do better than that," he told Merrick. "You can help us do what we have been planning long to do—to loose a revolt of the whole Dorta race against their Gur masters!"

"A revolt of the slaves? You've been planning for that?"

"Yes, for months!" Arlak exclaimed, eyes alight. "I told you we escaped Dortas had been making hundreds of ray-weapons—we have done so in hopes of arming the hosts of Dorta slaves inside the city and starting a revolt with them against the Gurs.

"Our difficulty has been that we could not get the ray-weapons inside to the Dortas. If we tried, the Gurs on the outer wall would give the alarm, and all chance of a surprize, which alone could give such a revolt success, would be gone. But with these flying-boats of yours you can take the ray-weapons in and distribute them to the Dortas tonight!"

"By the sun, it's a plan worth trying!" Holk declared. "Are you sure the Dortas would rise once they had weapons?" he asked Arlak.

"They would rise," Arlak said grimly. "And they would fight until either the Gurs or the Dortas were destroyed."

"We'll try it!" Merrick decided. "But we'll try first to find Narna.

"Here is the plan," he told the others. "We'll start tonight to the Gur city as soon as darkness comes, with the ray-weapons and as many of these Dortas as we can take in our four air-boats.

"We'll land in that outer circle of slaves as stealthily as possible and begin distributing the ray-weapons among the

Dortas. In doing so all of us will keep on the lookout for Narna among the slaves, and when we find her can get her out on an air-boat before we start the revolt."

AT ONCE, under Arlak's orders, the Dortas began preparing for action under Merrick's plan. There was little time left before night's coming, for already the huge red disk of Antares was sinking to the horizon. Excitedly the Dortas labored, bringing forth from hidden storehouses the hundreds of lantern-like ray-weapons they had fabricated and loading them on the air-boats.

When darkness came they still were working at the task, but soon after night's coming they finished. The air-boats were loaded from stem to stern with the ray-weapons. Without further delay the Corlans and as many Dortas as possible crowded onto the air-boats, Arlak and Shala taking places with Merrick and Holk and Jurul on the first one.

At Merrick's low order the four craft rose heavily into the darkness and headed over the lightless jungles toward the Gur city. Not far behind them towered the glowing death-wall toward the stars, casting a weird quivering light on the four air-boats. Merrick could see the terrific shining barrier curving away in the darkness, far away, enclosing completely this strange land by night as by day, the colossal wall's shining splendor enhanced by the darkness. Two red moons had risen.

Merrick looked ahead. They had not flown for long before they glimpsed a circular pattern of lights in the dark jungle. As they swept closer toward these, the lights of the city of the snake-men, Merrick saw that they and the city they outlined were several miles across. He gave order to rise a little higher.

Slowly the heavily laden air-boats slanted to a higher level, then as they neared the Gur city's lights moved more slowly so that their humming progress was scarcely audible. Merrick and Holk and Jurul, gazing ahead, could make out in the glowing light from the distant surrounding death-wall that the Gur city was as Arlak had described, composed of four concentric black metal walls that enclosed three concentric circular spaces.

There were lights at regular intervals round the outermost wall and he could make out the dark snake-shapes of guarding Gurs there. If these guards looked up they would see the air-boats passing above, Merrick knew, but he was counting on the fact that the Gurs would not be on the watch for aircraft.

His confidence was justified, for the four air-boats slipped almost soundlessly above the outer wall without any alarm from the Gur guards. Silently they descended through the darkness and landed in the deeper shadows of the outer circle. It held many long structures that Merrick guessed were the barracks of the Dorta slaves.

They disembarked, and Arlak and Shala entered the nearest slave-barracks. They returned in moments with a crowd of excited Dortas to whom they had explained the situation, and who despite their excitement came silently lest they rouse the Gurs on the wall. Quickly they were provided with ray-weapons, and as they spread to other slave-barracks increasing numbers of Dortas arrived, for weapons, from all around the outer circle of the Gur city. Soon some hundreds of them, dark shadowy forms in the darkness, had been furnished with ray-weapons, women among them as well as men.

Suddenly Holk's great dark figure moved and as he grasped one of the arriving slaves Merrick heard his whispered exclamation.

"By the sun, Chan Merrick—see whom I have here! It's——".

"Narna?" whispered Merrick eagerly, pressing toward him. "You've found Narna?"

"No! It's Jhalan!" Holk answered.

4. Through the Snake-Men's City

MERRICK stopped, dazed for a moment by disappointment, then went on to the two. His eyes, now accustomed to the darkness, made out Holk's great figure, hand on his light-sword's hilt ready to rip the weapon forth and destroy the man beside him. Merrick's face hardened as he saw for himself that this was Jhalan.

Jhalan, arch-traitor of Corla, the man who had tried to betray Corla to the Cosps and who had carried Narna north into this hell-city of snake-men masters and human slaves! Jhalan's strong, bearded face, his merciless eyes and mocking smile, were as when he last had seen them. But Jhalan had no light-sword now at his belt, dressed simply in black metal tunic like the Dorta slaves about him.

His eyes flashed with mocking light at Merrick. "The Chan Merrick from the unknown!" he greeted in a whisper. "So you have returned to Kaldar?"

"I've returned and I've followed you and Narna," Merrick said, his voice deadly. "Where is she, Jhalan?"

"She is, like myself, a slave of these cursed snake-men or Gurs," said Jhalan coolly, "though from the looks of things it seems that the Gurs' slaves are about to revolt."

"Where is Narna in this city?" Merrick asked. "I am going to kill you sooner or later, Jhalan, and it will be at once unless you speak truth."

"She is in the inner circle of the city—

that in which the Gurs have their quarters," Jhalan told him unperturbedly. "When the Gurs seized us, they put Narna among those Dortas who are personal servants to the snake-men. I saw her assigned to one of the Gur dwellings there before I was sent out to this outer circle."

"You'd know the Gur dwelling in which Narna is?" Merrick asked. "You could guide me to it?"

Jhalan nodded. "I'm sure I could."

"I am going to give you a chance to do so," Merrick said grimly, "and it is your one chance for life. If you'll guide me in there to where Narna is I'll give you a light-sword so you'll have a chance for your life when this revolt breaks. Without it you'll have none."

"In that case I'll guide you to Narna," Jhalan said. "This does not cancel the differences between us, though?"

"It does not," Merrick told him. "Once Narna is safe, you and I are going to settle our account once and for all."

"The arrangement is good," said Jhalan. "Where's the light-sword?"

Holk caught Merrick's arm. "Chan Merrick, you're not going in through the snake-men's city? And with this traitor Jhalan?"

"I've got to," Merrick told him. "Narna has to be got out of there before the revolt breaks, for hell will burst loose in this city when the Dortas rise. And Jhalan's the only one who can guide me to her."

"At least take us with you," Jurul whispered.

"Two of us will have a far better chance of making it than more, and every one of you will be needed here when the Dorta revolt starts," Merrick told him.

He turned to Arlak. "As soon as you've distributed all these ray-weapons, start the Dorta attack from all sides of the city, and press in on the Gurs before they can recover from their surprise. Holk, you lead the attack on the north side, Jurul on the south, Arlak and Shala on the west and east.

"If Jhalan and I are not back with Narna before the revolt starts you'll know that we've been caught. In that case, do everything you can to find Narna if you get to the inner circle, and get her safely back to Corla. Now give Jhalan a light-sword and we're off."

One of the Corlans unbuckled his light-sword and belt and Jhalan quickly put it on. He started then with Merrick through the silent but excitedly crowding Dortas.

Holk barred his way a moment. "Remember, Jhalan," he growled, "that if you survive this night and Chan Merrick does not, I'll be waiting for you."

"And I," added Jurul in a whisper, infinitely menacing.

Jhalan laughed soundlessly. "When tonight is over you'll have to wait your turn to be killed. The Chan from the unknown comes first."

With this mocking rejoinder he pushed past Holk and Jurul; and Merrick, after a brief hand-grip to the two Corlans, followed. In a moment they were out of the crowd of gathering Dortas, and looking back Merrick saw them only as a blur of dark shadows. There was no sound, for though the Dortas were gathering from round all the city to get the ray-weapons, they were moving with stealth and silence.

JHALAN led the way between the big long black structures that ordinarily held the hosts of Dorta slaves. He and Merrick made their way toward the inner side of the ring-shaped slave-circles, keeping in the deeper shadows always and out of the direct light of the three moons now overhead, and the less direct illumination of the distant surrounding glowing wall. Merrick looked back anxiously toward the lights up on the outermost wall, but no sound had yet aroused the Gur guards there.

They reached the wall separating the outer slave-circle from the second or midmost circular division of the city. Along it Jhalan led, and paused a moment later beside a narrow opening in the wall.

He and Merrick peered into the second circle. Merrick saw that it held looming machines and metal work-buildings instead of slave-barracks, and that though there were lights here and there in it, few moving forms could be seen. He and Jhalan moved into this second circle, heading across its great expanse toward the city's innermost circle. Their hands were on the hilts of their light-swords as they crossed it, keeping when possible in the shadows of machines.

When two-thirds of the way across it, Jhalan and Merrick had abruptly to crouch low as a party of Gurs approached from the right. They were moving through the silent second circle as though on a definite errand, five in number and conversing in hissing voices as they writhed forward in their hideous snake-fashion. As they neared the machine behind which Merrick and Jhalan were crouched, they separated, two continuing on through the circle while the other three started toward the inner part of the city, directly past the machine behind which were the two men.

Merrick knew they would be seen as the three Gurs passed, and he and Jhalan gripped their light-swords, drew them from their sheaths.

There was no need of plan. When the three Gurs writhed within a few yards of their hiding-place, Merrick and Jhalan sprang at them like uncoiling springs.

Merrick's light-sword touched and blasted one of the Gurs before the snake-man could voice an alarm. He spun toward the other two, to find that with incredible swiftness Jhalan had slain both.

"Quick work!" Merrick approved in a whisper, despite his hate for his companion.

Jhalan laughed coolly. "I just imagined those two were Holk and Jurul," he said. "Lead on."

"Lead on," Merrick said grimly. "The Dortas will rise at any moment, and when they do it'll be the end of stealth for us."

They threaded the mechanisms and structures of the comparatively deserted second circle and in a few minutes crouched by the wall separating it from the innermost circle, that of the living-quarters of the Gurs.

It was a circular space less than a mile across into which Merrick and Jhalan gazed. There were in it a great number of round squat structures of black metal, and from window-openings of many of these gleamed lights. A number of Gurs could be seen writhing occasionally from one structure to another, and also men and women Dorta slaves appeared at times, often with burdens. These, Merrick knew, were the personal servants of the snake-men.

He saw in at the circle's center a larger structure which he guessed held perhaps some center of government of the Gurs. Beside it he could make out a long low shape resting on the metal pavement, which he recognized as a Corlan air-boat.

Jhalan's eyes had followed his gaze. "It is the air-boat in which we came here," he whispered to Merrick. "The cursed Gurs seized it and us when we landed here."

"In which one of those Gur dwellings did you see Narna put?" Merrick asked.

Jhalan pointed to one of the round structures not far inside the circle. "That one. Whether Narna is still there I do not know."

"We'll soon find out," said Merrick. "Come on."

They moved through the opening and crept silently along the inside of the wall, two deeper shadows in its shadows. Merrick's thoughts were racing. It seemed unthinkably strange that he and Jhalan, the arch-villain he had pursued so far over Kaldar's surface with deadly purpose, should thus be acting in unison. But it was necessary — they must find Narna before the Dorta revolt which Holk and Jurul and Arlak were preparing out in the slave-circle broke upon the Gurs.

THEY left the wall's protecting shadow and moved out into the circle toward the structure Jhalan had indicated. There were lights showing inside, but no sound came from it.

Reaching the door-opening of the Gur dwelling, they sprang inside. They were in a bright-lit hall in which was no one else. It led into the structure's interior, rooms opening from either side. Merrick and Jhalan peered into these, light-swords in their hands.

There was neither Gur nor Dorta in the first two rooms, but in the third were two sleeping snake-men, their hideous serpent-bodies coiled and resting on cushions. They might wake at any moment, and Merrick entered with light-sword extended to destroy them.

As the shining force-charged blade reached toward the two coiled Gurs the eyes of one of them opened and stared squarely at Merrick. But in the next instant the sword had touched both and they were but scorched, blasted bodies.

Merrick was starting back to the hall

where Jhalan waited when through a door-opening at the room's corner came a sound of some one approaching as though alarmed by the slight sounds he had made. Merrick bounded to the door's side, light-sword ready to stab at any snake-man that came through.

But as a figure emerged he let the light-sword fall almost from his hand. It was no snake-man but a human, a girl, a red-skinned girl whose black hair matched the black of her tunic, who stared at Merrick with wide eyes——

"Chan Merrick!" Her exclamation was incautiously loud in her amazement. "Chan Merrick, you've come back to Kaldar!"

"Narna!" For a moment Merrick held her close. "Yes, I came back to Kaldar, and came north after you. And I've found you!"

"Quiet!" grated Jhalan from the hall. "You've been heard outside—Gurs are approaching!"

Narna stared unbelievingly from Merrick to Jhalan, as though unable to credit the spectacle of the two together, and not fighting.

"Holk and Jurul and I found Jhalan out with the Dorta slaves and he led me here to you," Merrick explained to her in a swift whisper. "The Dortas are going to revolt tonight and we've got to get back out to the slave-circle before——"

"Too late!" cried Jhalan. "The Gurs come!"

There was a sound of rushing snake-bodies in the hall and two Gurs appeared with short glowing rays stabbing toward Jhalan. Jhalan leapt to evade the rays and as Merrick jumped to his side their light-swords stabbed in and touched and destroyed the two snake-men.

Other Gurs pressed forward behind those, and Merrick and Jhalan fought them from the narrow doorway, their light-swords stabbing past the short rays and blasting the snake-men. Now a babel of hissing cries could be heard from outside and it was evident that news of the fight was spreading through the whole inner circle.

"Chan Merrick!" cried Narna. "They come through the other door!"

Two Gurs were writhing through the door in the room's corner through which Narna had entered.

Jhalan leapt back across the room, thrust under their rays and blasted the two snake-men.

"Hold that back door against them, Jhalan!" yelled Merrick over his shoulder. "If we can hold them for a little while, Holk and Jurul and the rest may get to us!"

Now Gurs were crowding into the building in scores and their very numbers hampered them as they sought to enter the room through the narrow door-openings defended by Merrick and Jhalan.

Merrick's light-sword wove a flickering net of death across his door-opening. The effective range of the Gurs' glowing rays was hardly longer than his sword, and as the rays could not affect the force-charged sword itself, sword and ray met on even terms. Merrick stabbed and struck swiftly, each touch of the deadly blade blasting one of the Gurs writhing to the attack.

He knew that they could not hold the room for ever against the crowding snake-men. A swift glance over his shoulder showed him that Narna was close behind him and that at the room's back door Jhalan had made a heap of scorched Gur bodies behind which he fought. The arch-traitor was using all the supreme swordsmanship Merrick knew by experience to be his.

The hissing outcries of the writhing Gurs drowned all other sounds. Glowing ray and shining light-sword crossed and clashed like flashing lightning. Merrick had now before him a heap of scorched snaky bodies like that Jhalan had made, but up over these writhed other Gurs to attack with their rays.

Suddenly there was heard over the hissing din a dull, distant roar of sound, swelling up from round the whole Gur city.

"Chan Merrick! What is it?" cried Narna.

"The Dortas are rising!" Merrick cried. "Their revolt has started!"

5. Battle's End

THE dull roar from around the city was increasing in volume each moment, and from the hissing outcries outside Merrick knew that the Gurs now realized that their human slaves were revolting, and that they were rushing out to meet the attacking Dortas.

Merrick had hoped that the snake-men attacking them would join the others to combat the Dortas, but they pressed their onslaught with even more fury, as though determined to dispose of Merrick and Jhalan so that they could join the other Gurs in the fight with the Dortas.

Merrick felt himself tiring as fresh Gurs crowded over the dead to stab with their rays at him. A glance backward showed him that Jhalan too was fighting fiercely to hold the other door. Merrick could hear the roar of battle drawing nearer and knew the Dortas must be pressing the Gurs inward toward the city's center, knew with what ferocity the human slaves must be falling upon their snake-men masters.

But would the Dortas led by Holk and Jurul and Arlak and Shala reach the inner circle in time to save Narna? It seemed to Merrick's racing thoughts that they could not, for though the din of battle

outside was ever louder as the Dorta attack crashed inward, he and Jhalan now were being assailed with reckless fury by the Gurs they held back. Merrick now could hear the yells of the Dortas as they fought into the central circle of Gurs.

The Gurs attacking Merrick suddenly changed tactics, sought by turning their rays on the metal wall on either side of the door Merrick defended, to widen that door! Merrick saw the metal crumbling under the glowing rays, knew even as he thrust to right and left at the swarming Gurs that in a moment more they would have an opening too wide for him to defend.

But the snake-men suddenly turned from Merrick, to fight Dortas crowding into the hall from outside. The rays of the Dortas mowed them down as with unhuman ferocity the slave-men crowded forward, wreaking vengeance for ages of slavery.

They crowded to where Merrick stood bewildered in the open doorway, and three of them leapt toward him. He recognized Holk and Jurul and Arlak, their faces aflame with excitement as they shouted to him over the din of battle still going on in the central circle outside.

"In the sun's name, we've loosed something here, Chan Merrick!" yelled Holk. "The Dortas have swept all the Gurs in the city into this central circle and are killing them—they've gone crazy!"

"Crazy with vengeance, yes!" Arlak cried, his eyes half mad. "Let them kill —no Gur escapes this night while a Dorta is left to kill him!"

"Chan Merrick, where's Jhalan?" Jurul cried. "And Narna?"

"Narna and Jhalan are here with me," Merrick said, turning. "Jhalan helped me—but they're gone!"

Gone! Neither Jhalan nor Narna was in the room, and at the back door Jhalan had defended there was only a pile of dead Gurs.

"It's Jhalan!" Merrick cried. "He killed the Gurs at that door and then took Narna while I was fighting here——"

With a bound Merrick leapt toward the back door of the room and through it before the others could follow. It led through another room and down a corridor out of the building. Merrick burst out, looking wildly about for Jhalan and Narna.

The central circle of the Gur city was a scene of madness around him. It was filled with combat, crowds of Dortas insane with blood-lust pursuing groups of the writhing Gurs and annihilating them with glowing beams. Merrick gazed despairingly for a moment around this hell of battle, light-sword in his hand.

Then he cried out. By the greater structure at the circle's center he saw the Corlan air-boat he had noticed when he and Jhalan had first crept into the inner circle, Jhalan's air-boat which the Gurs had seized. And Merrick saw now through the hordes of struggling Gurs and Dortas that Jhalan was running toward this air-boat, carrying Narna's hastily-bound figure in his arms.

Merrick yelled, sprang through the combat after him. He threw himself forward through a chaos of snake-men and humans and rays as he saw Jhalan drop Narna's helpless figure on the deck and spring to the air-boat's controls. Merrick heard the cries of Holk and Jurul behind him.

The air-boat was rising! Merrick, still a score of feet from it, flung forward in a desperate last spurt and then leapt forward and upward. His fingers caught the rail at the air-boat's stern and held, light-sword still in his right hand's grasp. He swung thus from the craft's stern as it shot up into the night.

As the air-boat shot out over the city of chaos where the Dortas pursued and slew the last of the Gurs, Merrick drew himself upward. He saw Jhalan turn, come leaping back along the air-boat's deck with light-sword drawn. Over Narna's bound figure Jhalan leapt and then his light-sword was clicking against Merrick's. They were fighting on the swaying deck of the air-boat as it rushed without pilot through the night.

A STRANGE calm held Merrick as his shining blade clashed with the other. He knew that the moment had come, that even as he had predicted to Murnal, light-swords were out for the third and last time between himself and Jhalan, and that one of them was going to die.

He thrust, side-stepped, parried, as though in the calmest of friendly fencing-bouts. Across from him Jhalan's dark, sardonic smile flashed at each thrust, but Merrick's face was set, his eyes brilliant. It was the strangest of duels, fought with deadly swords of shining light on the deck of the air-boat as it sped pilotless out through the darkness from the city of the Gurs.

Merrick took a step forward—another. The two shining blades flashed faster, needles of light weaving a web of death between the two men.

Again Merrick pressed forward. He was fighting as he had not known he could fight. Jhalan, his smile disappearing and his eyes becoming deadly, was wielding a blade that seemed everywhere about Merrick. Yet Merrick, as though filled with a force not of himself, was pressing him back toward the racing air-boat's prow. They passed Narna, bound and helpless on the deck, watching the fight silently and without fear in her eyes. They fought on as the craft rushed on over the dark jungles, and now to Merrick Jhalan's figure stood out dark against a glowing wall of light.

The air-boat, with no hand at its controls, was racing toward the mighty wall of glowing death!

Merrick realized it, and his shining blade flashed faster. Backward still into the craft's prow he pressed Jhalan but could not penetrate the other's marvellous guard. Feint, thrust, parry—click, click —each moment brought them nearer to the death-wall. Jhalan was in the air-boat's prow, could back no farther. His sword moved almost faster than eye could follow, yet Merrick's matched it as they battled on in this duel where a touch of either shining blade meant blasting death.

Now the air-boat was rocking in air-currents as it rushed closer to the towering wall of glowing death. Merrick read in the eyes of Jhalan that the other, with all lost, meant to fight on until they three had rushed together into death rather than surrender. The whole world before Merrick seemed dissolved in brilliance as with a rapier of light he fought as he had never dreamed he could fight. Jhalan's laugh rang suddenly.

"Chan from the unknown—I think we go into the unknown now together!" he cried. The air-boat was rocking in toward the deadly light-wall and in a moment would be in it.

"Not both of us—no!" Merrick cried.

He leapt in a mad last rush with the words, but at that instant the air-boat rocked violently and he was hurled from his feet to the deck. As he was thrown prostrate thus with sword still in his hand, Jhalan was leaping toward him with light-sword upraised and face gleaming with triumph.

Merrick knew it for the end but took the last slender chance open to him and with a sweep of his arm, from where he lay on the deck, hurled his own sword full toward Jhalan. His sword went dead and forceless as it left his grasp, but struck the upraised shining blade of Jhalan and knocked it back against the traitor's own shoulder. There was a flash as the sword's deadly force blasted its owner, and Jhalan fell in a scorched, lifeless heap.

Merrick leapt forward over him. Just ahead loomed the glowing death-wall, immense, walling the heavens with light. His hands slammed over the controls only just in time to send the air-boat curving away from the wall of death it had been about to enter.

M ERRICK, half dazed by the events of that night, staggered back and undid the bonds which Jhalan had hastily used to secure Narna. As the air-boat slowed and came to a halt in midair, they clung to each other in silence.

There came a cry from the night above them, and as an air-boat like their own dropped beside them, Holk and Jurul and Arlak poured over the rail onto their craft.

"Chan Merrick! Narna!" Holk cried, and then his eyes widened as he saw Jhalan's blasted, lifeless form. "Chan Merrick, we saw you leap onto Jhalan's boat and we followed in one of our own air-boats. And Jhalan is dead!"

"Jhalan is dead," Merrick answered dully.

"By the sun! To have missed the best fight in Kaldar's history!" swore Holk.

"Fought on the deck of an air-boat racing toward death!" Jurul cried.

"And that after helping us Dortas to sweep away our age-old masters!" Arlak exclaimed.

Merrick waved aside their excited praise. "Holk, you and the rest return to the other air-boat," he said. "Keep it alongside and I'll be with you in a moment."

Holk stared but obeyed, he and Jurul and Arlak helping Narna over the rail into the other boat. Merrick turned, stepped over the sprawled, prostrate form of Jhalan to the craft's controls, turned the air-boat and started it moving toward the glowing death-wall again. As it moved faster he stepped quickly into the other air-boat that had kept alongside, and as Holk brought that to a halt they all watched silently as the dark craft that bore Jhalan's dead form alone as crew winged on toward the glowing wall.

They saw it diminish to a dark spot as it neared the wall of light, and then Merrick, his arm across Narna's shoulders, glimpsed it rushing into the glowing radiations of the barrier, wavering for a moment to their vision, then disappearing as it and all on it were disintegrated by the deadly radio-active force. They stared in silence for a time at the glowing wall before Holk's great voice sounded.

"Battle's end for Jhalan, eh? Well, whatever else he was, he was a fighter."

Merrick nodded wordlessly, Narna close beside him. But Jurul had turned, was gazing back down at the Gur city where the wild uproar of the victorious Dortas was diminishing, the last of the snake-men slain.

"Back there, too," came Jurul's quiet voice. "Battle's end!"

6. Merrick, Chan of Corla

FOUR days later the four remaining air-boats of the Corlans, Merrick and Narna with Holk and Jurul on the foremost, rose from the Gur city. It was now the city of the Dortas, though, for the dead Gurs and the wreckage of the wild battle had been cleared away, and Arlak ruled now as Chan of the Dortas.

From Arlak and the Dortas they had parted, with promises of future visits and communications, and now Merrick's four air-boats flew out over the crimson jungles toward the eternal glowing barrier, climbed and climbed until the jungle was miles below, then shot as one through the weaker radiations at that height.

Steadily southward they flew, toward Corla, under the red blaze of huge Antares by day and under Kaldar's thronging moons by night. When they approached the great ring of black metal mountains encircling Corla, late on the third day, they were met by watchful Corlan air-scouts which shot at full speed to the city to take news of the return of Merrick and his friends.

So that when their four craft hummed down at last into the great central plaza of Corla it was to find plaza and streets and terraced pyramids massed with shouting men and women.

Up onto the dais of the Chan stepped Merrick, and there beat upon him stunning waves of sound as Corla's thousands hailed their Chan. When he stepped down from the dais to walk with Narna and Holk and Jurul toward the great pyramid of the Chan they moved through lanes of cheering, massed humanity.

In the chambers atop the pyramid of the Chan, Murnal greeted them, tears in his eyes.

"Chan Merrick! I knew that you would come back with Narna!" was all that he could say as he grasped their hands.

"So Jhalan is dead," he said when he had heard their tale. "And the great Gurs are no more. Truly, O Chan, you are of another world—none of this world could have done it."

"It was not I only, but Holk and Jurul and Arlak and the Dortas," Merrick replied. "Well, it was a bloody revenge that the Dortas took on their snake-men masters."

"Yes," said Jurul. "For once, I think, even Holk had enough fighting to satisfy him."

"Not I!" Holk exclaimed. "I'll go sorry until the end of my days that I missed that last fight between you, Chan Merrick, and Jhalan!"

When Holk and Jurul had left, Murnal between them and listening to their recital, Merrick and Narna turned toward the broad window, looked forth.

Antares, huge and crimson, was dipping its blazing rim behind the horizon, its red rays streaming in splendor over Corla's mighty pyramids and the throngs that crowded its streets and the air-boats that rushed and dived above them. Merrick, looking forth with his arm across Narna's shoulders, remembered how first he, a dazed adventurer from earth, had looked out from this very window on the same scene.

The last crimson light in the west faded and darkness rolled quickly across the scene. Lights gleamed out on the surrounding pyramids and on the humming air-boats, and laughter could be heard, and excited voices. Eastward Kaldar's green moon and two of its crimson ones were climbing already into the sky, but Merrick and Narna were gazing up toward the stars that gleamed in a canopy of jewelled light across the heavens.

Merrick pointed up to a faint yellow star. "The star and world from which I came, Narna," he said.

She gazed, silent. "You will be going back to it again, O Chan?"

He laughed, shook his head. "I couldn't now if I wanted to, for at the moment, a week after my return here, when I should have been down on the dais there to be drawn back, I was far north with you and the rest."

"Chan Merrick!" she cried. "To save me, then, you have lost your chance to return to your world!"

He shook his head, drew her closer. "No longer my world, Narna," he said. "I would never have gone back before of my own will, for I am Stuart Merrick of earth no longer. I am Merrick, Chan of Corla!"

Pale Hands

By E. HOFFMANN PRICE

An exquisite story is this, about an American who was one of Abd el Krim's agents, and how he was mocked by the witchery of love and absinthe

AS DAVIS LAWTON glanced up from the tall glass before him to gaze across the plaza just outside the gray-walled city of Bayonne, he saw that his friend Georges Joubert was approaching the table. Joubert was now a member of the *Sûreté Générale;* but instead of avoiding him, Lawton cultivated their wartime friendship. A subtle and audacious touch, that, maintaining cordial relations with a member of the French Secret Service!

"Sit down and have a drink," invited Lawton.

Although he declined the drink, as he usually did, Joubert accepted a place at Lawton's table.

"My friend," he began abruptly, after a marked and awkward silence, "there has been very much surmise about your connections, here in Bayonne, and else-where—in Morocco, for instance——"

Joubert paused again, groping for words. But further speech was not neces-sary to tell Lawton that his connections in Morocco were about to lead him to a stone wall in a courtyard, and a firing-squad primed with a stiff drink of cognac and grumbling with forced gruffness at small-arms practise at sunrise. Lawton knew that the *Sûreté* never made an open move until it had enough evidence to con-demn a man. The trial would be only a matter of form. But Lawton eyed Jou-bert very calmly: for in the beginning, Lawton had been a soldier and he would be one again, in the end.

"Very well, Georges," he replied. "Read me the papers."

"*Mon ami,*" came the answer, "I have no papers. That is, not yet. But I know that in twenty-four hours I shall have them. Maybe tomorrow morning. Some one has babbled. Not much, but more than enough. As for your being an agent of Abd el Krim, that is nothing to me, for personally, I don't think France has any right in Morocco. But once the informa-tion reaches me officially I shall be com-pelled to forget that day on the front, when you carried me to safety through that hell of machine-gun fire.

"So get out of Bayonne and across the border as soon after sunrise as you can. There is an early express to Spain.

"Yesterday's paper," he continued, "told all about Abd el Krim's successful advance all along the front. So if I have to arrest you it will be either a firing-squad, or Devil's Island, which is much worse. *Au revoir, mon ami!*"

Then Joubert released Lawton's hand, turned, and abruptly strode across the plaza toward the bridge of Saint Esprit.

"SOME one has babbled. . . ."

Joubert's words still burned into Lawton's brain like hot irons. But before making his escape, he would have to find out what or who had betrayed him. Per-haps Madeleine had said too much in a careless moment. At the very most, she knew very little; but that would suffice. Perhaps, in a flare of jealousy—but that simply couldn't be the case! Of all lovers, Lawton had been the most devoted. Madeleine wouldn't have betrayed him, though she might have been indiscreet. And even though he escaped the *Sûreté*, thanks to Joubert, he would have to face the unforgiving wrath of Abd el Krim for blundering and wasting time. The prob-lem of the moment was to find out who had betrayed him. Only the evening re-mained: but the Gray Goddess would tell him. She knew everything.

The law in France prohibited the sale of absinthe; but the Gray Goddess was subtle, so that she now materialized when the contents of two separate and distinct bottles, each in itself legal, were suitably blended. First a pony of *anis del oso,* then one of *cordiale gentiane;* and then the tall glass was filled with seltzer, which clouded, becoming gray and pearly. The result was insipid to taste, but when one had an abundance of time in which to court the lady of fancies, the innocuous flavor was worth enduring for the glamor that came stealing over one's senses.

Lawton paid for the afternoon's drink-ing, and then crossed the street to go up rue Port Neuf. He halted at a store near the corner, and after regarding its window display for a moment, stepped in. In a few minutes he emerged with a basket laden with all manner of exotic delicacies; and, among the several bottles of Oporto and Malaga, whose necks projected from their nest of parcels, there were as many more whose contents would insure the presence of the Gray Goddess during his last night in Bayonne.

Through continued evocation of the Gray Goddess, Davis Lawton had shaken off the fetters that bound him to earth and its restricting three dimensions. She had at last become a Presence, not visible, but none the less a distinct personality whose inspiration whipped Lawton's brain to uncanny agility, so that the most profound riddles became lucid as water. No reasoning was too intricate for his acuteness; and tonight she would tell him very certainly how he had been betrayed.

As he reached the head of rue Port Neuf, where the old cathedral lifts its tall spires like great, slim lance-heads, he wondered how much Madeleine had lost at Biarritz that day, and what new systems he would have to devise for her.

Madeleine lived in an apartment on rue Lachepaillet, a street that ran along the walls of the city, and overlooked the park whose broad, tree-clustered green rolled away from the moat, far below. The door opened before Lawton could pick the key from its companions on his ring.

"I've had the most thrilling day," said Madeleine between kisses. "I do wish you could have been along—but what's in the basket? Oh, aren't those grapes just wonderful! Why, you've brought *everything!* Tinned duck, and *confiture d'abricots,* and—you know, I've got a new way to fix that caviar, with little tomatoes —and even my favorite pastries. Looks like one of your large evenings! Do tell

me, have you had some good luck, too?"

Lawton smiled cryptically at that last. And as Madeleine, all enthusiastic about the indicated celebration, began her preparations for the feast, Lawton found a tall glass and mixed his libation to the Gray Goddess. To invoke her the more swiftly, he doubled the portions of liqueurs and diminished the quantity of seltzer.

"You know, the pelota matches were wonderful today!" chattered Madeleine. "And I won a bet of five louis from a charming old fellow. *Terribly* old, you understand, but he had the keenest eyes! Every once in a while he made a funny little gesture as if he were going to stroke his beard, then suddenly remembered that he was clean-shaven. He must have a history, that one, with the sudden shave he's not yet accustomed to!

"Oh, yes, and do you remember that bracelet we saw at Mornier Frères?" she continued as she set out an array of glasses. "That fascinating thing of green gold and platinum filigree, all set with diamonds and little sapphires—you didn't even notice I'm wearing it! You never notice *anything,* you with your pious meditations."

"It really is beautiful, sweetheart," admitted Lawton as he inspected the bracelet that glittered on her extended wrist. "You must have had a lucky day."

"You'd be surprised," replied Madeleine as she went on with her work. "But I'll tell you later. You'd never guess!"

And then the Gray Goddess, who had returned to Lawton's side, began whispering in his ear.

"Probably," she interposed, "she had it charged, so she can go back tomorrow with all her winnings and play them on double zero. You'll get the bill for the bracelet. . . ."

"I know it was terribly expensive," continued Madeleine, pausing long enough to run her slim white fingers through his hair. "But—no, I won't tell you, yet. That's going to be a surprise."

Lawton stared for a moment at her slender, exquisite hands. They had all had pale hands, that succession of ruinous adored ones of which Madeleine was the last. And each time that he rose from the wreckage of his duty they daintily plucked the foundation from beneath his feet again. Lawton sighed wearily, and felt very old at the recollection: but only for a moment. The Gray Goddess was weaving her web of sorcery and the Power was returning to Lawton. It pulsed and throbbed in his veins, and streaked in tiny flashes of fire down his spine, and tingled in his toes. The patterns of the Bokhara rug became exceedingly clean-cut, and then they clouded, islands of old ivory and deep blue in a sea of red that shimmered in the sultry glow of the tall floor lamp at his side. His head reeled ever so slightly with exaltation and all-knowingness.

"Tomorrow," Madeleine was saying, "we'll drive to Saint Jean de Luz. Do you remember that day——"

"That first day?" interpolated Lawton, ignoring for a moment the silver-clear syllables of the Goddess whispering in his ear.

"Our first day," said Madeleine, "when we paused on that crest and saw the gulf sparkling, far off, through a cleft in the Pyrenees?"

"Little stupid!" chided Lawton fondly; "do you suppose that I could ever forget? There was never such a day before. . . ."

There was a moment's silence, in which both she and Lawton half smiled to themselves at the memory.

"Do you know," she finally resumed, "I've often feared that some day you might leave. You're such a nomad. And

M. C.—8

I'm so glad that you remember. It might make you return, that memory."

"But suppose," suggested Lawton, "that I did return and didn't find you? Then what of remembrance?"

"Don't be absurd, darling," she reproved. "You know I'm perfectly foolish about you, and I'll always love you. But let's not even think of parting!"

To which Lawton nodded and smiled; for the Goddess at his side had taken form from the mist which always heralded her presence. She was tall when he stood, and she was tiny when he sat: always at a height just right for her to whisper in his ear, so close that no one else could overhear. And of course, no one else ever saw her.

Madeleine was chattering merrily. Lawton hated to cloud her gayety by telling her of his departure in the morning. The evening was too lovely to mar with bad news. Later, he would tell her; but now, he would respond to her high spirits. It was easy to smile, and have his lips reply for him. And this would be agreeable to the Goddess, for Lawton now spoke to her in the language of the little gray gods, some of whom were standing respectfully in the corners of the room. He could not see them, yet, but he could feel their presence.

Madeleine was eating now, picking dainty bits of tropical palm hearts from their garniture of mayonnaise. Her great, smoldering eyes regarded him amorously. Then she would smile, and murmur affectionate fanciful things as she offered him morsels of cold fowl, and jelly, and curiously adorned pastries and sips of Malaga.

THE enchantment was complete. He paid more and more attention to Madeleine, and yet was not distracted from the crystal-clear, thin voice of the

Goddess. Lawton knew that she was not offended because Madeleine did not offer her a bit of pastry or a sip of wine, or even one of those honey-sweet and honey-colored grapes from Spain. Goddesses did not eat; and neither did gods, but Lawton tactfully ignored his divinity long enough to accept the tidbits that Madeleine offered him; for that was their last night, and he wished to make it so memorable and perfect that she would never forget him, no matter who sought her during his absence.

"You've been so patient all evening," Madeleine was saying, "I'm going to tell you the secret I've been saving. I know you couldn't even guess——"

"Do tell me and end the suspense," Lawton replied with surprizing animation, in view of his speaking at the same time to the shadow presence at his side.

"I broke the bank today, really and truly! Can you believe it?"

As she spoke, Madeleine drew a great roll of Bank of France notes from her handbag, and then another, and still another roll, until the fine gold mesh, emptied, clung caressingly to her knee.

"Now, silly, aren't you sorry you growled so much about my playing roulette?" demanded Madeleine triumphantly.

"Sweetheart, that's perfectly wonderful, and I'm repentant already," replied Lawton. "Won't ever growl again."

The Goddess was still at Lawton's side, silent and smiling at her own thoughts. He could see her, without even turning his head, or lifting his glance from Madeleine's exquisite, slim hands and their rosy nails that glowed warmly in the rose-hued light. And then he saw that her eyes were amorous with heavy wine from Lisbon and the thin, ethereal vintage of France. In due course she would become very sleepy, and then Lawton could continue

his conversations with the Goddess: but in the meanwhile—the girl beside him was exceedingly lovely and desirable.

Lawton dismissed the riddles of the early evening. They would keep. Nothing in the world, either this one or the next, could compare with his love for this girl and her supreme beauty that was enriching their farewell. Then he remembered that his voice was deep and resonant; and so he sang:

"Pale hands I loved, beside the Shalimar,
Where are you now . . ."

As the last word passed his inspired lips, he leaned back against his cloud-bank of cushions and accepted Madeleine's ecstasy of approval, and her wine-perfumed kiss.

"Oh, but that was lovely! And now, do tell me what it means, that song in English."

He should have remembered that Madeleine did not understand English. He could compose long speeches in Tamil and Gujarati when he tired of Arabic; but he should not expect her to have his gift of language. So he translated.

"The words are lovely, too," said Madeleine. "And you really do love me that much?"

"Ever so much, and your pale hands also," replied Lawton, as he kissed her fingers one by one.

"And you won't ever leave me, you incurable wanderer?"

Lawton smiled, and his eyes spoke the lie that his lips could not achieve. Then a somber fancy possessed him, and he recited:

"When I am dead, open my grave and see
The smoke that curls about thy feet;

*In my dead heart the fire still burns for
    thee:
Yea, the smoke rises from my wind-
    ing-sheet."*

"That *is* beautiful," observed Madeleine. "Only, just a bit ghastly. You
have the strangest fancies, my dear."

"Nothing strange about that," murmured the Gray Goddess to Lawton.
"Very appropriate. You love her to distraction. And she's sold you to the
enemy, and then showed you the price of
your head. Only you won't be in your
grave when she opens it. But she did get
a good price for digging it, didn't she?
One of those rolls would have been
enough. . . ."

Lawton watched Madeleine stuffing the
notes back into the handbag, and saw her
smile at his audible words.

"That was clever," whispered the Goddess at Lawton's side, "getting all that
money as the price of your head. They
couldn't possibly have known how much
your head is worth . . . that's *our* secret."

"Maybe," continued that fine, thin
voice, "maybe they just wanted to make
an example of you."

"The chances are," suggested Lawton,
"that they suspected I'd completed a
rather brilliant plan to lead Abd el Krim's
troops all the way to the sea, and drive the
French out of Morocco. They must have
known I had perfected my plan while I
was pretending to be working on the
Communists to collect funds for Abd el
Krim. Shrewd fellows, to know that I
was squandering all that money as a blind,
and pretending to sit around the cafés,
everlastingly drunk. . . ."

"But you shouldn't blame her too
much," murmured the fountain of wisdom. "Think of the temptation! All
those thousands of francs! Anyway, she
knew you were clever enough to escape."

"But I object to the principle of it!"
protested Lawton.

THROUGH the swirling hazes before
him, Lawton saw the sparkle of a
bracelet.

"She's sold me out, and I'm not ready
to leave. Abd el Krim won't understand
that I spent all that money as a subter-
fuge. . . ."

Madeleine was clinging closely to him,
now, and her eyes were very dark and
lustrous. She was so near that he feared
she might after all sense the presence of
the Goddess, and be annoyed; so he cut
short the conversation, caressed Madeleine's hair, and kissed her full on the
lips. But he couldn't take too much time
from the oracle that murmured in his ear.

No, it was Madeleine who murmured
amorously as she caressed him.

"I'm not the least bit sleepy, sweetheart," he replied. "Well, then . . . but
I'll have another drink first. . . ."

With exquisitely precise gestures Lawton blended the final potion. That last one
would give him the power to cross the
Border and peer through ethereal vistas
deep beyond reckoning. He would see
with a keenness he had never before
achieved. Then She would reveal the
final secret.

Madeleine stood there between the
parted draperies, all shimmering in an
apricot-colored negligee. She paused for
a moment to smile at him as she drew the
drapes together. And then the Gray Goddess resumed her speech in a voice somewhat louder, now that they were alone.

"Lawton, you are still terribly stupid!
In just another moment she'd have
charmed you out of your senses, this fascinating girl who sold you to the *Sûreté*.
Think, Lawton, you will face a firing-
squad unless you leave by sunrise.

"But go into the next room," taunted

that thin, clear voice, bitter and vibrant. "You love her to distraction. Wake her and sing once more of the pale hands you loved——

"Of *all* the pale hands," concluded the Gray Goddess with venomous emphasis.

"No, by God! I'll not sing. I'll choke her!" retorted Lawton, stung by the memory of all his follies. "They've been my damnation all these past dozen years."

"But you can't change," murmured the Gray Goddess with a softness more enraging than the previous sardonic piping. "So leave quietly. Don't wake her, or her arms will hold you until Joubert comes in the morning to arrest you."

"No, Gray Goddess," replied Lawton solemnly. "For once you are wrong. This is the first one to take the price of my head. And this time I shall redeem myself."

His glance roved up and down the wall, and in the ruddy glow of the floor lamp he saw the picture he had once hung for Madeleine. Lacking wire at the time, he had used a cord of hard-spun silk, a relic of old days in Asia. Madeleine had shuddered as he told its history, and showed her the swift gesture used by Indian *dacoits* in their stranglings.

"Look, Gray Goddess, how simple it will be."

But she mocked him for a braggart as the drapes closed about him. Then she followed him, lest his courage fade before the loveliness asleep in the moonlight that streamed in through the drawn curtains and caressed the curved throat.

As Lawton knelt beside her, Madeleine stirred slightly and her shapely arms twined about his neck to draw him to her.

"Pale hands," mocked the Goddess at his side. "They will hold you for Joubert in the morning——"

A whiteness of searing flame swept through his brain as the hard-spun cord cut short the kiss that sought his lips.

"You have proved yourself, Lawton," exulted the Gray Goddess as they emerged again into the sultry glow of the floor lamp. "And there in that mesh bag is the price of your head. It will redeem you and your broken faith in the eyes of Abd el Krim. Now hurry, Lawton, hurry!"

The Goddess led him into a gray world. Lawton strode triumphantly down rue Port Neuf and past the deserted plaza, and across the bridge of Saint Esprit. Dawn was almost at hand. In the distance he heard the whistle of the express that would take him across the border of Spain.

LAWTON heard footsteps behind him. Perhaps it was Joubert coming to the station to assure himself that Lawton was leaving on time. He turned; but it was not Joubert who faced him. He stared for a moment, perplexed by the familiarity of the man who confronted him. Then he saw that it was Mahjoub, the right-hand man of Abd el Krim. No wonder that for a moment he had not recognized Mahjoub attired in European clothing, and without his long beard.

"Joubert didn't fail me," said Mahjoub. "By Allah! But I had to do it! You made such an ass of yourself. Abd el Krim gave me full authority; so I solved it my own way.

"Too bad it took that girl so long to learn to win," continued Mahjoub, ignoring Lawton's puzzled frown. "My heart stood still when I saw her take the winnings of the first play and stake them all on single zero. *But she won!*"

"What was that?" said Lawton, enunciating very slowly, like a mechanical toy that has just achieved speech.

"She won enough thousand-franc notes to stuff a saddle-bag. But——"

Mahjoub paused, and made a gesture of stroking his beard, then remembered he was clean-shaven.

"But I guess it was just as well that I did tell the *Sûreté*——"

"*You* told the *Sûreté?*" demanded Lawton.

His voice rang in his own ears as from a great distance.

"By Allah! Of course I did. Then I told your friend Joubert to scare you out of town. But Abd el Krim loves a good soldier, so he'll forgive a worthless secret agent."

"Then *she* didn't sell me?" Lawton's voice was husky and trembling. Exultation fought with despair, so that he could barely pronounce his question.

"No, she didn't," replied Mahjoub. "Nor did I. That was just the only way to get you out of town before Abd el Krim's wrath overcame him. If *he* had told the *Sûreté*——

"*Mafeesh!*" concluded the old man with a gesture of finality. "Finish for you."

The express was pulling into the station. But Lawton had turned, and was walking toward the bridge.

"Forgotten of Allah!" cried Mahjoub. "Where are you going?"

Lawton halted, faced about, but made no move to retrace his steps.

"I'm going back to town," he replied. His voice was strong and steady now, as though he commanded troops. "And my salaam to Abd el Krim!"

Then he turned and strode toward the bridge of Saint Esprit.

"Gray Goddess," he said bitterly, "you have mocked me. Her life is on my hands."

"Repentance is vain," murmured that sweet thin voice of the enchantress. "And you acted in good faith. So swallow your misery and your regrets. Be a man. Catch that express. Abd el Krim will give you a high command when he sees that money. You had reason to believe she betrayed you."

"Gray Goddess," replied Lawton, "I refuse to betray what little good there is left in me."

As he passed the second span of the bridge, his right hand swept out in a wide arc. A thick bundle of thousand-franc notes soared high into the morning light, fell into the river, and was sucked out of sight by an eddy. Then, as with lengthening stride he marched across the bridge, he sang in his rich, deep voice:

"*Pale hands I loved, beside the Shalimar,*
Where are you now . . ."

IT WAS but a short walk to Joubert's house.

"Georges," said Lawton to his astonished friend, "place me under arrest. And tell the Prefect of Police to call at 34 rue Lachepaillet. He will find her with a cord about her throat. I thought that she sold me. But I met an old man at the station, who told me——"

"I understand," replied Joubert, as he heard the final whistle of the express clearing the yards for Spain.

A Woman of the Hills

By ARREPH EL-KHOURY

*A dramatic story of the Arabs and the revenge of a woman who loved
her murdered Shaikh—by a young Syrian-American author*

THE village of Thouryah squatted on its slope, its whitewashed walls afire in the glare of the dying sun; and up in the palatial house of its late shaikh, a beautiful young woman sat on a divan in a large hall, looking through the opened window at the snow-covered hills. She was dressed in black, for her husband, Shaikh Tallall, the head of the village, had been recently killed in battle when he led his men against those of the village of El-Mizan.

Mrysh, for this was the young woman's name, looked at the hills, and her heart was heavy with grief. She had loved her husband, and his sudden death, just a few months after they were married, had struck a harsh note in the hidden recesses of her being. Her final resolve was never to marry again. Perhaps (and Allah is All-Merciful) the unborn would be a man-child to inherit his father's office.

How long Mrysh sat and looked at the disappearing sun on the summit of Mount Hermon, she did not know, but watching the sunset brought solace to her heart. Suddenly she heard a knock at the door of the hall. She left her seat on the divan, walked to the door and turned it open. In front of her stood her maid.

"Good omen, if it pleases Allah?" asked Mrysh.

"Shaikh Marouph is seeking audience," announced the maid.

Shaikh Marouph was the master of the village horsemen. He had fought at her husband's side in many a tight battle.

"Shaikh Marouph is one of us—admit him," said Mrysh to the maid, and returned to her seat. The maid departed.

It was not long until she returned with Shaikh Marouph dragging his broad, long simitar behind him. He was of gigantic height and broad of shoulders. His massive chest was like a deep drum, and his dash like that of a Tatar emperor. The maid pushed the door open and invited Shaikh Marouph to enter the hall.

Mrysh stood up and met him in the middle of the room. "May your evening be happy, O *Shaikha*," said Shaikh Marouph in his guttural voice.

At hearing Shaikh Marouph address her as a *shaikha* [wife of a shaikh], Mrysh smiled bitterly to herself, but the smile did not reach to her face and lips. "A dowager *shaikha* am I—and at the age of eighteen! Oh, the irony of Fate!" she said to herself. To Shaikh Marouph she said: "And may your evening be blessed, O Shaikh Marouph. Come, sit down," and she indicated the corner of the divan—the seat of honor in Arabic-speaking countries.

Shaikh Marouph walked to the corner and sat down. Mrysh came and sat near him. She wondered at this sudden and unexpected visit of Shaikh Marouph. But Shaikh Marouph perceived what was passing in her mind, and spoke. "I have come about a matter of great importance."

Mrysh surveyed him from the corners of her brown eyes. "A matter of great importance! What could it be, O Shaikh Marouph?" she asked.

"It is about the death of our late young chief, your husband—may Allah rest his soul," said Shaikh Marouph.

Her eyes were unblinking. "My husband and his death? O Shaikh Marouph, and for all I know he was killed in battle. Do you know other things concerning his death?"

"Yes."

"Tell me! Pray, tell me!" She seized his hands.

"I shall," was his answer. "Your husband was not killed by our enemies during the battle. He is dead and buried now (may Allah make paradise his dwelling), but——" Shaikh Marouph hesitated.

"But what?" darted Mrysh.

"But he should be avenged."

"Avenged? This is indeed strange! He was killed in a battle."

"This I know, but there are some hidden things about his strange death which none knows save Allah and myself."

Mrysh bit her lip and stared at Shaikh Marouph. "For Allah's sake, tell me all you know."

"Your husband was killed by our ally in that battle."

"Do you mean Shaikh Dirdar Ibn Dirdar? As I recall, he was the only man to ride with his men among your ranks."

"Dirdar Ibn Dirdar shot your husband in the back. I saw him with my eyes but could not say a word, fearing that if I were to speak, or kill Dirdar Ibn Dirdar, a schism in our ranks would be the inevitable result, and at that crucial moment the victory was falling into our hands."

MRYSH pondered a while, and remembered what had happened a year or two before she was married to her late husband. Dirdar had come from his village and dismounted in her father's house. He asked her hand in marriage and was politely refused, for her father had already pledged his word to her late husband. Dirdar Ibn Dirdar became very angry and left the house, threatening to take her by force or otherwise. Her late husband heard of Dirdar's threats, rode his swiftest mare and followed Dirdar to his village. He overtook him on the bridge, just a mile or two before Dirdar's village, gave him a sound beating and returned home. Upon hearing of this, Mrysh's father arranged for a peace between the two young chiefs and the incident was dead and forgotten.

"I see," said Mrysh thoughtfully; "then Dirdar killed him for the beating which my husband had given him."

"Not the beating, but that which hurts a man more than the swish of a bamboo wand."

"What is it?" she asked.

"Jealousy," replied Shaikh Marouph.

Suddenly Mrysh stood up and walked to the door. Shaikh Marouph followed her. "Where are you going, in Allah's peace?" he asked.

"I am going to summon the shaikhs of the village for a meeting and demand of them to avenge my husband," she said.

Shaikh Marouph thought her idea to be folly. "It is the logical thing to do, but alas! not practical," he told her.

"And why?"

"Simply because the minor shaikhs of the village would not declare war on Dirdar Ibn Dirdar. He is more powerful than we, and has just helped us win a battle. I shall be the first to oppose your suggestion, for I know our strength and his. To your presence I say this much: that if we were to make war on him it would mean a shameful defeat for us and an inglorious flight."

"Then what shall we do, O master of the horsemen?"

"Allah is All-Merciful, and He does not shut a door until He opens another. Be patient, O *Shaikha*. Wait and hope. The *bdui* [nomad] avenged himself after forty years and then said that he was too hasty. We are all descendants of the sons of the sand dunes."

"Verily, Allah is with the patient people," commented Mrysh.

Shaikh Marouph left her and went his way.

A MONTH later Mrysh was seated in her richly furnished court when one of her maids came announcing the coming of a visitor. This visitor was a village woman, named Khardalli. Mrysh told the maid to bring her inside.

Khardalli was an old woman whose wrinkled face appeared like a gnarled block of oak-wood. "May your evening be happy, O Mrysh," she said.

"And may your evening be blessed," replied Mrysh. "Come, sit."

Khardalli did not have to be invited twice; she sat on a rug near the brazier, which was filled with charcoal fire that glowed like a heap of ruby balls. Mrysh sat facing her. Khardalli's bleary eyes surveyed the corners of the place with a scrutinizing glance. The maid left.

Khardalli looked at Mrysh. "I have come," she began, "to pay my respects to you and ask you to do me a slight favor."

"Yob, old one," said Mrysh, "if there be a service which you may think I can render you, rest assured that to the fulfillment of it you will find me standing on the firmest of foot."

"May the All-Powerful grant you a long age, you to whom all good may come," said Khardalli. "I have come to ask you to accompany me to my humble house to write me a letter to my son—my only son, who, as you no doubt know, is serving his term in the Sultan's army."

"But we can do it here," replied Mrysh.

Khardalli shook her head. "Many things I want to tell him, and while I am saying them to you some one may hear us in this great house which is filled with servants, guards, slaves and peasants. In my house there is not a soul to disturb us, and I would be free to think and you would be free to write. Come with me (may Allah keep you!) and do this good deed for the Face of Allah," persisted Khardalli indefatigably.

Mrysh found it useless to argue with the resolute old soul.

"Very well then, to your house we shall go," she said.

So to Khardalli's house they went. On their way they passed by the village graveyard, and there, in the dark night, Mrysh saw the great tomb of her husband with its high alabaster dome shining crimson in the darkness. A pain surged in her young heart and tears rushed to her eyes. Slowly she moved until they were near Khardalli's house, when suddenly the latter stopped.

"May Allah forgive me!" Khardalli said apologetically.

"Why, what have you done?" asked Mrysh in astonishment.

"I forgot that I have neither ink nor paper in my wretched house," Khardalli muttered.

"Do not let that trouble you. I shall return to my house and fetch some," said Mrysh.

Khardalli grinned. "No!" she said firmly, "I shall borrow them from my good neighbor Oum el-Mouhseinein. Your house is too far away from here, and it will take me but a moment to go and come back. Here is the key to my house. Go and sit by the fire until I return, O daughter of the strong and free." She handed Mrysh the wooden key to her house and departed in the direction of the narrow, crooked alley at her right and soon vanished in the darkness like a gray, hunchbacked genie of evil.

MRYSH walked to the inner courtyard of Khardalli's house. She put the key into the lock and turned it around twice, then pushed the door ajar. She stood facing a long corridor illuminated by the dim oil-lamp that flickered dismally. She walked to the first door on her right, which she knew was the door of the winter quarter, in the meantime thinking that the place was a loneliness in which not even the wailing of *jin* was to be heard. But as she pushed this door open her brown eyes almost jumped out from the sockets. Before her stood Shaikh Dirdar Ibn Dirdar, the man who had killed her husband. On the threshold she stood panting. She knew that she had fallen into a trap.

Shaikh Dirdar Ibn Dirdar was tall, broad of shoulders, and fully armed. He carried two cartridge belts athwart his massive chest. Two heavy automatic pistols hung at his hips. His sash was decorated with a wicked, curved dagger. A long simitar swung at his side from silver cords with huge tassels. In his right hand he carried a whip with a golden knob. His left hand toyed with his black mustache that looked like the tail of a scorpion. He advanced toward Mrysh, smiling through half-closed eyelids.

"Welcome, O light of the two worlds," he greeted her.

Seeing him smile, Mrysh recovered from her first shock; she became a little cool and stopped panting. Her body was straight like a lance now, her head proudly erect over her supple shoulders. Her fright turned into anger.

"*Yoh!* O son of unmentionable begettings, back to the kennel!" she snarled at him.

Dirdar met her insult with a broad smile. "A year or so ago I came to your father; now I come to you——"

"And you shall be refused and discarded like an old dirty garment; and if the need arose the youngest of the village youths would give you a worse beating than the one you received at the hands of my late husband, who was stronger than you."

Dirdar seemed not to pay the least attention to her words. He went on: "I have come this time to take you away with me to my village, and there I shall make you my wife."

Mrysh grinned sarcastically at his words. "And it was through that old woman's intermediacy that you brought me to this house in a manner typical of a sniveling, slinking, sneaking fox, O vilest of Allah's creatures; and then you have the effrontery to order me to go away with you to be your wife as if I were a gipsy dancing-girl or a black slave-girl from Africa, O son of a burnt father! Away from my presence—away! and may the dirt-nosed pigs eat your last meal, O dog and a son of sixteen dogs!"

Her voice was high-pitched and her gestures were picturesque, but not effective enough to stop Dirdar from advancing toward her.

"Stop where you are!" her words stabbed at him.

"What would you do?" he asked.

"I would scream, and in but a glance the entire village would be at your throat."

"Do it then," and he advanced toward her. But she did not scream, for at that moment her mind flashed and the words of Shaikh Marouph rang in her ears: "*Allah ma ghalak baab ila fatah baab*" [Allah does not shut a door until He opens another].

"Why don't you scream?" asked Dirdar sardonically.

"I simply can't," she said meekly, with the air of one who is vanquished.

"Thanks be to Ailah!" he murmured,

and smiled broadly. The storm was subdued. She gave him her hand, and he covered it with kisses.

"Come, let us be going before the men of the village see us, for if I were caught they would cut my throat," she told him.

"Not while this rifle is in my right hand and this simitar is in my left," he said confidently and ran to the stable and brought his mare. He mounted, and placed Mrysh before him on the saddle-bow. They left the village unmolested.

Toward his own village they went. The north wind was riding a racked sky, but on they went until they reached the bridge below Dirdar's village. It was the same bridge on which her late husband had given Dirdar a sound beating. Under the bridge the roaring water of the melted snow surged up to a man's height among the granite boulders. Here Dirdar saccaded his mare and looked around. He had reached his own territory, where he was amir.

Mrysh looked at his face. She raised her left hand and began toying with his mustache. Her fingers moved like butterflies before his eyes. Her right hand was free. Feeling the warmth of her hand against his cheek, Dirdar was intoxicated with delight.

"Am I not fortunate to be alone with you—you who are so strong, so rich and so handsome that any woman might——"

Suddenly Dirdar saw something that had cut a silver streak before his eyes, and a shrill shriek like the bark of a hyena came from his throat. For Mrysh had swiftly lured him by rubbing her left hand against his cheek while with her right she had snatched his dagger from its scabbard and buried it deep in his heart.

"My husband is avenged!" she said, and Dirdar lived long enough to hear her words.

Quickly she jumped to the ground and watched him fall. His left foot was caught in the stirrup; she freed it and he fell to the snow-covered arch of the bridge. She seized him by the neck and dragged him to the edge.

"May the Merciful Allah never have pity on his soul!" she muttered, and tumbled his body into the roaring torrent.

She looked toward the East. Her left hand was pressed against her bosom, her right lifted the blood-smeared dagger skyward.

"Thou, O Allah, let this be a man-child, so he may sit in his father's saddle!"

She mounted the richly caparisoned mare of the dead shaikh and rode away toward her own village.

Indeed the Idols I have loved so long
Have done my credit in this World much wrong:
    Have drown'd my Glory in a shallow Cup,
And sold my Reputation for a Song.

Indeed, indeed, Repentance oft before
I swore—but was I sober when I swore?
    And then and then came Spring, and Rose-in-hand
My thread-bare Penitence apieces tore.
                                    —*Rubáiyát of Omar Khayyam.*

When China Buries its Dead

By JAMES W. BENNETT

A FUNERAL, in China, is not a trying affair. The mourners meet the guest at the gate with a brave smile which does not waver. They refuse to harrow the hearts of those who come to bid farewell to the departed. They offer food and wine in abundance. In this, they follow a time-honored custom. When a Chinese man-child is born, there is a banquet. When he arrives at maturity, there is another, and a third, when he reaches the venerated age of seventy. What, therefore, is more rational than this final banquet in which his spirit is thought to join?

Since the Chinese believe that ghosts prey upon the newly departed soul, they take precautions to frighten away such ghoulish phantoms. Crackers are fired and cymbals clashed. As the coffin is borne to its final resting-place, disks of silver paper are tossed in the air—to distract the attention of predatory demons.

There is one variety of ghost that the Chinese particularly dread at this time: the Fox Spirit. The Fox Demon is the wraith of some mortal who has lost his way along the journey to the distant World Beyond. It can only find peace by stealing the soul of one newly dead. The unfortunate ghost becomes a Fox Spirit, while the erstwhile Fox Demon wanders happily forward toward Paradise. Thus a vicious circle is set up.

The Sons of Han employ a certain, set, ritualistic method—guaranteed to circumvent the Fox Spirit. A rooster is brought

(Please turn to page 511)

THE SOUK

T HE MAGIC CARPET Magazine continues to make friends, and has gained thousands of new readers, as the excellence of its stories has become known to a wider circle. We appeal to you to call this magazine to the attention of your friends, so that it will be possible for us to issue the MAGIC CARPET every month, instead of four times a year as at present.

Assad Saud of Caracas, in the Republic of Venezuela, writes to the Souk: "I write to offer my congratulations on the general make-up of MAGIC CARPET. The new name gives the magazine a wider scope for taking the reader to the different parts of the world teeming with adventure. Though I enjoy the new stories, I have missed greatly in the last two issues the tales of the dragoman Hamed, by Otis Adelbert Kline. Please let us have more tales about Hamed."

"You certainly make no mistake when you get on your pages a story by H. Bedford-Jones, the dean of American fiction writers," writes Elwood W. Cooper, of Chico, California. "I never pass up any yarn of his. His name on the cover sells many a magazine. *Pearls from Macao* was great, and I enjoyed it from beginning to end. You have a fine line-up of authors, and a great variety of stories. I am sorry that you do not print your magazine monthly, but you know best and would probably be glad to do so if conditions warranted it."

Writes Robert Nelson, of St. Charles, Illinois: "Now, I don't want to bother you gentlemen any more than I have to, but I've just *got* to tell you that the July issue of MAGIC CARPET is wonderful. Congratulations for selecting such superb stories to appear in one issue. Chuck orchids, as Walter Winchell would say, to Seabury Quinn for his mystery tale, *The Bride of God*, which in my opinion is the best story in the July issue. But Howard's *The Lion of Tiberias* is a close second, and is the best story from the pen of this great writer that I have ever read. The battle scenes in this story read like some of the stirring episodes in Flaubert's immortal *Salammbo*, and very often, it seems, Howard goes Flaubert one shade better. Bedford-Jones's *Pearls from Macao* comes third in rank of the exceptionally fine stories in the July issue of MAGIC CARPET."

"Hurrah for more of Edmond Hamilton's stories about Kaldar," writes E. Brown, of Newport, Kentucky. "I like Hung Long Tom's poems too. Also like the cover get-up this issue."

A letter from Jack Darrow, of Chicago, says: "I like the new style of lettering for the title of the MAGIC CARPET, but the white letters do not stand out as they

(Please turn to page 510)

508

COMING NEXT ISSUE

The Shadow of the Vulture
By ROBERT E. HOWARD

A stirring tale of Suleyman the Magnificent, Sultan of Turkey, and the breath-taking events at the siege of Vienna, when Christendom stood at bay and a red-headed girl held the fate of Europe in her hands.

The Spider Woman
By SEABURY QUINN

A terrific adventure of Carlos the Tiger in the Netherlands, and a lovely woman spy who told him how to conquer a Spanish stronghold.

The River of Perfumes
By WARREN HASTINGS MILLER

She drove men to madness by her sheer beauty, this little maid of Indo-China—a fascinating Oriental tale of love, lust, and sudden death, and a wild adventure.

The Little Affair of the Eiffel Tower
By ARTHUR MORRIS CROSBY

Henri the Fox scorned to use the gross means of hired assassins, but his methods were just as effective—a tale of the Paris underworld.

Passport to the Desert
By G. G. PENDARVES

Algeria—a story of intrigue and a perilous adventure involving an American girl and an Arab bandit and slave-dealer.

Alleys of Darkness
By PATRICK ERVIN

A story of Singapore and Dennis Dorgan, hardest-fisted slugger in the merchant marine, and the maze of intrigue that enmeshed him.

Speed Planes for Moscow
By S. GORDON GURWIT

A thrilling tale of the Russian Five Year Plan and a romance that was surrounded with perils and death.

NEXT ISSUE  ON SALE OCT. 15

(Continued from page 508)

would if they were solid color. The whole cover, in fact, does not show up on the news stands as well as the latest WEIRD TALES. *Pearls From a Cow*—pardon me— *Pearls from Macao* by H. Bedford-Jones takes first place. I hope you will continue to have a story by this prolific author in every issue. This also goes for Robert E. Howard and Seabury Quinn and E. Hoffmann Price."

Warren Hastings Miller, author of *King's Assassins* in this issue, has a complaint to make. "One kick I would like to register," he writes, "is the cover of the current issue. It is very bad from a news-stand point of view; not the picture but the lettering. It is so faint in color that I spent ten minutes looking for it on the Gloucester stand without success. I finally gave it up, but my wife, who is more persistent than I, finally came out with a copy that she had discovered among the hundreds in the racks."

A vigorous objection to interplanetary stories in the MAGIC CARPET Magazine comes from E. L. Mengshoel, of Minneapolis. He writes: "I agree with Josephine Larson from Missouri, who says in the Souk: 'Let Merrick (and Hamilton) go back to Antares'—and stay there. Those stupid space-fantasies are just about as entertaining to persons with any amount of knowledge as would be some lunatic's harangue about happenings in hell. No, I say, let your MAGIC CARPET be mainly Oriental— terrestrial, at least. The best story I find in your last issue is *The Lion of Tiberias* by Robert E. Howard, with *The Forgotten of Allah* by Price as a close second. With the absence of the 'interplanetary' and 'cosmic' rot, that issue was good all through; every story was interesting and entertaining."

Readers, what is your favorite story in this issue? The most popular story in the July issue, as shown by your votes and letters to the Souk, was Robert E. Howard's superb historical tale of the Sultan Zenghi, *The Lion of Tiberias*. H. Bedford-Jones's thrilling tale of a perilous sea voyage, *Pearls from Macao*, came next.

My Favorite Stories in the October MAGIC CARPET are:

Story	Remarks
(1) _____	_____
(2) _____	_____
(3) _____	_____

I do not like the following stories:

(1) _____	Why? _____
(2) _____	_____

It will help us to know what kind of stories you want in the Magic Carpet Magazine if you will fill out this coupon and mail it to The Souk, Magic Carpet Magazine, 840 N. Michigan Ave., Chicago, Ill.

Reader's name and address:

_____

_____

_____

(Continued from page 507)

to the side of the bier. Its head is thrust to the ground and a cross traced there with its bill. The cross-marked spot is sprinkled with rice wine. The throat of the cock is cut and the blood allowed to mingle with the wine.

The death-watch itself is strict. No living domestic animal is permitted in the room. The Chinese believe that if a cat or dog is allowed to breathe seven times in the face of the cadaver, the body will be roused—not to life, but to a dreadful galvanic activity, exceedingly dangerous to the safety of the living.

The family of the deceased, next, make preparations not only for the journey of the soul into the Hereafter, but for its subsequent existence there. A house of paper and bamboo is fashioned. Servants of *papier maché* are placed in its rooms. It is stored with imitation food. Even a *papier maché* automobile is sometimes added.

It is the wish of every Chinese to be buried in the land of his birth and near the village of his immediate ancestors. Each ocean liner that leaves the Pacific Coast, or Hawaii, for the Orient, bears a cargo of Celestial dead. Each China river boat or coastwise steamer holds similar freight.

Very frequently in China there are families which have emigrated from the village of their birth to other provinces, yet which are too poor to send their dead on that last long journey back to the ancestral home. Nevertheless, the bodies *do* reach their native soil. The phenomenon strains our Occidental credulity; yet it has been attested so frequently that foreigners living in China have been forced to accept it.

A small sum is saved by the poverty-stricken family of the deceased and is handed over to a member of the Geoman-

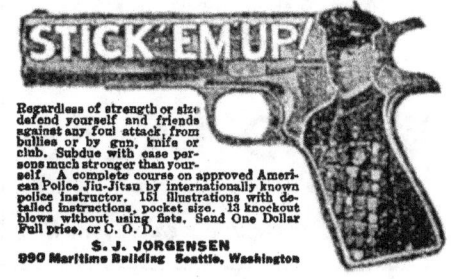

cers' Guild who is gifted with peculiar powers. As soon as he has collected sufficient money from enough families, he issues an order that their dead be brought to him.

What means he employs, no one in China—outside the Geomancers' Guild—knows, but he raises the bodies from their coffins and forces them to begin the long, overland march to their homeland. He travels at their head, a grim and grisly shepherd. The procession travels only at night, sinking back to a death-like state during the day. Speechless, unseeing, unhearing, they stumble cataleptically through the dark. Foreigners have come upon these macabre bands staggering through the blackness—and have been given a psychic shock from which they were weeks recovering.

When at last the group reaches its destination—at times, a thousand miles distant from its starting-point—the Geomancer who has been leading them releases the pressure of his will. Instantly the dead return to that slumber from which there is no further wakening. And their bodies peacefully mingle with the native dust from which they have been created.

The Pool
By HUNG LONG TOM

China is a great
Pool of learning
To which
For countless ages
Men have come
To drink.
If the waters
Now are running dry
Only the thankless
Complain about the dust.

M. C.—**8**